Broken Bits and Bobs

A Collection

of

What Ifs,

What Was,

and

What Never Should Be

Broken Bits and Bobs

A Collection

of

What Ifs,

What Was,

and

What Never Should Be

Darin Miller

ISBN: 979-8-9867566-5-3 (Paperback)

Library of Congress Control Number: 2023906801

Any references to historical events, real people, or real places are used fictitiously. Names, characters, and places are products of the author's imagination. No portion of this book was created through use of artificial intelligence (AI), nor may any portion be used to train AI.

Front cover photography by Nicki Miller.
Voracious reader portrayed by Chelsea Brooke Rose.
Shot on location in JD's Antiques, Books and More, Rivertown Antiques, 541 2nd St, Portsmouth, OH.

Printed by Kindle Direct Publishing, in Columbus, OH, USA.

First printing edition 2023. This printing edition 2026.

www.darin-miller.com

DARIN MILLER
WRITES

This is for Sheryl Davis
You caused all this!

(...thank you!)

Directory

Broken Bits

Bobs

PREFACE

I love short stories. Always have. Always will.

I grew up inspired by the amazing contributors to both *Alfred Hitchcock's Mystery Magazine* and *Ellery Queen Mystery Magazine*, and that, in itself, is a list so lengthy it could fill an entire book. The ability to engage, the efficiency of narrative, the agility to tap into very specific styles with relatively limited real estate—I have such tremendous respect for these authors whose deft storytelling lends itself to the medium. For those who are unfamiliar with these magazines, their stories often feature ill-fated protagonists who get their just rewards served up in an ironic twist in the final act. These are my humble attempts, and I hope you enjoy them, but be forewarned: most of these stories are darker than what you've come to expect from the *Dwayne Morrow Mysteries*. I have elected to divide this book into two sections:

Broken Bits—these are the stories that are darkest.

 Bobs—the lighter fare.

I am leading with a Bob and following with a Broken Bit and will continue that throughout the book to spread a little sunshine around, so to speak.

Almost all of these stories were written between 2000 and 2001, as a warm-up to writing the longer fiction which would eventually become the *Dwayne Morrow Mysteries*. Please keep this in mind and be a bit forgiving with stories like *"A Terminal Case"* where computer and chat technology has evolved so dramatically in the time since. Smartphones weren't really a thing, either, but I mean—who knew?

The stories are about a little bit of everything, and most have a little "gotcha!" in the end. There are tales of love grown cold, meddlesome neighbors and a mother's worst fear. You'll meet the ladies of Buena Vista and have pizza with Grandpa—there's even a tiny bit of toilet humor within. (There will *always* be a thirteen-year-old boy inside me...) There are stories to warm your hearts, and stories to keep you on the edges of your seats.

The final three stories were written within the past year, and I couldn't be happier with the last one, *"Best Laid Plans."* Garry Sexton, Jr.—I will miss you until the end of time, my brother.

With that being said, grab a drink of your choice, gather 'round the fire and snuggle beneath your favorite blanket.

It's story time.

DINNER, THEN A BEDTIME STORY

"Melissa spilled juice on the pho-one!" Billy shouted, racing from the kitchen and into the hallway on legs of lightning, the soles of his shoes screeching in protest as he abruptly changed direction and bounded into the living room.

With a sudden snort, Hal Walker was wrenched from his nap, sitting bolt upright in his blue suede recliner. He knew he had missed something, but for the life of him he didn't know what it was. Then Billy flung himself into the old man's ample lap and pulled himself upright using the old man's neck for leverage.

"Melissa spilled juice on the phone," Billy repeated urgently.

"It's not polite to tattle on your sister, young man," Hal chided.

4

"But Grandpa!" Billy's face was contorted with anguish, so real for the boy, so comical to the man. "Mom said we could have pizza tonight. She left money and everything. All's we got to do—"

"All we've got to do," Hal corrected.

"—uh-huh, all we've got to do is call for dee-livery. But now the phone don't work—"

"Doesn't work."

"Grandpa! For Superman's sake, won't you let me say anything?" The boy rolled his eyes upward in exasperation before dying of mistreatment in Hal's arms. Hal couldn't help but grin. In little Billy Dryden, Hal could see the impish qualities that had made the boy's mother, Molly, such a special child at that age. Billy's tousled brown hair (which desperately needed washed) lay in clumps across his forehead, his clothes bore skid marks from the better part of the yard, and something that glowed red in the dark had stained the corners of his mouth. He was adorable. He also was quite the showman, apparently subscribing to the notion that presentation is everything.

After a moment without getting a response, Billy cautiously opened one eye. "May I speak now, sir?"

"You may."

"My wonderful sister has spewed juice on the phone. Pizza! Pizza!" And he was off, racing back down the hallway to rejoin his sister in the kitchen.

Hal sighed and pulled himself up from the recliner. The last thing he needed was for Billy and Melissa to really go at each other. A six-year-old hyperactive boy and a five-year-old spoiled princess could be a deadly combination in the right climate. He lumbered down the hall after the retreating thunderclaps of Billy's Nikes.

"Why do you only have one phone, Grandpa?" asked Melissa innocently as Hal entered the kitchen. Aha! In her typical fashion, Melissa was laying the groundwork for this whole incident to be Grandpa's fault because he had been too shortsighted to see the obvious need for a cell phone or alternate extension. It was really amazing the way her mind worked. Hal figured she would either become a brilliant litigator or a criminal genius. Nothing was ever Melissa's fault, as she saw it.

"There's only one of me," Hal replied. "Why would I need more than one phone? Let me see that thing."

Melissa handed the receiver of the wall phone to Hal with sticky fingers that matched the red at the corners of Billy's mouth. Hal gave Melissa a stern look as he gingerly accepted it.

"I told you she spilled juice on it," said Billy.

Melissa gave him a quick punch on the arm. "Did not!"

Hal treated Melissa to another of his patented glares, the one that acted like truth serum.

"Well," she said, pouting, "I didn't do it on purpose."

"Doesn't matter!" shouted Billy. "You still did it." He punched Melissa's arm, and the two were off, Billy running for his life while Melissa pounded along the hardwood floor after him.

It was difficult for Hal to even feign consternation with his grandchildren. Their personalities were so distinctly different, and their interaction was often more entertaining than prime time television. Hal wished Alice had lived to see their grandchildren, but she had passed early on; Molly had only been fifteen at the time. Molly had met her husband, Rob, while attending Ohio State, and they had married shortly after graduation. Rob was a good man—ambitious, but not to the point of neglecting his family. He had just earned an executive managerial position at his investment firm and tonight, he and Molly were celebrating the promotion with an evening on the town. Hal was more than happy to step in as babysitter.

Sure enough, the juice had leaked down into the crevices which surrounded the buttons on the handset, and none of them responded when pressed. Hal chuckled as he realized he'd have to buy a new phone. How does someone spill liquid on a wall-mounted device? Hal simply shrugged.

Several moments later, Hal stepped out onto the porch of his townhouse, scanning the yard for the children. They were wrestling in the front corner, near the rose bushes.

"You two behave out there!" yelled Hal, stooping to pick up the evening paper. He settled onto the porch swing and flipped to the sports, rocking gently in the warm summer breeze. He loved evenings like this. It reminded him of when he and Alice had bought the house, so many years ago, and watched their own daughter play with the neighborhood children. Clifton Lane hadn't changed much in all the years—well-kept two-story houses lining both sides of a wide roadway which saw little more than local traffic.

By the time he had finished with the sports, the comics and the sales flyers, Billy and Melissa had returned to the porch. "Grandpa!" wailed Billy.

"Yes?"

"Pizza! Pizza!"

Melissa giggled and chimed in, "PIZZA!"

"Oh, you want pizza, do you?" asked Hal, carefully folding his newspaper and placing it beside himself on the swing.

"Yeah! Yeah! Yeah!" Billy said, running from one end of the porch to the other and back again. Melissa leaned against the porch rail like a dainty sculpture, nodding her head earnestly. Billy added, "I'm about to starve my pants off."

Hal raised an eyebrow and looked at the boy. Billy couldn't keep a straight face to save his life and collapsed in a series of giggles. "You're a silly little man, do you know that?" Hal asked.

"Well, duh!" said Billy, rolling his eyes and giggling some more.

"Well, would you look there," said Hal, pointing out toward the street. A compact Chevrolet, comprised mostly of interlinking rust particles, was pulling into the driveway. A lighted dome rested on the flaking top of the car, advertising Maloney's Pizza Shack, 555-YUMM.

Billy's eyes were wide with wonder as a lanky, pimple-faced teenager emerged from the vehicle, a large box held horizontally at his side. Melissa squealed, clapped and ran out into the yard to meet him.

"I thought the phone was broked," said Billy.

"Broken," corrected Hal. "And it is."

"Then how—?" Billy's voice trailed away as the pizza man reached the porch.

"So how did you do it?" asked Billy, with mozzarella cheese stringing down his chin.

"Do what?" Hal asked, having long since lost the thread of conversation. He had been watching Melissa, who was dissecting each piece of pizza into its individual components before eating them one at a time. She had pizza sauce halfway up her arm with a little streak tinting her long blonde hair.

"How did you order the pizza?" asked Billy, sighing with exasperation.

"I called," said Hal, patting at the corners of his mouth with a paper napkin. "How did you think?"

"But the phone is broked—um, broken!" said Billy, tossing his fork to his plate with a clatter.

"Ah, yes," said Hal. "So it is. Maybe it was magic."

Melissa's eyes brightened while Billy's rolled upward again. "Magic?" she asked wondrously. "Really?"

"No, stupid!" said Billy.

"Don't call your sister stupid," chastised Hal.

"Well, it sure wasn't magic. That's dumb," said Billy. "That's TV stuff."

"All right, then how did I do it?" challenged Hal.

Billy folded his arms across his chest and deliberated. After a moment, he sighed. "I don't know. Tell me."

"It was magic," insisted Melissa.

"It sure was," said Hal, smiling at his granddaughter. He turned to Billy and winked. "I'll tell you later," he whispered.

Even though Molly allowed the children to stay up until 9:30, Melissa inevitably dropped off around 8:30, no matter how hard she fought it. Billy, on the other hand, could have probably gone on until 11:00 without missing a beat. His energy was exhausting to watch. Hal found it most efficacious to tell the boy stories. He supposed it was a sort of hypnotism, lulling the child to the brink of consciousness and then pushing him over the edge.

Billy liked adventures. He also liked scary stories. His favorites were a combination of the two. Hal always made his selections carefully; he didn't want the boy to have nightmares, for Superman's sake! He hoped he wouldn't be pushing the envelope tonight. It was a good thing Melissa had already fallen asleep. She had nightmares at the slightest provocation.

Hal inspected Billy after his shower and sent him back to brush his teeth again. (Pizza sauce was still evident on the boy's breath.) Afterward, he tucked him into his bright red-white-and-blue bed, pulling the Superman sheets up to the boy's chin. Hal had long ago set up a room for each of the children in his big, empty house.

"So, tell me," Billy said.

"Tell you what?" asked Hal, settling into the overstuffed armchair that was positioned near the head of the bed.

"Grandpa!"

"Oh, all right! Let me dim the light, and you get settled," said Hal, reaching up and darkening the desk lamp that hung its head out like a goose from the headboard.

"It was in a neighborhood very much like this one that it happened. As a matter of fact, it was a family very much like this one."

"What are you talking about?" asked Billy, struggling to his elbows. "How does this explain how you ordered the pizza?"

Hal looked at him sternly. "It's my way or goodnight to you, young man."

Billy flopped back on his pillow and stuck his bottom lip out a little. The corners of Hal's mouth curled upward almost imperceptibly. "Okay," Billy said. "Go on."

"All right then. Where was I? Oh, yes. It was a hot summer, very much like this one. The family was called Pitts, I think. Yes, that's it. A mom, a dad, a brother and a sister. Anyway, on a particularly hot day, wouldn't you know the air-conditioning went out. Mr. Pitts was at work and the kids were at the swimming pool.

"Mrs. Pitts had a big party planned for that night—lots of important people, like Mr. Pitts's boss and the president of the company, too. It wouldn't do to have the air-conditioning broken, now, would it?"

Billy shook his head.

"So, Mrs. Pitts called for a repairman. They were very busy. Apparently, lots of folks' air-conditioners had broken down that week, but they said they would send someone out as soon as possible.

"Mrs. Pitts—I believe her name was Prunella—went about her business, tidying the house and preparing the main course in the slow cooker. The house was every bit of ninety degrees, and she had opened the doors and windows so fresh air could get in through the screens. As she was dusting the mantel in their living room, she saw a fellow in a dark green uniform approaching the front door. He was carrying a metal toolbox—you know, like the one I keep my screwdrivers in—and Prunella went to meet him.

"'Oh, thank heaven!' she said to the man. 'Maybe my party will be saved after all! Come on in and see what you can do to get that blasted thing running.'" Hal's voice went comically falsetto as he imitated the woman. Dropping back

13

to his normal inflection, he added, "If Prunella had been paying attention, she might have seen the momentary look of confusion on the man's face, but she was lost in her own thoughts, worrying about how quickly time was getting away from her. She had to have time to make herself presentable too, you know. So, she pointed to the door of the basement and returned to her chores."

Billy sighed impatiently. "The phone, Grandpa, the phone."

"I'm getting there," said Hal. "Anyway, over at the pool, the children swam until they couldn't swim anymore. The girl, Melinda—about the same age as your sister—was going home with a friend to spend the night. The boy, Charlie— about your age—was going to a Cub Scout meeting and was staying the night with a fellow Scout. Trouble was, as Charlie started collecting his things from his locker in the changing room, he realized he hadn't brought his uniform with him. He told his friend he would have to stop by his house first and get it before he came over.

"When Charlie approached his house on his bicycle, he saw that all of the doors and windows had been closed. Apparently, the air-conditioner repairman had been able to get the unit working again. Charlie laid his bicycle on the sidewalk by the porch and bounded up the stairs, giving the doorknob a quick twist as he propelled himself forward. Guess what happened?"

Billy shook his head, not caring to hazard a guess.

"The door didn't budge, and Charlie ran right into it. WHAM!" said Hal, clapping his hands together loudly.

Billy laughed and echoed, "WHAM!" He clapped his little hands, too.

"Well, Charlie didn't think it was too funny. He had stubbed his nose and nearly fallen down! Besides that, Prunella never kept the door locked, and Charlie knew she hadn't planned to go anywhere that day. He guessed she must be upstairs taking a bath and had decided to lock the door while she was in the tub.

"The Pitts kept an extra key hidden along the underside of the porch swing, and Charlie knew just where to look. He let himself into the house and was immediately greeted by a wave of sweltering heat."

Billy interrupted, "Sweltering?"

"Yes. Thick like a big wool blanket," said Hal.

"Okay."

"Anyway, he walked through the living room, past the dining room, and then into the kitchen, but there was no sign of Prunella. The slow cooker was still cooking away on the counter, the heavenly smells of roast beef wafting through the hot air. Steam rose from other pots on the stovetop, and Charlie immediately sensed that something was not right. Prunella would never have left the stovetop on if she had to go out.

"So, careful as he could be not to make a sound, Charlie slowly climbed the stairs," said Hal, pausing for dramatic effect.

"Was she dead? Did he find her dead?" asked Billy, his eyes twinkling in anticipation.

Hal narrowed his eyes and looked at the boy. "Dead? What kind of babysitter do you take me for? Would I tell you a story about a dead mother and send you off to bed? I don't think so."

"Well, where was she?"

"Hold your horses, I'm getting there. When Charlie got to the landing of the second floor, the feeling that something was amiss had grown, and he wondered if he should turn around and run away. But he worried about his mother, and he felt like he should make sure she wasn't somewhere in the house, hurt and unable to respond.

"Careful not to make a sound, Charlie tip-toed down the hall toward his parents' bedroom. The door had been pulled to, and Charlie lightly tapped a knuckle against it. 'Hello?' he whispered.

"He jumped when he heard a thump from the other side of the door, like something somewhat heavy had dropped to the floor. Before he lost his nerve, he twisted the knob and threw open the door. What do you think he saw?" asked Hal.

"His dead mother!" exclaimed the boy.

"I told you that I don't tell dead mother stories," said Hal.

"Oh, right. Um, a pirate?"

"What would a pirate be doing running loose in a residential neighborhood? Pirate stories tend to be set at sea."

"I don't know! Tell me!" implored Billy.

"Well, it was his mother, alright," said Hal. "She was bound to one of the dining room chairs by furnace tape, of all things. She also had a big strip across her mouth. She had managed to lift her feet a little and drop them back to the floor, which was the sound Charlie had heard.

"Charlie crossed the room and, as gently as he could, pried the tape from his mother's mouth. 'Charlie!' she whispered. 'There's a burglar somewhere in the house. You have to get out of here. Go get the police!'"

"A burglar?" Billy asked incredulously.

"That's right," said Hal, leaning back in his chair and crossing one leg over the other. "The air-conditioning repairman was no air-conditioning repairman. Prunella had been so anxious to get hers fixed in time for her party that she didn't ask to see any identification. The gentleman had been staking out the neighborhood for hours, and Charlie's house, with its doors standing open and all its windows raised, was too much temptation for the thief to resist. He had to at least have a look, you see. Well, wouldn't you know that Prunella had spotted him when he had least wanted to be spotted? She invited him right in. He returned the favor by forcing her to haul one of the dining room chairs up to her own bedroom where he promptly bound and gagged her, and then scavenged the house for things to steal. What's more important, he was still in the house. Fortunately, Charlie hadn't crossed his path downstairs, but that had only been dumb luck.

"Charlie started to pick at the tape on his mother's wrist, but she told him, 'No! There's no time. You have to go and get the police!' Charlie's eyes wandered to the phone, thinking it might be best to place a quick call to 911, but he could see from where he stood that the face of the phone had been entirely smashed. Without further protest, he turned and left the room. He hoped his mother would be safe until he returned.

"It was once he was in the hallway that he heard the movement downstairs—heavy footsteps against the hardwood floors. He knew that the thief was walking right below him, near the foot of the stairs. There was no way for Charlie to get past him without being seen."

Billy's eyes were wide, and his mouth was open—just a little. "What did he do, Grandpa? What did he do?"

Hal smiled. "Our lad Charlie was a clever little fellow. First, he checked the telephone extension in the hallway. The face of that phone had been smashed, as well. He lifted the receiver and heard a dial tone, nonetheless. He pressed the jagged plastic which had once been the '9' button, but there was no tone in his ear. The dialing mechanism had been destroyed."

"Just like Melissa did to the phone in the kitchen!" Billy noted excitedly.

"More or less," said Hal. "But by now, Charlie hears the heavy sounds of the man's work boots climbing the stairs. As far as Charlie knows, the burglar doesn't even know that he's inside the house. If nothing else, he should have the element of surprise on his side. Still, Charlie was a six-year-old boy, and the intruder was at least of an appropriate age and stature as to impersonate, even if unintentionally, an air-conditioner repairman. This meant that a physical altercation might prove unwise."

"Altercation?" Billy asked, his nose scrunched up inquisitively.

"A row, fisticuffs, a fight," said Hal, watching the boy's expression as it reached enlightenment. "So, Charlie had to outthink the villain. As the footsteps continued to near,

Charlie sneaked down the hallway to the guest bedroom at the rear of the house. Prunella always kept the room ready for unexpected company, and she had decided some time ago that as a matter of courtesy, guests should have access to the telephone without having to leave their room. In other words, there was another phone extension in there.

"Charlie hoped for more dumb luck, that the phone might still be in one piece, but alas—it was not. Its face had been caved in, too. Still, Charlie grabbed the phone and crawled underneath the bed, dragging it with him."

Hal uncrossed his legs and raised his elbows, linking his fingers behind his head, smiling at his grandson. "That's some story, huh? Let's turn the lights off now and send you off to sleep."

Billy sat straight up. "What? No! You have to tell me what happened."

"What happened?" Hal asked absently.

"To the Pitts! What happened next?"

"Oh, all right," said Hal, unclasping his hands and leaning forward in the chair. "About ten minutes later, the police arrived and arrested the burglar. Turns out he had been doing his afternoon robberies for several weeks in that area, and the police were mighty glad to have finally caught up with him."

He volunteered no more information and watched Billy's face go from bewilderment to ponderousness to impatience, all in a span of about ten seconds.

"How did he make the call?" Billy begged.

"Very simple," said Hal. He got up from the chair and crossed the room to where Billy's desk was. Hal had furnished it from garage sales, building a "play" office for his grandson (although it turned out Melissa most often used it). There was an ancient desk lamp, a cast iron manual typewriter and a gutted rotary telephone he had bought for a quarter. It was the telephone in which he was interested, plucking it up and carrying it over to the bed.

"Have you ever heard of Morse Code, Billy?" asked Hal.

Billy sighed. "I'm a Cub Scout, for Superman's sake! Of course, I've heard of Morse Code."

"Don't get snippy. I was just asking," said Hal. "See, nowadays, folks are used to fancy gadgets of all sorts. Did you know that early automobiles were started by turning a crank that stuck straight out of the front of the car?"

"No way," said Billy doubtfully.

"Yes way," insisted Hal. "I would not kid my one and only grandson."

"Would you kid Melissa?"

"You bet. There are lots of things that we just take for granted today. Take for instance, did you know that a television set used to only come with twelve channels and a UHF band?"

"UHF?" asked Billy.

"Oh, it doesn't matter—you could never get anything on it anyway. Point is, most of your TV came in on channels two through thirteen, and since cable wasn't around, you had to rely on an antenna. This meant you really only got about three to five TV stations. Can you imagine that?"

Billy shook his head, his mind trying to picture a world before Nick Jr.

"What's more, if you wanted to change the channel, you had to get right up off of your lazy butt and turn the knob."

"The knob?"

Hal chuckled. "That's right, the knob. Everything's done on circuits, nowadays. You want to change the channel? You press a button. You want to change the channel from where you sit on the couch? You press a button. You want to fix dinner in the microwave? You press a button. Do you see where I'm going with this?"

Billy's face was comically vacant, apparently still disturbed with the notion of prehistoric television.

Hal placed the phone on the bed in front of Billy. "What do you notice about this telephone?" he asked.

Billy studied it then said, "It doesn't have no buttons."

"Any buttons," corrected Hal. "And you're right, it does not. It is a telephone with a dial."

"I've seen those before," said Billy. "On television."

"That's right," said Hal. "I'm sure you have. And they operate on today's telephone systems just as well as the pushbutton phones to which we have grown far more accustomed. You just put your finger in the hole that corresponds to the number you wish to dial and turn the dial clockwise until you meet the metal stopper. See?"

"Yes, Grandpa," said Billy impatiently. "I could figure out how to dial a phone, I should think."

Hal chuckled again. "I suppose you could, my boy. Listen very carefully while I dial a '5'." Hal put his finger into the dial and turned it. "Do you hear the clicking sound? It's not Morse Code, but it's a similar concept. Listen carefully while I do it again." He repeated the maneuver, slowing the dial's counterclockwise return by leaving his finger in the hole. Billy counted five clicks.

"What you probably didn't know is that those five clicks can be replicated like this," said Hal, lifting the receiver and tapping the plungers upon which it had rested five times in quick succession. "When the plungers are down, such as when the telephone is hung up, the line is disconnected, but with the receiver lifted, when you group a series of clicks together on the plunger, it is just like dialing the number on the face."

"So that's how Charlie used the phone?" asked Billy.

"Exactly," said Hal, standing and returning the phone to the little desk. "That's also how I called for the pizza this evening. Charlie simply lifted the receiver and tapped the plunger ten times. He had learned how in the Cub Scouts, from one of the troop leaders. When the operator answered, he quietly explained that he needed the police immediately, and she dispatched them right away."

Hal leaned over the bed and kissed his grandson on the forehead, pulling his sheets up and then turning off the gooseneck lamp. "I shall have to replace my telephone tomorrow. Melissa really did a number on the keypad with the spilled juice."

"She breaks everything."

"Billy."

"Well, she does," said Billy, nestling deeper into his pillow.

"So did you learn anything from my little story?" asked Hal.

"Never let anyone into your house unless you are absolutely sure who they are," said Billy firmly.

"Right-o," said Hal. "And you should never make that decision. Always get your mom or dad. Anything else?"

"Always keep your doors locked," said Billy.

"Good, good," said Hal. "Anything else?"

Billy grinned, his eyes glistening in the near darkness. "Yep. I know what I'm going to do for the science fair this year. Can you find me an old phone that's gots more guts than that one?"

"That has more guts than that one," corrected Hal.

"Grandpa!"

"Good night," Hal said, smiling to himself as he closed the door.

BORN UNDER A BAD SIGN

Some folks have a run of bad luck; a plague of misfortune if you will. I believe my birth must have been signified by some extraordinary unholy alignment of the planets, the like of which happens only once in a millennium. That night, as the skies filled with lightning and thunder, and rain poured forth, I'm sure a jackal laughed, somewhere far in the distance. I really believe I must have been born doomed.

My name is Matthew Roderick Gentry.

My mother had died during childbirth. You go ahead and try to tell me that isn't a horrific burden to bear from the moment of your first innocent breath up to and including the present day. My father has silently blamed me from the beginning. It was always the look in his eyes. I don't recall him ever actually putting it in words, per se, but the look in his eyes was unmistakable. I had two older brothers and an older sister. He never looked at them that way. I had taken his beloved wife away, and the resentment he felt for me had always burned the air between us. For the most part, I steered clear of him, learning those lessons early in life and keeping a low profile until after I graduated high school. I never saw him much afterwards. He now sits in a retirement home where he's been for the past fifteen years, rocking in a chair, staring out the window. The home's probably not five miles from here, but I don't see the point in going. I went once, early on in that first year, because Garnett, my sister, and Nina, my wife, had tag-teamed me in the kitchen one morning over breakfast.

"The doctors say Dad's best chance for recovery is for us to spend time with him. Talk to him or read to him. I know it seems strange, like he doesn't even know we're there, but the doctor said we could be getting through subconsciously," Garnett said as she sipped coffee. "Roger and I have gone with the kids no less than three times a week, and Jack and Larry have been by several times with their families and grandkids, but I really think you're the missing link." She fixed her eyes on me.

"Honestly, Garnett," I said. "You make it sound like we're having a séance over the old man to bring him back from the other side." It was lame and pretty cold, but I really didn't know what else to say. Garnett, Jack and Larry had never understood the void between Dad and me. They thought I was imagining it, martyring my own cause. Surely, my father's serious medical condition could only worsen. The man was seventy-five and had suffered a series of strokes. For heaven's sake, I was forty-six myself and pouting like a petulant child who hadn't gotten his way in decades. My entire family believed this about me, and I was ashamed of the man I had become.

"Matthew," Nina said, her voice cutting the morning air like ten-inch fingernails across a mile-long blackboard. "You're being an ass. Grow up! Your brothers and sister need your help, and so does your father. You'll go."

And that was that. Nina had spoken, and I would go. And go I did, that very evening. But only once. I didn't care what they thought of me after that.

My father sat in his wheelchair, aimed as always at the window. It was raining that night, too, I think. Funny how the soundtrack of my life so often seems to be borrowed from some cheesy old horror flick. I hadn't been in the same room with the man since my wedding. He sat at the back of the church, not in front with the family. I found that disturbing. Wouldn't you? That had been twenty-six interminable years ago. What was I supposed to say?

I don't remember exactly what I did say. I'm sure it was some prattle about the weather, or "How 'bout them Browns?"–something equally vacuous and meaningless. It was the breadcrumbs with which we turn a half-pound of ground beef into a pound-and-a-half of meatloaf.

The sight of the old man was disturbing. He seemed to have shrunk, and not just a little. His once powerful arms were thin and spindly with loose flesh sagging beneath. His once firm and chiseled face was lined and hollow. His eyes had sunken into his head, and he had no teeth, real or otherwise. He had had his own teeth at my wedding, I think. I can't really remember.

Anyway, I turned his chair around to get a good look at him. A bolt of lightning had lent a brief pulsing light to his profile. I really couldn't bear it. He couldn't say a word, or blink an eye once for yes, twice for no—oh no, nothing like that. Instead, his face was frozen in that look! The only communication he could offer to the whole wide world was directed at me and only me. It was a reminder I wasn't off the hook yet.

I left immediately. To hell with Garnett and the others. Once the bad seed, always the bad seed. I haven't seen my father since, but he has thus far refused to die, so I suppose he still sits in the window, sending that look out in search of me.

29

I really hadn't wanted to go home. Nina would be there. She was always there. Why I had ever married that woman, I'll never know. The only thing about our marriage I still enjoyed was our anniversary. This was because each year, in celebration of that black day, I have tried to kill her. Each year she had avoided the Grim Reaper, and each year I would try again.

Oh, no, not at first, I suppose. If it had been this horrible in the beginning, I would never have subjected myself to her interminable whining and bitching. We had met when we were in college. Nina had been a voluptuous girl, studying theater. She had large breasts, full hips and a slender waistline, just the sort of woman featured in movies and on magazine covers. Her mousy brown hair had been bleached to a Marilyn Monroe blonde and styled similarly. She was self-confident and self-assured. She was going to go to Hollywood and be the next Big Thing. The problem was, she couldn't act. I wasn't much better myself, fake plastic smiles painted across my face whenever she would ask for a critique of any of her completely uncharismatic performances.

We were cruelly pulled together by the Fates one fall semester by, of all things, a play I had written. It was my purpose in college. I had daydreamed my childhood away. My fantasy was to become a writer. No one needed to know anything about me. In my writing, I could become someone else, maybe someone with a mother. Having never met my own, there has always been a cold, empty space deep inside me, a space that should have been filled with memories of the woman who would protect me with her life, if necessary. This space for me was a black void. I had always envied the other students just a little. Okay, maybe a bit more than a little.

Nonetheless, Nina was the star of my little piece of claptrap, and she had been difficult from the onset. She frequently wanted to change her lines because she had not felt her character would say such things. I often wondered if it was because she could not pronounce such things, but I was green, and she was the star. Even if it was just a community college theater production, it was the most important thing in the world to me at the time. It's funny how we can convince ourselves we are far more important in the Grand Scheme than we truly are. Here I was, this twenty-year-old kid, thinking I was on the fast track to the Big Time. I had actually successfully completed a play and was certain anyone with any connections whatsoever who read it or saw it would run screaming to New York declaring its insightful brilliance. Surely there was bound to be someone with connections in the audience at least one night during the play's run.

But I'm getting off track. Nina worked with me on these last-minute script changes almost nightly. She had been such a hard ass with everyone on set, but with me, in private, she flirted and batted her eyes and cooed like a sweet little bird. She asked if I wouldn't mind too awfully terribly if she changed this or that, and I told her, "Shucks, ma'am, you just do any old little thing you want." I was cattle being corralled.

On the opening night of the play (which, by the way, received a rather chilly reception), Nina and I ran into each other at the cast party. The party was lively enough, considering Caroline, the woman who played Nina's mother, had forgotten roughly half of her lines, and Nina had chewed the scenery into submission. The champagne that the cast and crew collectively purchased was free-flowing, and there was a certain heat in the air. Nina and I found comfort with each other that night.

The play closed after only two weeks. I didn't see Nina for a while afterward. I had sequestered myself in my dormitory room, seeking inspiration for my next work. I had been savaged by the critics, the thin skin of my ass still baring fresh bite marks. I truly believe my creative self committed suicide one of those evenings. I haven't had an idea worth putting to paper since then.

I really never expected to see Nina again. I knew our night together had not really meant anything. It had been alcohol inspired. Hell, Nina had probably already forgotten my name. So, I was very surprised to see her standing at my dormitory door one stormy afternoon, about four weeks after the play had closed.

She looked terrible. Her blond hair was hanging around her shoulders, dripping rainwater in the hallway. She had applied mascara earlier in the day, but it had bled into skidmarks under her eyes. I couldn't tell if they were caused by the rain or her tears, but she had been crying. The skin beneath was puffy and red.

"Nina?" I asked. "Are you all right?"

"Do I look all right?" she snapped. "No. I'm not all right. You're not all right. Nothing is ever going to be right again." Her eyes were dull and empty, and tears were flowing again.

I smiled stupidly at her, unable to grasp the depth of her despair. "Whatever it is, it can't be that bad."

"Not that bad?!" she shrieked. "Our lives are over."

My stupid smile would just not go away.

She went on, "I'm pregnant."

Pregnant. My smile finally bid adieu.

There was no question whatsoever of what to do. In those days, a man took responsibility for his actions. I had no desire to disgrace Nina's family nor my own, so we quickly made wedding plans.

I didn't return to college after that semester, and neither did Nina. Our individual fates had been unexpectedly altered and jammed roughly together. I had taken a job as a milkman for the local dairy while Nina sat on her ever-widening ass and watched television all day long. We barely made enough money to keep our heads above water. Our finances were more an obstacle course than a budget, and I had no idea how we were going to manage once the baby was born.

It was a needless worry. During the sixth month of Nina's pregnancy, as a particularly angry thunderstorm raged against the night sky, Nina had gone into premature labor. She had been in excruciating pain. Since we could not yet afford our own, I had to borrow my brother's car and drive through sheets of rain with Nina screaming in the backseat the whole way.

By the time we had reached the hospital, we knew things were going terribly wrong. The doctors worked feverishly, but the baby was stillborn, and Nina had almost died from hemorrhaging on the table. In the end, the doctors had been forced to do an emergency hysterectomy to save her life. The hysterectomy became my second albatross. Nina's career was over. Nina's chance of motherhood was over. It was all my fault.

At first, the bitterness toward me wasn't apparent. Oh, sure, Nina had a blue spell when she first returned home from the hospital. But then we had what was probably the most satisfactory period in our entire marriage. Nina's need to be a mother and my own need to know the mother I never had perverted into a single need to fulfill a parent-child relationship. Nina had taken care of me, and I had allowed myself to be taken care of. It was kind of nice. Of course, it didn't last.

I really thought I was keeping my end of the bargain. I plodded off to work every morning, eventually becoming a supervisor at the dairy. Nina had discovered how to spend proportionally to my income, and you know, I really didn't care. Nina could have everything if she would just take care of me.

It started with the nagging. Her warm, theatrically trained voice had given way to a nasally sort of bark. "Matthew! For heaven's sake, stop leaving your underpants on the banister!" Or "Matthew! I damned well nearly broke my foot on this bowling ball of yours. Why can't you put anything away?" She always said my name as if it were two words, and it frankly irritated the hell out of me.

Everything had an assigned place in the house. The underpants belonged in the hamper, and the bowling ball belonged on the top shelf in the closet. The newspaper belonged in a wicker basket beside my recliner, not around the base of the toilet. The dirty dishes belonged in the sink, not tucked under the edge of the couch.

I really don't want to give the wrong impression. I wasn't born a slob. But these funny little habits develop if they're allowed to, and in the first five years of our marriage, Nina's maternal sheltering had enabled me to turn into a rather lazy fellow. Oh, sure, I see it clearly now, but then I had been completely oblivious.

It was at our fifth anniversary party when I received quite a rude awakening. We rarely had company over, but Nina had gone all out. She invited my brothers and sister, my boss and several co-workers. She invited her bridge club and several women whom I did not know. Our little house was filled to capacity. We had rented one of those eight-foot folding tables and set it up in our living room, pushing all of our threadbare furniture back against the walls.

Dinner, I believe, was roast turkey and all the things you might expect with it. My sister had commandeered the kitchen and wouldn't let Nina do a thing. As we settled at the table, Nina had tapped her fork against her wineglass, and everyone quietened. Through the table's pressed wood surface, I felt the rumble of thunder rolling outside.

"I would like to make a toast," she said. She raised her glass and looked down at me. I had never seen her look at me quite like this, with such disgust; it was very reminiscent of the gaze my father had so perfected. "As you all know, Matthew and I are celebrating five long years together." She had paused and looked at me, a smile borne of pity playing at her lips. "I have high hopes for the coming year." She patted me on the shoulder. "I hope this is the year you get the promotion that cheap bastard of a boss won't give you." She smiled smugly at Mr. Penrod, my boss, who was deep crimson red from the collar of his shirt to up and over the top of his bald head. "I hope this is the year we can afford a flat screen television. I hope this is the year you learn to stop peeing on the rim of the toilet. I hope this is the year you stop using the banister as a tree for hanging your filthy underpants!" Nina slammed her wineglass down and stormed off to our bedroom, leaving in her wake a roomful of stunned guests and one mortified spouse who had just decided that his wife must die.

You might wonder why I wouldn't just divorce her and be done with it. Nina was born and raised a devout Catholic. The concept of divorce was an abomination. We had made a vow, and we would see it through. Until death us do part.

It isn't as easy as they make it look in the movies. I am really a very quiet and gentle man. A man like me doesn't suddenly become homicidal overnight. It wasn't as if I had immediately headed to the basement to load my shotgun and emerge in a blaze of gunfire. No, instead, I decided to carefully ponder the possibilities. I would make a bit of game of it.

Three hundred and sixty-four days a year, I was my normal, meek self, plodding off to work on weekdays, bowling on Tuesday and Thursday evenings, listening to Nina pick and pick and pick at my many failures every day. But on that one magical day per year, our anniversary, I would attempt to kill Nina. It would be an annual venture until I finally got it right.

Anniversaries six through ten, I tried the same method, which was inspired by Russian Roulette. Early on the mornings of those anniversaries, I crept into the kitchen and emptied the silver saltshaker from our dining room table. I refilled it with rat poison and returned it to its normal position. Then I had waited. Nina frequently salted her food and would surely use the tainted receptacle. However, each of these five anniversaries had gone by without incident. The morning after each, I had emptied the poison, washed the container, and returned its normal salt content.

Of course, I would have been caught had the poison succeeded. I didn't say I was any good at this. But at this point, the part of me that wanted her dead was willing to sacrifice the part of me that would serve the sentence. After five failures, I needed to pause and regroup.

I have to admit, by then I was a little obsessed. I decided with a full year to plan, it was ridiculous to needlessly expose myself to prosecution. I had been an imaginative fellow once, and surely, I could do a better job of trying to protect myself. I began going to the library regularly, reading every murder mystery I could get my hands on. Reading these bits of pulp revived a specter of the writer in me. Many of the devious plots were too complex for consideration. A surprising number I found entirely implausible. Ultimately, I decided I should script my own plot, in perverse tribute to my former ambition.

In theory, this is all well and good, but I was still suffering from the same blasted writer's block that ended my career so many years beforehand. For the next several years, every scheme I cooked up had been so riddled with holes I found myself at the last minute swapping the contents of the salt container when the exalted day arrived. Again, I realized should my plan succeed, I would undoubtedly be caught, but Nina had an unerring knack for being particularly cruel in the weeks before each of these anniversaries. I didn't care if I got caught. It would have been worth it.

Nina and I had been married for twenty-five years by the time I finally had a decent idea. I determined that whatever happened, it should appear to be an accident, of course. Anyone who has read anything knows the bereaved spouse is always the first suspect, should the corpse be bullet-riddled, strangled or stabbed. Although brutal, random murders most certainly do occur, as a motive, they constitute a relatively small percentage of all homicides. Apparently, the larger percentage is committed by the very same person who had once loved the victim with all of his or her heart. I find that ironic.

At a glance, accidental death may seem to be an easy undertaking. It surprised me how many factors played into an "accidental" death. It wasn't at all like those old cartoons, where an anvil would be precariously perched atop a cliff ledge to be sent plummeting to the earth just as that crazy Roadrunner came zipping up the road underneath. The question was where to place the anvil, if you will. I could suspend an ax from a hook over the front door, rigged to swing down when the door was opened and plant itself in her now-plump midsection as she entered the house. But you tell me, how many houses have you been in where an ax is suspended by hooks in the ceiling by the front door? Me, I don't think I've seen one. It was a matter of plausibility. Every detail had to seem natural. The accident had to seem like a cruel twist of fate and nothing more.

Just last year, the day before our twenty-fifth anniversary, I realized I had been overcomplicating the whole process all along. The more elaborate the plan, the easier it would be to fail. On that morning, I got out of bed a little earlier than usual, reaching the downstairs before Nina. We had maintained separate bedrooms for some years by then. It was a Sunday morning, and I knew Sunday was Nina's normal day for doing laundry. Our machines were located in the moldy and damp basement, another source of annoyance for Nina. I decided to take a length of very fine fishing line and stretch it across the path of the rickety stairs. Nina always trundled down the stairs with the clothes hamper in front of her. She would never see the line and, with any luck at all, would break her neck when she tumbled to the concrete floor of the basement below. I would creep up to my own bedroom and go back to bed, waiting for the colossal disturbance of Nina's girth bouncing down the stairs. Once I heard the joyous sound, I would race down to the basement, quickly remove the fishing line and then continue down the stairs to my poor sweet Nina's aid. It would be deemed an accident and I would live in

41

blissful peace for the rest of my days, a mourning widower. I sigh to this day just thinking of the simplicity.

Ah, but nothing ever goes according to plan, does it? After stringing the line and giving myself a smug pat on the back, I crept back up to my room with visions of sugarplums dancing in my head.

As the next half hour crawled by, I sat on my bed, awake and alert. Then came the sounds of Nina shuffling out into the upstairs hallway, dragging the clothes hamper from her room. She was getting closer to my room, so I slipped back under the covers and feigned slumber. She threw the door open and entered briskly, stooping here and there to collect my various garments which were strewn across the floor. She muttered under her breath the whole time as she tossed them into the hamper and slammed the door behind her.

I pulled myself out of bed and pressed my ear to the closed door. I almost held my breath, waiting for that last glorious shriek. It occurred to me I would not have to shed crocodile tears at her funeral; my tears would be real tears of joy.

And then it had come. There was a shrill cry followed by a series of thumps. I froze in place, unable to fully comprehend what had just happened. After all these years of planning, after all my failed attempts, was this finally the year I succeeded? I was afraid to check. I stood there giggling softly.

After what I'm sure was only a few minutes, I found my arms and legs again, and exited my bedroom, heading toward the downstairs with what I hoped was a look of concern on my face. The look fell away quickly enough once I reached the bottom of the stairs. Nina was lying on the floor near the door to the basement, a rather angry red spot forming on her shin. She was propped up on an elbow, her dirty dishwater blonde hair spilling over blazing eyes. Clothing was scattered in all directions and the hamper had nearly slid all the way down the long hall to the kitchen. Tangled at her feet was my bowling ball.

"Do you see what you've done?" Nina asked pointedly.

I stood there stupidly. She was supposed to be at the bottom of the stairs, her head staring back at me, grotesquely and at an impossible angle. Yet here she was, fixing me with that look.

"I have been telling you for twenty-five years to put this bowling ball in the closet where it belongs. Can't you just do that one little thing right? When I think of everything my life could have been, everything that I could have had. Sometimes I think the only rest I'm ever going to get is when I kick the bucket," she said, struggling to her feet. Oh, if only she had known... "You can do your own damn laundry, mister. I can't be near you right now."

She left then and didn't come back for two days. I gathered the clothes, put my bowling ball on the top shelf in the closet, unstrung my fishing line and then proceeded to turn all my whites a bright pink in the wash cycle.

I had been so sure of myself. I couldn't believe things had gone so horribly astray. I was miserable, and many months passed before I even had the inkling of an idea for this year's diabolical plot. As a matter of fact, so many months passed that my anniversary was practically upon me, and I was about to revert to the old standby, the spectacularly unsuccessful rat poison scenario. It's hard to believe that was just last week.

I was on my way to work Monday morning when the brake light in the instrument panel of my old Chevy blinked red. It really pissed me off. Our mortgage was due, and it was the worst possible time to need car repair. I dropped the car off at a service station across and up the road from the dairy and walked back to work.

After I punched out that night, I walked back to the station to hear the verdict. It wasn't pretty. The master cylinder was leaking brake fluid with each pump of the brake pedal. The burly, greasy mechanic said a new master cylinder would be required and when he told me the price, I laughed hysterically.

"Buddy, there's no way I can afford this right now," I said. "You guys offer any kind of E-Z payment plan?"

"You kiddin'? We don't even take checks," he had replied. "I don't recommend you drive it any farther, though. If the cylinder goes dry, you won't have any pressure behind your brake pedal. You won't be able to stop the car."

"I'll have to take my chances," I said. "Top it off with brake fluid, and I'll take a couple extra quarts for the road."

"Whatever you say, Mac. Don't say I didn't warn you." The mechanic then headed to the rear of the shop to retrieve the brake fluid.

On my drive home, something kept niggling at my subconscious. A new plan was forming, and I didn't have much time before our next anniversary the following Monday. I spent the next several days testing the speed with which the car was expending brake fluid. By the fourth day, I determined it wasn't losing fluid quickly enough. I decided to throw caution to the wind and help it along a little.

Three days ago, on Sunday, I went out to the garage as I frequently do when I'm of a mind to avoid Nina. Nina was particularly unpleasant on laundry day. This time, however, I had a mission. I slipped into an old set of coveralls I wear when I change the oil in the cars. I used a pair of pliers to loosen the line from the master cylinder. I tested the reaction by pumping the brake pedal and was rewarded with substantial oozing of brake fluid at the point where the line was coupled to the cylinder. Now I just had to ensure Nina would use my car instead of her own.

Nina had been doing volunteer work with Meals on Wheels for the past several years. On Mondays, Wednesdays and Fridays, she took trays of unappealing slop to the elderly in nearby convalescent centers. I suppose it gave her some sense of purpose. She had an old VW station wagon in which she tooled about town. Every Monday, Wednesday and Friday evening, I had to listen to Nina complain about what a bomb the car was. Truthfully, it was a sad sight. Rust had dined on all of the wheel wells, and what had once been shiny dark green paint had dulled and peeled in the many years since we had bought the car, secondhand even then. The engine was reliable, however, but that little fact was entirely overlooked by Nina, who was far more focused on how embarrassed she was for her friends to see her piloting this glorified lawn mower.

"I know we can't afford a different car. Hell, you barely make enough to keep the roof over our heads," Nina had said. "But for heaven's sake, don't you think I could at least have a decent radio put in the car? I spend all afternoon in that heap, three days a week. I have sung to myself until I am sick of the sound of my own voice!"

Aren't we all, dear?

The radio in the station wagon was original AM equipment. It emitted a high-pitched squeal through the tinny little squawk box imbedded in the dashboard. You could tune it until your arm dropped off and only receive varying pitches of static and interference.

I decided I would tell Nina I needed to swap her cars on Monday so I could have her anniversary gift installed. I had a buddy at the dairy who had been trying to sell an old radio for some time. He advertised it on a small index card posted in our break room. It wasn't very nice, but it came with two little speakers and could at least pick up a station or two. Most importantly, it wasn't very expensive. I would need to buy the radio and have it installed just in the off-chance Nina might survive the crack-up in my car. The terrain of our little town was very hilly, and I hoped it would stack the odds in my favor that she would not. Nina drove like a bat out of hell, too, which further increased my chances for success.

Have you ever had the feeling that you know something big is going to happen? Well, that's how I felt about my anniversary this year. In the past, I had hoped my plans would come to fruition. This year, I knew I would succeed.

On Sunday evening as we sat down to dinner, I told Nina, "I need for us to trade cars tomorrow."

"What in the hell do you need my car for?" she demanded, one eyebrow raised suspiciously.

"I've got a surprise for you," I said while blowing on a steaming forkful of Hungarian goulash.

"Matthew," she whined. "Don't you think you're a little old to be playing stupid little games with me?" I raised my eyebrow in response. "If you want my car, you'll tell me what this nonsense is about."

"Well, if you really must know, I'm having a radio put in tomorrow, just like you wanted. It was going to be a surprise for our anniversary, but I guess not now," I said with exasperation. I can't help but feel any other woman might have found the suggestion of an anniversary surprise to be romantic. Not, Nina, though. Oh no.

"Well, finally," she said. "It does have a cassette player in it, doesn't it? It would be awful to be at the mercy of those foulmouthed deejays all of the time, playing the same songs over and over."

I lowered my head into my hands and began to laugh. The radio I bought didn't have a cassette player. Of course. And if it would have had one, then she would have expected a compact disc player. And if it had one of those, she would have wanted a goddamn band in the back seat, taking

48

requests. I wanted to snatch up the iron doorstop that sat beside the door to the basement stairs and bash her head in with it. I wanted the experience of pounding the life out of her. But no, I would wait...

"What's so funny?" she asked.

"'Does it have a cassette player?'" I mimicked savagely. I was surprised at both the venom and volume of my own voice. "No, it doesn't have a cassette player! It's just a simple radio. Wanna know why? That's all I can afford! I have listened to you go at me, time and again about what a failure I've been to you, how I've disgraced you to both your family and friends, how I never apply myself at work and how I'll never make enough money to see middle class with binoculars. Well, I'm sick of it! Do you hear me? Sick of it! Has it ever occurred to you that our station in life could be dramatically improved overnight if you actually went out and got a job? You do all this volunteer shit anyway, so you might as well get paid for it. Oh, but no, that would taint this saintly image of yourself you have constructed for the sole benefit of impressing your friends. Gracious lady, volunteering her assistance to the poor and the elderly. Well, I hate to tell you, but we are the poor and the elderly," I slammed my fork down and stood abruptly from the table, glaring down into Nina's shocked expression. "You will accept this damned radio with all the phony graciousness you can muster in that cheesecake-bloated body of yours. I will leave my keys by the door in the morning."

With that, I stormed upstairs to my room and slammed the door. Inside, I was all atwitter. I had never said anything so bold or forward in all my life, and it felt better than I had ever imagined. I was surer than ever my plan would finally succeed this year!

The next morning, we ate breakfast in silence, Nina never once looking in my direction. It was just as well. I was afraid she could peer into my eyes and see what I really had planned. I left for the dairy in her old rattletrap, hoping and praying I would never have to lay eyes on the woman again.

It was a glorious day. The sun shone bright and warm as I dropped Nina's VW at the service station to have the radio installed. I had purchased the radio the day before and brought it with me.

The mechanic remembered me from last week. "Did you get your brakes fixed?" he asked.

"Not yet. Soon," I replied, handing him the radio from the rear of the wagon. "I'll just pick the car up on my way home tonight."

"Roger dodger. It'll be ready," he said, already climbing into the cabin of the car.

At work, Mr. Penrod was in an especially good mood, complimenting my reorganization of the delivery routes. He intimated I might be up for a salary increase very soon. For the rest of the day, I went through the paces of my normal routine with a big dumb smile on my face. Quitting time seemed days away, but it eventually arrived, just as the sky began to cloud over.

By the time I collected the car and drove home, rain had started falling, first softly before gaining momentum. Lightning and thunder pierced the evening sky as I pulled the VW into the driveway. The Carpenters were singing wholesomely over the tinny twin speakers that had been installed.

Immediately, I knew something had gone wrong when I opened the garage door. My Chevy was still parked where I had left it that morning. I cannot describe the disappointment I felt just then. I felt so helpless. I would never be free of this woman. I suspected if I were to actually succeed in offing her, she would simply reincarnate and reattach to me like a poltergeist, whining and hounding and nagging me until I was cold in the ground myself.

I unlocked the front door and peered into the dark house. The living room was immediately to the left, and straight ahead was the hallway which led to the kitchen. Both were inky black. It was unlike Nina to leave all the lights out. As a matter of fact, it was unlike Nina to leave any of the lights out. The electric bill was not her concern. As I closed the door behind me, I pulled the chain of the standing lamp just inside, which filled the area with artificial light.

I was startled to find Nina, lying in a heap in the hallway. Her arms and legs were splayed out unnaturally, and she was not moving. I crept closer and could soon see her head was resting atop the iron doorstop that held the basement door open. Her head was bloody and pulpy, and the doorstop seemed to be slightly implanted. The top of her scalp was lacerated, too, with little ribbons of blood streaking through her hair and down her forehead. In one clasped hand she held my car keys, and in the other was a set of jumper cables. I noticed my bowling ball was in the back floor of the closet, a tiny bright red splotch covering the giant "B" for Brunswick.

I impulsively reached for the ball and pulled it out. It suddenly became clear what had happened. Nina had been ready to leave this morning, and my damned car wouldn't start! She had come back into the house to get the jumper cables we keep in the top of the closet and probably to call one of our neighbors for a jump-start. When she had pulled the cables, she had inadvertently pulled my bowling ball down, too. For once, I had put the ball into its rightful place. It had come down on her head, knocking her senseless. When she had fallen down, she had finished the job by impaling her temple on the doorstop. The house filled with my convulsive laughter. Nina was dead, and I hadn't done a thing!

I dropped the bowling ball back into the closet with a start, realizing I shouldn't tamper with anything. After I felt sure I could suppress any inappropriate giggling, I called 911 and an ambulance was dispatched.

At last, I was free.

When the emergency squad arrived, they confirmed her demise and transported her body away. The police appeared on the scene somewhere during the squad's resuscitative efforts and a Sergeant McElroy asked a seemingly endless stream of questions. I had the newfound confidence of innocence to bolster my ability to play the part of the bereaved husband as I proffered my theory of what had happened. When McElroy left, he offered perfunctory condolences and some mumbo-jumbo about how most deadly accidents happened at home. If there were any further questions, he would give me a call.

I slept the night through like a peaceful baby. No more would I have to listen to the sound of that woman's voice, telling me how worthless I was. It's hard to believe that was just last night.

This morning, I ate ice cream for breakfast, right from the container. I changed clothes and left my dirty underpants on the banister. I said to hell with the toilet and peed right into the bathtub. I phoned work and told Mr. Penrod what had happened, and he told me to take however much time I needed. I was entitled to five paid days off, and I planned to take them all. I spent the early afternoon driving the VW around town, the crappy little radio blasting its happy songs from the little soup can speakers and me singing off-key the whole while.

When I returned home about an hour ago, I was surprised to see a black-and-white parked in the drive. Sergeant McElroy was waiting in the driveway with a younger man who I found out later was Deputy Loomis.

"We'd like to ask you some more questions about your wife's death, Mr. Gentry," said the sergeant, in a most officious manner. "Can you come down to the station?"

Although surprised, I couldn't imagine I had anything to fear. After all, I hadn't done anything. "Certainly, Sergeant McElroy," I said. "I don't need my lawyer, do I?" I added with a laugh.

Sergeant McElroy wasn't laughing. "That might not be a bad idea."

I was stunned. I didn't say a word as the officers directed me to the cruiser. What was going on?

I was taken downtown and placed in the small holding room where I am now sitting, waiting for the next round of interrogation. The room is a white box with a window looking out over the parking lot of the police station. I was read my Miranda rights and have, for the moment anyway, waived my right for legal counsel. I don't want to appear guilty, you see. I didn't do anything!

Sergeant McElroy entered the room, his dour expression still in place. After reactivating the tape recorder with which he had been recording my interview, he took the seat across the table from me and stared, long and hard.

"You and the missus didn't get along terribly well, did you?" he asked after a lengthy silence.

"I suppose we got along as well as anyone who's been married for as long as we have," I said, unable to control the fidgeting I was beginning to do.

"Hmmm," he said, his eyes fixed and unblinking. "Why did you take your wife's car yesterday morning?"

My confidence was fading, but I desperately needed to retain the appearance of innocence. "It was our anniversary," I said. "I was having a radio put in Nina's car."

"Hmmm," he said again.

I wasn't sure what the sergeant was driving at, and my patience was running thin. "You can't tell me you think I killed her," I blurted out.

"That's exactly what I think," he said.

"How in the world—? I was at work all day! You can call my boss, Alan Penrod, at the dairy. He can verify that," I protested.

"Oh, we have," the sergeant said. "We've been checking out quite a few things, actually. You and the missus had quite a row the night before the 'accident,' didn't you?"

I remembered yelling those vindicating phrases at Nina as she had interrogated me as to why I needed her car. How could the policeman know this? Tentatively, I answered, "I wouldn't say it was a row, Sergeant. It was an animated discussion."

"Well, your wife apparently thought it was more than that. When it was over, she called a Mrs. Abernathy," he said, consulting his notes. Mrs. Abernathy was the coordinator of the Meals on Wheels crews. She and Nina had been close friends for decades. "Your wife told Mrs. Abernathy she had never seen you in such a state. She said she was afraid for her life."

"Afraid of me?" I asked incredulously. "She has never been afraid of me!"

"Funny, that's not what she told Mrs. Abernathy. She said she was afraid you were going to kill her. Mrs. Abernathy thought your wife was being overly dramatic, although Nina had spoken frequently to her about how unhappy your marriage had become. She's kicking herself

56

right now because she didn't take Nina's story more seriously," he said.

"All right, sergeant," I said. "Why don't you tell me just exactly what it is that you think I've done."

"Do you know anything about car repair?" he asked. I could feel the color draining from my face.

"I suppose I've picked up a thing or two," I said.

Sergeant McElroy sat back in his chair and crossed his arms over his broad chest. "You wanna know what I think? I think that you wanted your wife to use your car because you knew it wouldn't start. The interior light had been left on and drained the battery. You knew when she went for the jumper cables in the closet, she would pull down the bowling ball you had perched on top of them. C'mon, now Mr. Gentry. Who puts his bowling ball on the top shelf of a closet?"

"That's ridiculous!" I exclaimed. "That is totally circumstantial, and there's no way you can prove a crazy thing like that."

"Perhaps not," the sergeant said. "But I think your plan was a little more complex. I don't think you had confidence that the bowling ball would definitely do her in. I think you had a backup plan, an insurance policy, so to speak. I've spoken with a mechanic at Bill's Auto. You ever use Bill's Auto?"

"Yes," I said indignantly. "That's exactly where I had the radio installed in my wife's car."

"And it's also where you were informed last week that your own car had developed a nasty little braking problem. This was the very same car you instructed your wife to use yesterday. Did you have the car fixed? No need to answer. We've examined the car. The brake lines have been loosened," the sergeant continued.

"How does this implicate me?" I asked.

"Let me ask you a question. Do these coveralls belong to you?" he asked, holding up the protective gear I always kept in the garage. There were a series of drip marks on the right sleeve, running toward the elbow. "Do I need to tell you that these stains are brake fluid? Mr. Gentry, I think you should call your lawyer."

The fight had left me. As badly as I wanted Nina dead, as surely as I would have done it myself, I truly was innocent.

As I wait for my court-appointed lawyer to arrive, I see the evening sky fill with lightning. There is a crash of thunder, and the rain is falling, yet again.

THERE GOES THE NEIGHBORHOOD

"What in the world are they *doing* over there?" George sprawled over the back of the couch, his round, ruddy face pressed against the window. He was short and fat, and the maneuver was awkward and undignified.

"Oh, for heaven's sake, George!" exclaimed Jessie, drying her hands on a brightly colored dish towel as she entered the living room. "Would you get down from there? You're going to break the back of the couch!"

"*Shhhh!*" George growled, waving absently in Jessie's direction.

She sighed, scowled and put her hands on her hips. Her husband, the always irate George Templeman, was thoroughly displeased with the real estate transaction which had recently transpired next door. The Jordans had

59

decided after fifty-odd years of living in their beautiful two-story Colonial to move to a retirement village in Florida. Harley Jordan had put the house on the market at rock bottom prices with easy terms, interested in unloading it, not making a profit. George always knew Harley Jordan had cotton balls for brains when it came to business, but this was proof positive.

The house had been snatched up immediately by Lance and Patsy Appleton, a New Age pair of middle-aged hippies without a cause. They had been moving in all morning, and George had left his post only once when his bladder threatened to give way.

"Have you ever seen so many freaky things?" George wondered aloud. "I can't even tell what half of it is! I'll bet they're into witchcraft or something."

Jessie rolled her eyes and stepped up behind George to peer over his shoulder. Patsy and Lance were carefully walking a large painting that looked like a sneeze on canvas up the long gravel drive toward the house. She wore a free-flowing paisley wrap made of gauze, and a large, floppy hat shielded her from the sun's harmful rays. Jessie couldn't help but notice the woman had enormous feet with long grubby toes straddling rubber thongs. Patsy was pencil thin and rather tall but looked wiry and strong. Lance, on the other hand, was short, round and covered with hair at every possible exposure. Heavily bearded, hairy armed and hairy backed. His chestnut mane was fastened in a braid which hung all the way down to his derriere. He wore faded jeans with holey knees, a poorly patched rear end and a t-shirt which vulgarly displayed his rounded belly and floppy breasts and the scrunched-up body hair which covered it all.

"It's just a painting, George," Jessie said, patting her husband on the shoulder.

"You call *that* a painting?" George asked with a snort. "I wouldn't use it to wipe my shoes on."

"It's modern art, dear," Jessie said. "I think it's interesting."

George whirled from the window to gape at his wife. *"Interesting?* Oh, help me out here, Jess—that's *garbage.* I'll bet that Amazon gypsy painted it with her feet."

"Oh, no, dear," Jessie said. "It's very much in style in all the bigger cities."

"Don't get me started on that," George groused. "New York, L.A., Paris—*woo-hoo!*" He twirled a finger and rolled his eyes. "Just places for all the weirdoes to gather." He turned his attention back to the window.

Jessie couldn't believe what a sour old grump George had become over the years, especially since he had retired. They had married young, when she was fifteen and he was eighteen, on his way into the Army. They had gone to school together since the first grade and had always known they would marry and raise a family of their own. George had been athletic in school and quite dashing, with a thick thatch of jet-black hair slicked back with pomade. Time had been cruel to our boy George. After his tour of duty in the Army, he had returned to Burkett, Ohio to become an official representative of the U.S. Postal Service. Years of trudging along his same route had left an undeniable mark on the man. His body had widened with age, his hair had lessened with age, and his temperament had gone out the window with age. Jessie struggled to find the boy she had once known in this troll-like man, pressed to the window and looking to start a fight.

Not with her, of course. Oh, no. Never with her. He had always been gentle as a lamb with Jessie. They had raised three wonderful children, a boy and two girls, and theirs had been a very happy home—well, except for when George had too much to drink, which truly wasn't all that often. But when he did, it was just as well to stay clear of him.

"I should put together a plate of my special orange cookies and take them over," said Jessie, turning and heading for the kitchen. "Welcome them to the neighborhood."

For only the second time that morning, George left his post by the window. He was on his feet in a second, bathrobe flapping loosely over his boxer shorts and t-shirt, wisps of his remaining gray hair dancing wildly in a ring around his head. "You'll do no such thing!" he said.

"Oh, for heaven's sake, George," said Jessie. "It's just cookies. It would be the neighborly thing to do—"

"I said no, and I mean no!" he said. "What's the matter with you, woman? Don't your head work right? Look at them Looney Tunes out there. They're probably a branch straight off the Manson family tree."

"George!" gasped Jessie, putting a hand to her chest. "What a thing to say! You don't even know these people!"

"And I can tell you right now, I'm not going to know 'em anytime soon, neither. And neither are you. And that's *final.*" George folded his beefy arms over his chest and jutted his bottom lip out stubbornly, like an insolent toddler.

"You can be such a ridiculous man sometimes," Jessie said. "What do you think they're going to do, meet me at the door with a ball bat and beat my brains out?"

"Sacrifice."

"What?"

"Well," said George, rubbing his chin. "I see you more as a sacrifice. They would probably overpower you just as soon

63

as you cleared the rose bushes—maybe with chloroform—or maybe a ball bat."

"Oh, stop it, George!"

"Then they would sacrifice you under a full moon, eat your carcass for dinner and drink your blood in the name of Beelzebub."

"George Templeman!" Jessie said, putting her hands to her ears. "That's enough!"

"Fine," said George, turning back to his perch on the couch. "But no cookies, and I mean it."

"Fine," said Jessie, turning and retreating to the kitchen.

On the third day, the animals began to arrive. George watched in amazement as countless dogs and cats began investigating their new home—as well as the Templemans' adjoining property.

"Jessie!" he bellowed, fogging the pane of glass in front of his face. "You have got to *see* this!"

Jessie was running the vacuum cleaner, but so accustomed had she become to the pitch of George's booming voice that she immediately clicked off the appliance. "Did you say something, dear?"

He gestured for her, and she crossed the room to peer over his shoulder. "Have you ever seen so many blasted animals?"

"Mmm," said Jessie. "It does seem like quite a few."

"What in the world are they running over there, a wildlife preserve?"

"Oh, George," said Jessie. "So, they're animal lovers. Big deal. Are you telling me that you hate animals now, too?"

"Of course not!" he snapped. "But I've lost count of how many they have. It's a lot, though. Oh! *Oh!"* His attention snapped back to the activity outside. "I can't believe it."

"What, dear?"

"A cow. They are bringing a cow down out of a trailer."

"Are you sure, dear?" Jessie followed George's gaze to the neighbor's drive. *"Mmm.* It *does* appear to be a cow, doesn't it?"

"There have to be laws against this! People can't just go turning their yards into Old MacDonald's Farm!"

"Well, maybe you can call Petey Markham down at city council. He should be able to help. But really, George. Is this the first impression we want to make on our new neighbors? Ask the city to zone them out? They're liable to think we're unfriendly."

"Who gives a rat's rear end what they think?" said George, exasperated. "Did they come and ask our opinion about their little jungle? *No!* What's more, they haven't even fenced off the yard! Those creatures will be all over our yard, digging holes and destroying my garden!"

"Oh, for heaven's sake, George," said Jessie. "Why don't you just go *talk* to them? I'm sure they are reasonable—"

"There is nothing whatsoever reasonable about what's been going on over there," said George. "Petey Markham is out of town on a bowling tournament. He won't be back for five more days."

"Is that so awfully long?"

"An eternity."

Jessie looked outside again and had to admit that George was right about this one. The Appletons were running a small-scale Noah's Ark, and it was rather presumptuous of them to do so without first installing appropriate fencing. Jessie sighed. She hated the thought of her lovely yard being split down the middle by a fence. In all the years that the Jordans had lived in the neighboring house, the two large yards had always flowed together, along with the Moritzes beyond the Jordans and the Wrights beyond the Moritzes. It gave a sense of warmth and neighborliness, qualities which were rare in the modern world. But still, a *cow?* Yes, a fence would be required.

"You could speak to Petey at our barbeque this weekend," she suggested. "Then he can see firsthand what's going on with all their animals. Still, I wish you'd let me go over and have a little chat with the missus. I'm sure we could resolve this silly mess over a cup of tea."

"Absolutely not," said George, his voice firm and unyielding. "I forbid it."

"But George, we could get this whole thing under control before it gets out of hand."

"It's already out of hand, or have you already forgotten the zoo outside? No, I'll talk to Petey on Saturday. Hopefully, we won't get trampled in a stampede before that." George turned back to the window. "I don't believe it."

"What? Another cow?" asked Jessie, straining to peer over George's shoulder.

"It's a goat, Jess, a *goat!* I *told* you they were into witchcraft! Doesn't a goat have something to do with the devil? Goats are sacrificed, too, I think—"

"Oh, for heaven's sake, George!" said Jessie. George was right about one thing, anyway. It *was* a goat the Appletons were leading up the drive.

By Friday morning, activity next door had slowed. The Appletons had finished moving in their bohemian belongings, and were apparently focusing their attention on the interior, positioning bean bags just so and such. George hadn't gotten a proper night's sleep since the Appletons had brought the animals, their mooing and bleating and barking maddeningly endless and endlessly maddening.

Bleary-eyed, George stumbled down the stairs and went into the kitchen, absently pouring himself a cup of coffee from the waiting coffeepot. Jessie was standing at the counter spreading dough with a rolling pin. One more quick swipe, and she reached for her biscuit cutter, deftly cutting circles and leaving little waste behind.

"Where's the Sports?" he grumbled.

"Sorry, dear," said Jessie, wiping a runaway strand of silver hair out of her eyes. "I haven't made it out to get the paper yet. Be a dear and go fetch."

After more grumbling, George headed for the front door, opening it and gazing out onto his lawn. The newspaper was supposed to be on the stoop, just outside the door, but the Newsome kid threw like a three-year-old, and the paper was more often than not in a bush near the front of the yard. George proceeded out onto the large country porch and down the wooden steps to the sidewalk. He could hear dogs growling ahead of him, and as he rounded Jessie's prized rose bushes, he saw two of the Appletons' mangy curs playing tug-of-war with what was left of his newspaper.

"Shoo! Get out of here!" barked George, waving his arms and stomping his feet in the general direction of the dogs. They growled instinctively, before making a hasty retreat to their own property. His newspaper was mauled, lying in pieces about the lawn. George could feel his blood pressure rising, filling his temples with heat. He took a step toward the paper's remains, and his foot encountered something soft, slick and ripe. George didn't possess the reflexes of his youth any longer, and he toppled to his bottom in the smelly pile.

Blinded by the rage of a warrior bound for battle, George struggled to his feet, scooped up several fragments of the paper and stormed across the yard to the Appletons'. Patsy was seated on the ground in the side yard, her legs folded impossibly over one another. Her eyes were closed, and her clasped hands were pressed vertically to her forehead as if she were contemplating something very important. Lance was hauling a bag of unidentifiable animal chow around from the other side of the house, his round, bearded face inflating and deflating with labored breath. When he saw George storming across the yard, he released his grip on the bag and approached, wiping his dirty hands on his equally dirty blue jeans.

"Howdy, neighbor!" he called, smiling and waving.

George couldn't find any words, sputtering and grunting instead while he shook his newspaper pompom at Lance.

"I'm Lance Appleton," Lance said, choosing to ignore George's histrionics. "I don't think we've had the pleasure of meeting. And you are?"

"I'm ticked off, that's who I am!" George finally managed. "Do you see what those dogs of yours have done? Look! *Look!*"

"Oh, no," said Lance apologetically. "I'm so sorry. Let me get my paper for you. Hold on."

"No!" said George. "I don't want your paper! I want those dogs behind a fence!"

"*Mmm,*" said Lance, running his fingers through his scraggly beard. "I'm afraid we can't do that."

"*What?*" George's blood pressure had skyrocketed into stroke territory, but he refused to give this hippie the satisfaction of dying in his yard.

"*Mmm,* no. Patsy—that's my wife—Patsy and I don't believe animals should be pent up. It's against the natural order."

"The natural order? The natural order of *what?*" George asked.

"Well, the natural order of the universe, of course. How would you like to spend your life in a cage? You wouldn't, of course."

"Hullo!" It was Patsy, unfolded from her lotus position and floating across the lawn in a loose-fitting tunic. Her feet were still grubby, still in sandals. She was a tall woman; the top of George's head was level with Patsy's shoulders. She walked right up to George and wrapped her bony arms around him, giving him a warm hug while he fidgeted and squirmed and looked for a way to escape. "I see you're uncomfortable with brotherly love, my friend. Please—it's just an expression of respect from one human being to another."

"Look," said George, finally breaking free from Patsy's grasp. "You whacked-out hippies can preach this free love all you want, but in the meanwhile, you'd better get a fence up. I will not tolerate your dogs chewing up my paper and crapping all over my yard."

"It's so good for the land, though," protested Lance. "It's fertilizer in its most natural state. You should consider yourself blessed."

"I'm telling you, you'd better get a fence up, you'd better keep those dogs behind that fence, and if you don't, I can't be responsible for what might happen. I've been known to leave a pan of antifreeze in the yard," said George, aiming a finger like a revolver in their general direction.

Patsy gasped and raised a hand to cover her gaping mouth. She quivered on her beanpole legs as if she were about to faint and turned her head to the side, lifting the back of her hand to shield her eyes. "I'm sorry, Lance. I need to go lie down. This gentleman has a particularly dark aura, and it's dampening my life force."

"Oh, baby," Lance lamented, concern wreaking havoc with his pudgy countenance. He extended an arm to steady his wife. "Will you be alright? Should I make you a cup of herbal tea?"

"That would be lovely," she sniffled, turning and walking toward the house. "If I don't look directly at him, it's almost bearable."

"What in the world is that fruit loop yammering about?" asked George, staring at Patsy as she retreated to the house.

"That 'fruit loop,' as you so eloquently put it, is my wife, and I would thank you to stop disparaging her," said Lance, his voice still even and warm.

"I didn't lay a hand on her!" said George, mistaking disparaging for molesting. Lance rolled his eyes in response, but George plodded on. "There are animal control laws in this area, Mr. Appleton. Either you take care of this, or I will."

George walked away in a huff, unaware of the amused smile on Lance's face. Jessie was waiting at the front door as he stomped up the porch stairs, her eyebrows raised in puzzlement.

"Those people are *unbelievable*, Jess. Couldn't care less that their dogs ripped my paper to shreds. Couldn't care less that they're doing their business in my yard. Oh, no!" ranted George, his voice then slipping into a high-pitched sing-song, *"Animals shouldn't be caged, it's against the natural order."*

"Oh, for heaven's sake, George," said Jessie, her cheeks tinted pink. She stepped forward and took George's arm, guiding him back into the house. "Would you get in here? You're running around in your *underwear!"*

George hadn't noticed that in his hurry to get the paper, he had forgotten to don his bathrobe. He had presented himself to those free loving hippies in his boxers and t-shirt. Lord only knows what kind of ideas he had given them.

Saturday was a beautiful day. The sun was shining and the temperature, although high, was not full of the sticky humidity so common to Ohio summers. George spent the morning making preparations, cleaning the grill, checking and rechecking his charcoal and lighter fluid supply, and monitoring Jessie's progress in the kitchen, where she was busily forming hamburger patties and assembling cold cuts and cheese in attractive geometric patterns on serving trays.

Twice per year, George and three of his fellow postmen collected for an outdoor cookout, bringing their wives and spending the afternoon eating, drinking beer and sharing the same old stories of life in the Service—the Postal Service, that is. Bill Myers and Petey Markham, had retired around the same time as George, which was nearly five years ago. Forrest Dickerman was in his last year of service, bringing new stories from the trenches at each of these gatherings. The men took turns hosting the events, and this time it was George and Jessie's honor.

Jessie watched from the kitchen window as George fumbled about, scanning for any canine residue which may be mining the back yard. She really didn't care much for these events. The wives were supposed to amuse themselves while the husbands exchanged tired stories, but she wasn't particularly fond of any of the women. She wished she could invite Rosie Dixon, her best friend for the past forty years, but George insisted these events be closed to outsiders, and that was how he considered anyone who wasn't a U.S. Postal Service employee, active or retired, or the wife of one or the other. Years before, these events had included the families of George's co-workers as well as his own children, but the affair had grown smaller as children graduated and married and moved away. Now, Jessie was left to her own devices for passing the time with these bitter gossipmongers, and she couldn't wait until the whole thing was over. She sighed and returned to her tasks, folding lunch meat into perfect little wedges and fanning them out on a large serving platter.

At least the Appletons had shown signs of complying with George's wishes. Rolls of chain link fencing had been delivered late Friday afternoon, and Lance and Patsy had spent the morning digging holes for the fence posts. Jessie had hoped for a nice wooden fence, perhaps painted white, but in any event, George should be satisfied that the Appletons had heeded his warning. She knew how difficult George could be and wished that he would let her go talk to the neighbors. She felt confident that she could smooth over the rough edges. Although the Appletons were no spring chickens themselves, they would surely outlive the

Templemans. She didn't want to be at odds with her next-door neighbors for the rest of her time on the planet.

Guests began arriving shortly afterward and soon enough, Jessie found herself seated at a round metal table on the brick patio, holding a tumbler of dice and preparing to take her turn at Yahtzee. George, Bill, Petey and Forrest were playing horseshoes under a tree at the far end of the long lawn, tossing back beers and getting louder as the afternoon progressed.

Beatrice (Bitzy, to her friends) Myers stubbed out a cigarette and promptly lit another. "You're dawdling, Jessica," she said.

"I'm sorry," said Jessie absently, tossing the dice to the table. "I was wondering if I should remind George to get the hamburgers on the grill."

"Are you kidding?" laughed Jane Markham, fluffing her rust-tinted beehive hairdo. "The boys are veterans at this. They'll tell us when it's dinnertime, not the other way around."

"It doesn't matter to me one way or the other," said Lana Dickerman, always bored and bothered. "I like to keep *my* figure."

"Just what are you implying?" screeched Bitzy, ever-sensitive to her bell-shaped hips.

Lana rolled her eyes. "I'm not implying anything, Bitzy— or should I say Buttzy?"

Lana and Jane burst into raucous laughter while Bitzy's face bloomed like a rose. Jessie's attention had drifted over to the Appletons', where Patsy had resumed a lotus position in the backyard, oblivious of the world around her. *She looks so calm and serene,* Jessie thought. *I'll bet she's never had a headache in her entire life.*

One by one, the other wives' eyes followed Jessie's over to the neighbors. "What in the world is she *doing?*" asked Lana, her hand fluttering to her chest, appalled.

"Maybe she has fallen and can't get up," suggested Bitzy.

"I believe it's some type of yoga," said Jessie, returning her attention to the dice tumbler and hoping to draw the others' attention away from the Appletons.

"What's she *wearing?*" asked Jane, scrunching up her nose in distaste. "Some sort of hospital gown?"

"It looks like a bed sheet with a drawstring," said Bitzy.

"And a dirty one, at that," added Lana, and the old hens began to cackle.

Jessie became aware of George, bellowing and stomping around at the rear of the yard. Bill, Petey and Forrest stood in a semi-circle around him, looking at the ground. An errant horseshoe, apparently tossed skyward in a fit of rage by George, dropped to the ground nearly crowning poor Forrest.

"What in the world—?" said Bitzy.

"I've never known George to be a sore loser," said Lana.

"Apparently you haven't been paying very close attention," mumbled Jessie. The women pushed their chairs back and trotted back to where the men stood, George still fussing and cussing.

"What's the matter, George?" asked Jessie.

"I'll show you what's the matter!" he roared, lifting his foot and displaying the sole of his shoe, caked with what was undoubtedly animal excrement. "It's all over the damn yard!"

"They're working on fencing the property," said Jessie.

"Not fast enough! It's our turn to host this get-together once every two years, and now it's *ruined!*" said George.

"Oh, for heaven's sake, George!" said Jessie. "The day is only ruined if you let it be. Why don't I get the hamburger patties from the refrigerator, and you and the boys start cooking?" She didn't offer him time to protest, trotting off in the direction of the house. She could hear George berating the neighbors in a loud voice, sure to pierce through Patsy Appleton's meditative trance.

The other wives returned to the patio, leaving the men to commiserate over what a sad state the world was in, when the sanctity of a man's property could be violated by the wrong type of neighbor.

"I'll drop over before we go home, George," said Petey. "Remind them that they should have put the fence in first. Suggest that we might have to take the animals if it isn't done right away."

"Thanks, Petey," said George. "I can't believe Harley Jordan did this to me. After all the years we lived next to each other, he sold me out without a single thought. You can bet I'd be hearing about it if I had done the same to him."

"Harley never was much for usin' his head," said Forrest, offering a twig with which George could clean the tread of his shoes.

"I'd march right over there and tell 'em to keep their dogs over there before one of 'em ends up full of buckshot," said Bill, scowling and glaring across the yard at Patsy, her focus apparently unbroken by all of the hubbub.

"You can't just go around shooting people's dogs, Bill," said Petey. "It'd cause more trouble than it would be worth."

"Besides," added Forrest. "It ain't like the dogs did anything."

"The hell they didn't!" said George. "They're using my yard as a toilet!"

Forrest shook his head. "It's still the fault of the owners. If they had a fence in place like they should've, this wouldn't have happened."

"Alright then," said Bill. "I'd start shovelin' it back over onto their property. Turnabout's fair play."

George's eyes lit up. "That's not half-bad," he said. "They call it nature's fertilizer. Let's see how they feel when it's piled up in *their* yard."

"George!" Jessie called from the patio. "How about putting a match to this charcoal?"

*

"Oh, for heaven's sake, George!" said Jessie, putting her burger back on her plate. "Can't we talk about something else?" George had refused to let go of the topic throughout the entire meal, despite the inappropriateness of the occasion.

"Really," said Lana. "It's very unappetizing."

"I can't help it," said George, shooting a hostile glare toward the Appletons. Patsy had unfurled from her lotus position and was now stretching her legs out in front of her, touching her dirty toes with her extended fingers. "I swear I can *smell* it!"

"Let it go, buddy," said Petey. "Everything will be fine soon enough." Petey had made a first-rate councilman, even tempered and highly effective, even with irate folk such as his old buddy George.

"Oh, that's what *you* say," said George, ketchup running down his chin. *"You* don't have to live next door to them."

"I think everything's getting blown out of proportion," said Jessie. "I'm sure I could resolve everything with a little neighborliness."

"Are you out of your mind?" asked Bitzy, her eyes wide with revulsion. "I've heard stories about people like them. They're like sixties rejects. Next thing you know, you'll be at the airport pushing flowers and recruiting for the commune."

"It's not a commune, Bitzy," said Jessie. "It's just the two of them."

"And about fifty million animals," added Jane.

"I'll bet they have the morals of horny monkeys," said Lana.

"And you are a fine one to talk," said Jessie, her temper finally getting the best of her. "If I'm not mistaken—and I'm *not*—you and Forrest were already expecting Tommy when you got married—or have you forgotten? Quite scandalous at the time, if I recall."

Lana's face glowed crimson and she sputtered like she was running out of gas. "Well, I *never!*" she finally managed.

"Come down from the pedestal, Lana. Glass houses and all," said Jessie, pushing her chair back and leaving the table. The other guests sat in shocked silence, a mouth or two hanging open in disbelief. Just as Jessie reached the back door, she heard the telltale sounds of several of the Appletons' dogs. She turned just in time to see them attack the plate of extra burger patties which rested beside the grill. George was on his feet as fast as he could pry himself from the patio chair, but not nearly fast enough to salvage the burgers. The dogs had claimed their prize and already returned to their territory by the time George reached the grill, swearing and kicking.

Jessie sighed as she went into the house. George's ranting followed her in, and she gladly shut the door on the whole day. For her, this little get-together was over.

"You didn't have to be so rude to our friends," said George, pulling on his tennis shoes and lacing them up. The Markhams had finally departed, and Jessie had emerged from the house only afterward. She collected paper plates into a large plastic bag, wiping the surface of the metal table as she went.

"They're your friends, not mine," she said.

"Oh, now, Jess!" George said, sitting back in the patio chair. "We've been friends with them for as long as I can remember."

"Bunch of snooty blabbermouths, the whole bunch of them. I can certainly respect your desire to remain friends with your fellow coworkers, but I would prefer not to be in the company of their wives any longer," said Jessie, tossing the garbage bag into one of three metal cans which stood in a line by the back door.

"I suppose you'd rather be squatted down in the grass with the freaks next door," said George, the contempt in his voice barely below the surface.

Jessie whirled and glared, her eyes sparkling angrily. "Maybe I would. I cannot tell you how tired I am of hearing about the Appletons when no one has even taken the time to say hello to them." She turned and strode defiantly into the house, no longer wishing to discuss the matter.

George stayed behind, mulling over Bill's suggestion. It would certainly serve the Appletons right if he slung all the dog droppings back onto their property, but after seeing his cookout ruined by the uninvited and unexpected canine guests, George thought he should do something more substantial. The Appletons would probably be grateful; it was, after all, nature's fertilizer.

Suddenly, his eyes glimmered.

Of course! he thought, struggling to his feet and going into the house. Jessie was standing with her back to him at the sink, washing the utensils from the cookout. He nudged her aside and reached into the cabinet below, retrieving a large garbage bag.

"What are you doing?" asked Jessie. "I already rounded up the trash."

"Never you mind," said George, going back out into the yard.

Jessie followed and peered through the storm door. George was ambling back toward his work shed at the rear of the property. *Good,* she thought. *If he gets busy with one of his projects, he'll forget all about the Appletons.*

Deep down inside, she knew better.

Daylight had slipped into twilight, and twilight was slipping into night. Spotting the little piles had been easy at first, but as the light dwindled, George feared he might have to get a flashlight. This was no good, as he didn't want the Appletons to notice his busywork. With a gardening trowel, he scooped pile after retched pile into the plastic garbage bag.

When the sun had finally lowered enough to obscure the lawn in shadow, George decided to forgo the flashlight and call it an evening. He was surprised that the bag was only maybe a sixteenth full, if that. It seemed he had been stepping around and occasionally into the messes all day long. One thing for sure, there would be more tomorrow.

One more thing to do before retiring to his own house.

George crept over into the Appletons' yard, hauling the trash bag with him. The Appletons' house had originally been equipped with a coal burning furnace. Every fall, Harley Jordan had ordered truckloads of coal, having it dropped through a chute along the house's foundation. The basement was only large enough for the furnace, the pile of coal, and the utensils Harley used to feed and stoke the fire. About ten years ago, Harley had finally invested in a gas furnace, having it placed where the old coal burner had stood. The small, rectangular trapdoor which covered the coal chute had never been removed, and Harley had never bothered to lock it. George figured that the Appletons had yet to investigate the basement; it was too small for storage.

Dogs howled as George crept across the lawn. A lesser man might have turned and run, but George refused to be dissuaded. The damn things howled all the time anyway; the Appletons wouldn't even investigate.

George grimaced. His foot had encountered another soft spot in the ground. He considered adding it to his collection but decided he should finish his business and get home. He reached the coal chute and squatted down, carefully lifting the trapdoor open. A large, animated collie poked its long, golden nose in George's face, eager to be of assistance. George flapped his arms like an angry duck, sending the confused dog running for cover in the shadows of the backyard.

George quickly shoved the contents of the plastic bag through the chute and into the Appletons' basement. After carefully lowering the trapdoor, George hurried across to his own property, suppressing the urge to giggle as he trotted along. He tossed the empty garbage bag into his work shed.

Step One complete.

Although not happy about it, the Appletons continued with the construction of the fence, stretching chain link fencing across the median of the properties and securing it to galvanized steel posts. The fence was completed after two days of hard work.

In the interim, George made nightly visits to the Appletons, dropping a fresh delivery through the coal chute. Each evening's payload had been considerably less than the night before, so by the third day, George actually spent some time retrieving ammunition from the deepest reaches of the Appletons' own yard, back where the cow grazed. It was like hitting pay dirt.

Tuesday morning, George was occupying his customary position in the front window, grimacing as he studied the new fencing.

"What is it now, dear?" asked Jessie, descending the stairs with an empty clothesbasket in her hands.

"That fence looks awful," George groused.

"Oh, for heaven's sake, George," said Jessie. "You're the one that made them put it up. Now you don't want it?"

"Well, I figured they would put up a nice fence, you know? What did we get? Chain link. It's like living in a trailer park."

"These people cannot do a thing to please you, can they?" asked Jessie.

"Nope."

Jessie sighed and continued into the kitchen. George was transfixed, watching Lance and Patsy Appleton practiced yoga. They squatted down in the middle of the front yard, knees touching, and eyes closed. They wore matching off-white tunics which looked as though they badly needed a washing.

George had intended to stop filling the Appletons' basement as soon as the fence was complete, but now that the day had arrived, he was sort of melancholy. How he'd love to see the expressions on their faces when they turned their heat on this winter and the house filled with the collective scent of canine excrement. Ah, but at least there was three nights' worth festering below.

A tremendous backfire sounded from down the road, followed by the roar of a non-muffled engine. Soon, a rusted VW Vanagon wobbled down the street, tilting and swaying on shocks that had seen better days. It slowed before turning into the Appletons' drive, spewing gravel and a plume of dust in its wake. It came to a stop, its brakes protesting loudly, and three couples descended from the van, joining Patsy and Lance on the front lawn in a rambunctious display of affection.

George was nauseated.

Apparently, the house was to be used as some sort of flophouse. The new arrivals carried duffel bags in, presumably filled with all their worldly belongings. George could feel the blood pressure intensify in his temples, making his head throb with each heartbeat. There was no way he would stop with his plan now. He would drive these 'people' out if it was the last thing he ever did.

"Oh, for heaven's sake, George!" chided Jessie, clearing the kitchen table. "Face it, you were *wrong*. They were just visitors, not cult members."

"They *could* have been cult members," said George sullenly from behind his newspaper. He really hated it when he was wrong.

"*Mmm-hmm,*" said Jessie absently, placing a stack of breakfast dishes in the sink. "And the Pope himself gives me my markers every Wednesday at Bingo."

George dove for deeper cover behind his newspaper, grunting in response. Even though the strangers had only been visitors, George had continued with his nightly deposits through the coal chute. Of course, his entry and exit to the Appletons' property was hampered by that damned fence, but at least Lance and Patsy had been considerate enough to put a gate at the back of the yard. George was certain that before winter settled in, ex-hippies from the four corners of the earth would converge at the Appletons' for a festival of debauchery, or whatever it was that ex-hippies did. He had detected the funny-smelling cigarettes wafting their pungent odor across his lawn, overpowering Jessie's fragrant rose bushes. Soon they would be selling drugs right out of their living room, no doubt.

It had been three weeks since George had begun his project, and so far, the Appletons hadn't noticed his prowling about. George was also certain that they hadn't discovered his gifts yet; the stench that greeted him when he lifted the coal chute was becoming more and more overpowering.

Jessie was getting a little suspicious, though.

Over the past few weeks, George had broken a long-standing habit of watching television each night, wearing only his t-shirt and boxers and stuffing his face with Cheezits until it was time for bed. He had passed it off as a project in his shed, but it was only a matter of time before Jessie wanted to see results of some sort. George debated buying a birdhouse from Craftmart, but he hadn't actually done it yet. Come to think of it, three weeks' worth of work would produce a pretty big birdhouse. He would have to think about that tonight when he was making his rounds.

A week later, George was returning from Craftmart, an elaborate wooden dollhouse loaded into the bed of his truck and covered securely with a blue plastic tarp. Bill Myers had suggested the dollhouse. Jessie had collected antique dolls and various accessories throughout the years. Bitzy Myers was positively green with envy, her own meager collection of dolls paling in comparison. Because of this, Bill was made constantly aware of Jessie's interest, Bitzy spending more money than Bill liked each year just trying to keep up, with the ultimate hope of one day surpassing her. She had become especially focused on this goal since Jessie had snubbed the group at the cookout. Apparently, Bill hadn't realized that a dollhouse to placate Jessie would eventually lead to a dollhouse to placate Bitzy, but that was of no concern to George. It was a believable three-week woodshop project—provided he remembered to take the price stickers off.

Sirens swelled behind George, and he pulled his truck over to allow the county fire engine to roar by. It had been a dry summer, woods catching fire if given half a chance. The fire engine had become a familiar sight, bells clanging and sirens screaming.

As George neared his property, he could see a thick, black column of smoke rising into the dusky sky. The Appletons' yard was a flurry of activity, firemen running from one end to the other, dragging long tendrils of thick hose as they went. George's heart filled with joy as he saw the old Colonial engulfed in hungry flames. He pulled into his own driveway and ran to the porch, pushing his head in through the screen door.

"Hurry up, Jess!" he called. "You've got to *see* this!"

He turned and ran across the yard, pushing his way through Jessie's rose bushes which had already been partially trampled by the firemen. He saw Darby Rogers, the county's sheriff and principal law enforcement officer, speaking with a distraught Lance and taking notes on a clipboard. George wandered about the yard, trying to stay out of the way and still yet absorb information from conversations floating around him.

"They didn't even have insurance! Can you imagine that? That'll teach old man Jordan to sell on land contract. Now he's gonna get stuck with the ruins," a teenage boy said.

Yay! No insurance! No repair!

"That's pretty cold, Alex," said another spectator, presumably the boy's mother.

"Well, you know what I mean."

"*Still*. I hear the woman's dead."

George froze. He had wanted the Appletons out of the neighborhood, but he hadn't wished *this* type of misfortune upon them. He walked up to the two spectators, recognizing them as the Moritzes from two doors down.

"What happened?" he asked, easing himself into their conversation.

"Oh, George!" said Tricia Moritz. "What a mess this is, hunh? I guess it's really bad. Some sort of explosion."

"An explosion?"

"Uh-hunh," said Alex. "It was really *cool!*"

"*Alex!*" Tricia said sharply. "I guess it was something in the basement. It blew the kitchen right off the house, and the fire spread pretty quickly after that. I hear the woman was killed."

George's heart sank. "Are you sure about that?"

"They carried someone out on a stretcher, but when the ambulance left, it wasn't running its sirens," said Alex.

George staggered away from them, trying to locate Sheriff Rogers. It had only been a prank. He hadn't meant any harm, but the pent-up methane must have been ignited by the pilot light of the furnace.

Firemen, policemen and gawking neighbors filled the yard. Dogs ran underfoot, yapping from all the excitement. Lights from the fire engine cast a roving red eye around the yard. Sheriff Rogers was nowhere to be seen.

Suddenly, George felt a hand come to rest on his shoulder. He turned and was quite surprised to see Patsy Appleton's concerned face looking back at him.

"Oh, thank God!" George exclaimed, involuntarily pulling the woman close for a quick, unanticipated hug. "I heard you had been—well, never mind. I'm so glad to see you're alright." Relief poured through him, dousing the red-hot anxiety that had been welling since he first heard Alex Moritz speak of the ambulance and its unidentified cargo.

Unidentified?

George pulled back, holding Patsy at arm's length. Lance had emerged from the crowd and was standing behind

Patsy, the look on his face...was it sympathy? Sheriff Rogers was just behind Lance, with a similar expression.

"We're so sorry, Mr. Templeman," choked Patsy.

"Mrs. Templeman brought over cookies to welcome us to the neighborhood," added Lance.

"We had gone into the living room to select one of Lance's handcrafted vases to give the two of you in return—you know, to say thank you. And that's when...that's when—" Patsy was all tears and sobs now.

Sheriff Rogers looked on with consoling eyes. There was nothing he could add to what the Appletons were already saying.

"If there's anything we can do at all, Mr. Templeman," said Lance. The Appletons were sincere in their gesture, their concern a tangible thing. They seemed completely unaffected by the total loss of their new property.

George felt his chest tighten and heard his own pleading voice, begging for a revised version of the story that was unfolding before him. Jessie, the beautiful girl whose pigtails he had pulled in the first grade, the mother of his children and his constant companion for the past fifty-three years, had been right all along about the new neighbors, and George had been wrong. Dead wrong.

Oh, how George hated it when he was wrong.

THE CHIP ON MARGARET'S SHOULDER

Margaret Traeger slowed the station wagon at the entrance of the garage and depressed the button on the automatic door opener. As the old chain clattered and the door raised, she placed the remote in the center console and noticed the crumbs from the Butterfinger candy bar that had showered across her silk blouse, leaving little grease spots from the chocolate and crumbly goodness inside. Not like Howard would notice, anyway.

Howard didn't look at Margaret anymore. They had been married for thirteen years, and the bloom was definitely off the rose.

They had been an odd couple, even then. Howard was athletic throughout his school career, playing basketball in both high school and college. He had dark hair and shiny blue eyes that could pierce through total darkness. He was neither short nor tall. His smile, complete with cheek-dimpling action, could calm the ocean. The girls wanted to be with him, and the boys just wanted to *be* him. He was perfect.

On the other hand, Margaret (then Brinkman) had been an introverted and studious girl, never on the cutting edge of anything. She was slender; arms, legs and eyes all appropriately positioned. While Miss America would never lose sleep worrying about what Margaret was wearing to the prom, she was attractive in a rather ordinary way. With Howard, she had come *alive*. With Howard, she would do the right things and find the right words to say. With Howard, she had become whole.

She had been surprised when Howard first asked her out, way back in the eleventh grade. He could have had his pick of any of the cheerleaders, with their voluptuous bodies, perfect hair and straight teeth. Oh, and their bodies! Doing the splits, tumbling and scissor-kicking their way into the dreams of the entire male student body. To be completely forthright, Howard *did* date several of the cheerleaders prior to going out with Margaret. He had earned quite the reputation as a ladies' man. Inexplicably, he then asked Margaret out.

Margaret had said no. It had to be another stupid joke. Darla Drake (head cheerleader and bitch extraordinaire) must have some elaborate scheme cooked up to embarrass and crush Margaret. Or Buck Turlane (all-star sports everything) must have won a bet with Howard. "If I can drink ten beers in thirty minutes, you have to ask Freaky Margie out." There were a million underhanded possibilities. No, make those probabilities. Margaret may not have been the lowest rung on the ladder, but she could see it clearly from her foothold.

Yet Howard had been persistent, and eventually, Margaret had pensively agreed. She remained quiet for most of that evening, waiting for the floor to fall out from under her. Even if the joke wasn't an obvious one, it *had* to be a joke. If not, then there was only one thing Howard could possibly have on his mind. Her mother had warned her about eager fellows. "They're sneaky as snakes! They'll say anything, and I mean *anything*, but sooner or later it's the hands that do the talkin'!"

Howard had been a complete gentleman. He filled what could have been awkward silences with his viewpoints on this, that and the other. He had dreams, hopes, and plans, and they didn't end with getting ripped at Eichman's Pier every Friday night. He had told Margaret every joke he knew, and she laughed and laughed, thinking Howard might be the funniest man on Earth. Cupid had locked Margaret in his sights and taken aim.

After that first perfect date, her every waking moment was filled with thoughts of Howard. Surprisingly, his thoughts seemed to be of her, too. He made her feel safe and strong, two things she had never felt before. She even found the super-bitch Darla was now leaving her alone. Howard liked to go to his friends' parties with Margaret on his arm, and she almost felt like she belonged.

They married right out of high school. Howard enrolled in college, studying computer programming and engineering, and playing basketball in the evenings. Margaret attended business college, studying office management. After graduating, she took a clerical position with a law firm in town, and although she was very good at what she did, her co-workers kept her at a cold distance and soon, the old Margaret had reemerged. Conversations would cease when she entered the room, and she knew they were talking about her. *Why? She hadn't done anything wrong!* She compensated by spending time with the good folks at Hostess. She gained fifteen pounds.

*

Howard's graduation signified the dawn of a new era in their relationship. He worked long hours at the offices of Byte for Byte, Computer Programmers, and advanced quickly through the ranks. As his earnings increased, so did their savings and soon enough, it was time to shop for a house. Margaret had fallen in love with the Evans' old family farmhouse, thirty miles outside of town with the nearest neighbor two miles down the old country road. The bank had foreclosed on elderly Mrs. Evans three years before, and the house had been standing empty. There would be no prying eyes or gossipy neighbors. It was ideal.

Howard, who liked the farmhouse (*and* the price tag, thank you very much), was not nearly as enchanted with the solitude. He liked to be around people, and no wonder, what with the charisma he oozed from his hair follicles to his black patent leather wingtips. But it wasn't a *long* drive into town, and he agreed to give it a try.

It was at the Byte for Byte Christmas party ten years ago that things took a turn for the worse.

Margaret had befriended Howard's assistant, a slender little waif named Dixie Patterson. Dixie helped Margaret find appropriate attire for different occasions and offered social advice to help boost Margaret's confidence at those dreaded company banquets. Dixie invited Margaret to play bridge with her friends. For the first time in her life, Margaret had found a *friend*. Sometimes, when Howard was out of town on business, Dixie would stay overnight at the farmhouse, and she and Margaret would sip wine on the back patio until the wee hours of night, discussing politics, religion, celebrities...you name it.

It was all the more surprising when, at this fateful Christmas party, Margaret, who had not seen Howard for some time, stumbled upon him and Dixie using the top of his desk in a manner not intended by the manufacturer.

Margaret's world disintegrated. Betrayal is such an ugly thing, making people question things they should never have to. This betrayal was of the worst kind. It wasn't just her *husband*, it was her husband and her best friend. She didn't even have anyone to talk to, no shoulder to cry on. Margaret had no siblings, and her father had died when she was just a child. Her mother had been in a nursing home for three years now, debilitated after a massive stroke. Margaret was utterly alone in the world, with social skills best described as embryonic.

Her new best friend was Sara Lee. She gained twenty more pounds.

Ultimately, Margaret elected to stay with Howard. He and Dixie swore on Bibles stacked to the moon that it was an isolated incident, inspired by the free flow of liquor at the Christmas party.

Howard had some unconventional ideas about fidelity, anyhow. At least, these ideas were unconventional to Margaret, likely more normal for the average man. For Howard, sex was an act of pleasure, while love was an act of commitment. Although Margaret could understand his viewpoint on a clinically detached level, she found the notion morally reprehensible. Sex and love, like peanut butter and jelly, should *never* be separated. If a man was dissatisfied with his home life, he found sex elsewhere. For Margaret, it was just another matter of being Not Good Enough. Howard held her and cried with her, swearing he understood how deeply he had hurt her, and he would never, ever hurt her again. She mewed like a wounded kitten, wanting desperately to be strong and send him away, but just one look in those magnetic eyes sapped her resolve.

Afterward, life for Margaret and Howard was never quite the same. Margaret would have gladly donated a lung to be able to step back in time before the Christmas party and keep Howard at her side. Since this was impossible without the intervention of science fiction, she instead severed all ties with Dixie and told Howard that he must do the same. It was a little hairy at first, as Dixie was Howard's assistant, but three months after the incident, Dixie received a promotion and was transferred out-of-state. Margaret would have preferred it if she had been hit by a bus, but as an alternative, it wasn't bad.

Margaret found herself checking up on Howard all the time. She would call the office at odd times throughout the day just to ensure he was where he was supposed to be. She would take her lunch hour at different intervals and sneak home unannounced, knuckles turning white on the steering wheel as she silently crept into the driveway, prepared to see Dixie's little sports car tucked up behind Howard's. They were never there.

Although Margaret tried to keep her surveillance on the Q-T, Howard wasn't long in figuring out what was going on. One evening, he sat down beside Margaret on the couch and took her hand into his. He told her she was the most important person in his life. He was grateful to have been given another chance, but if she didn't back off—just a bit—this jealousy would turn into an insurmountable obstacle for them. Damnedest thing was, she knew it was true. She *had* to learn to trust him again. But what if...

As the years passed, Margaret learned a nifty little trick that seemed to help. Diversion. She immersed herself in sitcoms, books and little organizational projects that kept her occupied.

Three years ago, Howard had begun what he called "the biggest project of his career" at Byte for Byte. He put in a lot of overtime. He had a new assistant, and Margaret was elated to discover that *his* name was Mike Powers. Little Mikey, they called him. He was fresh out of school and had a real knack for computer programming. Howard looked at Little Mikey as an apprentice and took him under his wing, both professionally and personally.

Little Mikey was as green as the grass on a well-kept lawn. He had never been on a real date before, but unlike Margaret, he was *burning* to learn the social ropes. Howard considered it his duty and obligation to teach Little Mikey what he knew. Little Mikey idolized Howard as the big brother he had never had.

One evening over dinner, Howard told Margaret he wanted to start going out to the clubs in town with Little Mikey. Her eyes narrowed, looking for the hidden meaning in the words. Howard explained how shy Little Mikey was and how he needed Howard for support if he was ever going to get a date. Besides, Howard missed the nightlife. Since that Black Christmas, Howard had entirely given up going out on the town. He had come home from work night after night, dozing on the sofa as the evening sitcoms played, waking in time for the evening news and going to bed directly afterward. He and Margaret didn't talk like they used to. Ironically, this was more her doing than his. Her busywork had grown proportionally with time, and now she found herself looking forward to this evening time where she could spend the night with the cast of *3rd Rock from the Sun* or *Friends* or *Frasier*, or immerse herself completely in a torrid romance novel, or alphabetize and categorize the disinfectants and cleaners underneath the sink...the possibilities were endless.

It helped immeasurably that Margaret liked and trusted Little Mikey. There was a quality about him that made you want to help him out if you could, because he was so endearingly helpless. His mind was sharp as a razor with anything computer-related, but his common sense and coordination were sorely lacking. Odds were good he would trip over his own feet while walking down the street because his shoes were on the wrong feet and the shoelaces were hanging loose and free like a waiting, tentacled monster. The instinctive reaction was to put him on an allowance and hire a nanny.

Therefore, she agreed to this new arrangement. Howard went out with Little Mikey twice a week. In all fairness, Howard asked Margaret if she wanted to go *every single time*. Margaret was sure that this was to alleviate any remaining jealousy because Howard knew she wouldn't go. It may as well have been a million years since the days when

Howard had taken Margaret to his friends' parties during high school. Margaret couldn't remember what it felt like to even *want* to go. Two years ago, her desire for social interaction had met an untimely demise.

That time, she had *almost* gone. It had been a Tuesday, one of the boys' normal nights out. Margaret had decided over the weekend she might just give it a try. The thought had nauseated her. After gaining those last few pounds, crowded rooms had given her a bit of a panic attack. The only contact she had outside of home was her job, and she had been there long enough that people mostly left her alone. She was the crazy aunt in the attic. Her co-workers were familiar, if not friendly, and the panic remained at bay while she was there.

Other places were different, though. That Tuesday, she had gone shopping at the North Avenue Mall to find an appropriate outfit to wear. I may have mentioned she had gained a little weight. She worked her way to the center of the mall, looking as much at the floor as anything else to avoid the stares of the passersby. And they *were* staring. All of them. Some looked genuinely repulsed. Savage teenaged laughter floated down the mall corridor. They could only be laughing at Margaret. The sound encircled her, swirling and swirling, taking little bites of her hide as it began to constrict and force the air from her lungs.

Margaret veered into the clothing store as quickly as possible. Within the smaller confines of the shop and after a few minutes, her breathing returned to normal, and her perspiration dried. After slowly sifting through the first rack or two, Margaret had completely forgotten about the incident and immersed herself in the project at hand. She rummaged through rack after rack of evening wear, looking for something not too casual, yet nothing too dressy, either. She found a slimming black pantsuit with a matching blouse which was trimmed with silver spangly things. They looked like diamonds in the light. Margaret removed her size from the rack and approached the dressing rooms.

There is nothing more discouraging than to find that the size you once knew as your own is now a distant memory. Margaret had to go back not once, but twice, each return trip causing her face to turn a deeper shade of crimson. Once she finally had the right size and suited up, she gave herself a once over in the mirror. *Not too bad,* she thought. *Not too shabby.*

She decided she would wear the new clothes home. The mall shoppers would find nothing to laugh about when she looked so much better. Feeling more confident than before, Margaret collected her receipt, shoved her street clothes into one of the boutique's plastic handle bags and stepped back out into the mall corridor. She held her head higher, sure if anyone were looking at her, they would be merely studying her in silent approval.

The world turned askew as she had passed a section of the mall corridor that was covered with mirrors. Margaret froze in place, dropping her plastic bag beside her. The creature that returned her gaze in the mirror was a stranger, not looking remotely like the image she had just seen in the boutique dressing room. The new clothing accentuated Margaret's midsection weight gain. Had her head always been this *big?* Her throat and jowls bulged out like a frog preparing to croak. Her ruddy forehead had a dusting of acne that she hadn't noticed before. Her hair had gone as flat as a serving platter on the top. *No!* Nose hair. *Nose hair!*

Margaret began to experience tunnel vision. The rumble of conversation of passersby echoed from far, far away. Out of the unintelligible murmur, the sound of laughter gained volume. Soon, all Margaret could hear was vicious laughter, booming from one end of the mall corridor to the other. The exit looked as if it were five miles away. She started walking quickly, moving toward it. Soon she was running, sweat pouring down her brow. She couldn't seem to catch her breath. After what had felt like an eternity, Margaret burst through the doors and into the parking lot.

Once Margaret finally reached her station wagon and lowered herself behind the wheel, she quickly adjusted the rearview and side mirrors up toward the sky. She didn't want to see that creature again. Ever. Tears rolled down her face as she exited the mall parking lot, nearly mowing down a pedestrian.

Margaret did not go out that night, nor any thereafter.

As the years between then and now passed, Margaret realized that she and Howard were only having one-sided conversations with each other. She prattled on about the synopses of her favorite shows, foods she thought she might try preparing for them, sale prices from the grocery store, etc., and Howard might as well be speaking a foreign language to her: Gigawhozits and megabiters. He was always so excited, and yet Margaret's eyes were always blank. And that was *if* he was home at all, between the nights he worked late and the nights he went out with Little Mikey.

One of those evenings, as Margaret was doing laundry, she came across a scrap of paper in Howard's work trousers. It read, "D.P. - 555-9009" *Dixie Patterson!* That son of a bitch was messing around again! He probably had been carrying on with her the entire ten years following the Christmas party. What a *fool* Margaret had been. Everyone at Howard's office probably knew about the ongoing affair. She could hear them now. *Howard's such a nice-looking man. It's no wonder he needs a diversion with a wife like* Margaret. *I wonder why he even stays with her?*

Although furious at the thought of having been made a fool, Margaret was startled to realize she wasn't jealous. Not even remotely. She *was* angry, however, but at herself. She no longer trusted people. Everyone had a secret agenda. While many may dream of winning the lottery, Margaret had reached a place in her life when all she wanted was to be left *alone.*

She contemplated divorce but realized how financially devastating that would be for her. She never had a head for money and had always let Howard take care of such things. All their combined property and holdings were in Howard's name. Despite her distrust of Howard's fidelity, she trusted him implicitly with money. Allowing him free reign spared her the collective years he would have had to spend explaining debits, credits, money markets and tax shelters. She had never considered how vulnerable this left her if they were to split. They had no children, so there could be no child support. She still held her position at the law firm which, although not nearly as lucrative as Howard's career, could certainly keep a roof over her head and food on the table. Oh, yes, Margaret could have pursued alimony or other forms of restitution, but this really had nothing to do with money. She didn't want to sell the house and split the proceeds. She loved the house. She loved the hermit-like existence she had carved out for herself and all the goofy little routines it included. The world would be a perfect place, if only Howard was dead...

For the next few months, Margaret was filled with thoughts she had never imagined possible. While preparing a meatloaf, her hand would hover over the collection of cleaning products under the kitchen sink, postulating the effect of a cup of Drano in the meat and vegetable concoction, or perhaps a little dilution of Howard's evening nightcap with a finger or two of Windex. But to commit murder and get away scot-free were two entirely different matters. One was easy, one...not so much.

Margaret lacked imagination. She found most of her murderous ideas originated from ill-conceived notions in paperback mysteries and movie matinees. And in the end, the murderer was always caught. This was no good. She held her breath every time the phone rang, or the door chimed. Hopefully, it would be some nice police officer whose unpleasant duty it was to inform Margaret her husband had been flattened by a motorcar or had fallen down the thirty-two flights of stairs at Byte for Byte. She wouldn't even have to feel guilty.

Margaret sighed and pulled the station wagon into the garage, absently flicking the switch to close the garage door behind her. Today, providence had smiled in her direction. She looked in the passenger seat and spotted the twin prescription bags she had just collected from Mr. Hagerty, the octogenarian pharmacist with whom the Traegers filled their prescriptions for years. Both Margaret and Howard had two medications apiece they took daily. Margaret kept her thyroid and blood pressure medication on her nightstand. Howard kept his pill bottles on the kitchen counter, and as part of his daily routine, he scooped his blood pressure and acid reflux pills into his palm and tossed them down his throat with a quick drink of coffee. Then he would go to the bathroom and insert his contact lenses.

Margaret developed an upper respiratory infection that week, and her doctor gave her a prescription for penicillin, a medication to which Howard was severely allergic. Since she would be making the trip to town, Margaret elected to refill Howard's reflux medicine while at the Hagerty pharmacy.

Each pill bottle was contained in a slim paper sack which displayed the prescription information and side effect warnings. Margaret paid for the prescriptions and thanked Mr. Hagerty, then bought a can of Pepsi from the vending machine at the door and headed back to her station wagon. She figured she may as well go ahead and take her first dose. The sooner she started, the sooner she could breathe freely again. She settled into the driver's seat and pulled open the bag labeled with her name. She removed the little orange pill bottle from the bag and started to pull off the safety seal Mr. Hagerty always applied. She stopped suddenly, holding the bottle up and examining the contents in the sunlight that had filtered through the orange plastic.

These were not her pills. Her name read clearly on the computer-generated label. It also clearly said, "Penicillin." The pills in the bottle were unmistakable to Margaret. They were the familiar black and pink Prevacid pills Howard took to control his acid reflux. Margaret jerked her fingers even farther away from the safety seal, as if she had been burned. An idea was forming. She carefully opened the second prescription bag and examined the pill bottle. The label bore Howard's name and declared the contents to be Prevacid. The pills filling that bottle were penicillin. The safety seal was intact.

Margaret had driven home in a daze. This was The Opportunity. It could not have been more perfectly planned had it been deliberate. All she had to do was place the refill on the kitchen counter with Howard's medication. He never looked at the pills. Just scoop, scoop, swallow. Even if he looked, he probably wouldn't notice the difference. He wouldn't be wearing his contacts, and the pills were approximately the same size. He had two remaining pills in his old bottle. Then he would crack the seal and swallow his last pill ever.

Margaret went into the house and set her plan in motion.

Margaret fixed a special dinner that night. She thought that Howard deserved one last special dinner. She prepared lasagna, Howard's favorite, with salad and a homemade cheesecake for dessert.

Howard seemed distracted through dinner. Margaret studied him through the light of the single candle she had placed on the dining room table. He usually expressed his delight when Margaret served lasagna, but tonight he was a million miles away. Probably thinking of that bitch, Dixie.

"Your day okay?" Margaret asked, unable to bear the uncomfortable silence any longer.

"Busy, busy." Howard scooped another bite of lasagna into his mouth. "As a matter of fact, I was just thinking that I should head back down to the office after dinner. I've got a project on the front burner that needs a little attention."

Dixie.

"I see. Well, I'm finishing a really good book, so I probably wouldn't be much company anyway," she replied.

"Hmmm." But Howard's attention was already gone. She could almost hear the steady clicking of the wheels working in his mind.

After ten more minutes of awkward silence, Howard folded his napkin on the table and pushed his chair back. "Well, I'm going to head back and get it over with," he said. He stood behind her chair for just a moment, resting his hands on her shoulders. His touch had once been warm and soothing; now her shoulder muscles knotted, and she had to force herself not to recoil. "I've got a little surprise in the works for you, Margaret. In a day or so, I should think..." He pecked the top of her head and drifted toward the living room.

Margaret raised a disinterested eyebrow at that. The last "surprise" Howard had brought her was a deluxe, self-propelled vacuum cleaner. *Whoopee!*

"Funny you should say that," she said. "I've got one for you, too. In about a day or so..."

On the third morning, the Emergency Medical Squad was dispatched to the Traeger farmhouse. There, they discovered a man in his mid-thirties, severely convulsing on the kitchen floor. A round woman in a bathrobe stood in the corner of the kitchen, nervously watching the man writhe.

A short, stocky, no-nonsense female EMT asked for details.

Margaret said dazedly, "He just fell down. I don't know. He just fell down."

Margaret watched the attendants work feverishly to stabilize Howard. He was not breathing anymore, and his skin had taken on a slightly blue pallor. His tongue lolled forward, protruding slightly from between his teeth.

Please, please, please, please, prayed Margaret.

Howard's funeral was four days later. Margaret could not shake the feeling she was trapped in a surreal dream. She didn't feel guilty. She hadn't done anything. Well, almost nothing. No one else knew she had seen the bottles had been incorrectly filled. Matters were further simplified the very same day Howard died. Old Man Pratt who drove the county school bus had a fatal reaction to another of Mr.

Hagerty's pharmaceutical mistakes. Margaret still hadn't opened her own prescription, having determined if the police should intimate she had switched Howard's medicine, she would have proof of her innocence since hers was still safety sealed. Later, she worried they might find it suspicious she hadn't started taking her own prescription. She needn't have worried.

Mr. Hagerty was forced to retire, and his malpractice insurance company was eager to negotiate healthy settlements for both Margaret and Old Man Pratt's widow.

Margaret began to emerge from her fog two weeks later. She had taken a leave of absence from work to reorganize herself.

Although the settlement from the insurance company wasn't anywhere near finalized, it became abundantly clear Margaret would likely be able to retire once it was. She spent a week sleeping late, reading in bed, and watching television in her bathrobe. It was heaven. Her eating patterns changed, now that she wasn't expected to have dinner ready when Howard got home. She began to lose a little weight. She could spend day after day after day curled up in her recliner, doing anything and everything exactly as she wanted and exactly when she wanted to.

The mornings were difficult, though. Margaret was surprised to discover how much she missed Howard in the morning. Their daily routine was so set she had taken it for granted. He always told a joke at the breakfast table. The jokes were always very corny. Margaret would groan outwardly, and Howard would grin at her. Often, he would repeat the same joke every couple of days, which made Margaret's groan even louder. He had a favorite that involved a preacher, a teacher and a can of corn. How appropriate.

Every afternoon at precisely one o'clock, Howard would call Margaret at work, just to ask how her day was going. She would tell him about the maniacal morning drivers who had attempted to assassinate her as she navigated the roadways into town. She followed up with the latest devious plot with which her co-workers hoped to thwart her. She didn't remember ever once asking Howard how his day was going, but surely, she must have. Now, one o'clock came and went, her phone forever silent.

Every evening, just before bed, Howard would wordlessly take position beside her on the couch, pulling her feet into his lap. He kneaded them firmly and tenderly the entire duration of the evening news. Now, Margaret did not watch the news, because it hurt her feet too much.

One month after Howard's death, as Margaret sipped her morning coffee, she was beginning to realize being completely alone was not exactly as she had envisioned it.

Three rapid taps at the kitchen door startled Margaret. She wasn't expecting anyone; she hadn't had uninvited company in over ten years. She had isolated herself from the rest of the community years ago and none of her neighbors would even think of stopping over now.

Margaret gathered her robe around her and retied it. She peered through the window in the door. It was Little Mikey. He was shifting from foot to foot as was his trademark nervous habit. He lifted his right hand up and waggled it from side to side in Margaret's direction. His goofy grin covered the lower quarter of his face.

"Mikey! How have you been?" Margaret asked as she opened the door.

"Fine, fine. Thanks. The company asked me to come down to talk to you. Can I come in?"

"Of course." Margaret stood back as Little Mikey passed. In his left hand, he had a briefcase which he had set on the table. "What's up?"

Little Mikey fumbled over condolences, just as he had at the funeral. "You know Howie and I were best buddies, hunh? Well, I wanted to be the one to come and tell you. I think he would have liked that."

"Tell me what?" Margaret asked, hoping to keep alarm out of her voice. Could Little Mikey know what happened? That would be impossible!

"First, I wanted to bring you this check. It's from Howie's life insurance policy. His agent's card is attached if you need anything." Margaret's eyes dropped to the name on the card. Daniel Petrie. 555-9009. The blood drained from her face.

Little Mikey slid an envelope from his briefcase and handed it to Margaret. She eyed it for a moment, her dumbfounded mouth hanging open. She lifted the flap of the envelope and peered inside. The check was for $2,000,000 and made payable to Margaret Traeger, as Sole Beneficiary of Howard Traeger. A small squeak escaped her lips. She felt the fog settling back into her mind. She knew Howard had life insurance, but it never occurred to her in what amount. Howard always took care of those things. Little Mikey was taking great pleasure in the presentation.

"You know that Howie was putting in a lot of overtime lately, too, right? He was working on a top-secret project for Byte for Byte. He was finished with all the technical stuff before he.... you know." He grinned sheepishly. "Anyway, Byte for Byte is preparing to launch the product next week. It's big. I mean *real* big. Gonna change the way computers are built."

Now Little Mikey was getting swept up by his own enthusiasm. Margaret had a vague sense of déjà vu as memories leapt to mind of Howard prattling endlessly on topics constructed of computer-speak, his eyes sparkling like those of a child at Christmas.

"I'm sure it was brilliant," Margaret said flatly.

"Oh, yeah, yeah. It's a model for a new CPU microprocessor. It leapfrogs both Intel and AMD by, like, sooooo much. It's *twenty-five* times faster. We have both Dell and Hewlett-Packard on board to distribute and that's just the beginning!" Little Mikey's cheeks were flushed with excitement.

"Wow." That's all Margaret could manage. Twenty-five times faster than what? To ask would be an invitation into the realm of the unknown, where Little Mikey would attempt yet again to explain to her how megabytes related to hard disk space and why the appropriate random-access memory (or RAM, don't you know) made all the difference when running a graphics program. Translation: *Blah, blah, blah-blah, blah blah blah.*

Little Mikey suddenly realized he was babbling and the flush spread over his entire face, coloring the end of his nose and the tips of his ears a bright, angry red. "Sorry. I always get carried away. But I haven't told you the best part."

"Best part?"

"Oh, yeah, yeah. Even though Byte for Byte owns the controlling rights to the hardware, Howie had retained a healthy residual percentage for future sales. Everyone who has *seen* the processor understands what kind of money we are talking about! Now that Howie is...you know, the money will go to you."

Margaret's mouth was still hanging open. "Money? What money?"

Little Mikey giggled. He took her hand in his. "So much money you could spend like a wild woman and still have more money than most people see in a *lifetime*. A *lot* more money."

"I...I don't understand."

"Sure, ya do! You're stunned. Who wouldn't be? Howie was planning all this as a big surprise for you." Margaret remembered the special lasagna she had prepared...had it only been a month ago? *This* was the surprise of which Howard had spoken.

"There's one more thing," Little Mikey said, still uttering an occasional nervous giggle. He paused for dramatic effect. "He named the processor after you."

"Hunh?" When, oh when would Margaret ever close her mouth?

"Oh, yeah, yeah. It's called the MCP, or 'Margie Cyclonic Processor.' Company fought him like hell over that one. They said it didn't flow from the tongue. But let's face it. Howie came up with the damned thing and could call it anything he wanted. He wanted more than anything to name it after you."

Margaret's mouth finally snapped shut. She looked up at the ceiling, which had apparently sprung a leak. Her cheeks were wet. With her fingers, she traced the source of the wetness back to her eyes. Howard hadn't been cheating. He had been working.

Howard had immortalized Margaret. For his time and trouble, Margaret had allowed Howard to die.

PERKS

Armed with a newspaper, Mike hurried into the stall, latching the door behind him and nearly soiling his trousers before having the opportunity to clear the way. His stomach was turning inside out. That piece of chocolate dessert wasn't sitting well. Or maybe it was the ribs. Or the popcorn shrimp. Maybe it was the combination of everything. There had been a lot of leftovers tonight.

Jill was covering Mike's tables while he was incapacitated, and he hoped his tips wouldn't suffer too much because of it. Jill was a fat, lazy frump of a girl who had all the personality of a wooden two-by-four. He could hear her now, sighing in exasperation while Mrs. Kramer sampled her coffee, clutching Jill's beefy arm with one of her spindly, blue-veined hands, excusing the waitress only

126

after she was thoroughly satisfied that the coffee wasn't too cold/hot/strong/weak. Mrs. Kramer was a fussy old bird, but in Mike's mind, she had earned that right, offering a substantial gratuity whenever the service warranted one. Apathetic Jill had never seen a substantial gratuity in her depressingly long tenure as a waitress.

Not for me, thought Mike. *Work my way through school, then I'll be the one leaving the tips—or not, if my waitress is even half as bad as Jill.*

Of less concern were the Pendletons at the five-seater in the corner. They were 'new' money, as the Kramers might snidely call them, a young husband and wife and their three ill-mannered offspring. They were easy—hell, Mike could probably screw up their entire order and still receive twenty percent. *Geez!* If he didn't hurry and get back out there, Jill would snatch the guaranteed money right out from underneath his nose.

Another wave of cramps reached its crescendo then abated in a loud burst of flatulence. Mike's face reddened, and he was glad he was the only person in the restroom. A public restroom is fine for a quick piss, but not at all suitable for the humiliating sounds of a difficult bowel movement.

Mike scanned the headlines of the newspaper, his stomach gurgling as the discomfort faded. His attention was lost as the bathroom door opened, and he heard the sounds of hard-soled shoes on the tile floor. The gentleman entering was in mid-sentence, apparently talking on a cell phone. "— I *told* you that, Annie. —No. —No. —Tell her whatever. No, look, it's *your* problem. She's *your* sister, not mine. —Fine."

Mike could hear the man muttering as he disconnected the call. Running water, tearing paper, then the door again.

Silence was restored, save for the next burst of flatulence, which would have been funny had it not hurt so badly.

Mike's eyes returned to the paper. Stock market down. New ozone concerns. Middle East tensions escalating. Nothing good at all. He flipped to the comics.

The door opened again. "Mike? You alive in here?" It was Timmy, the high school kid *Monte's* had hired to bus tables.

"Yeah," Mike grunted. "I'll be out in a minute."

"Okay," the kid said dubiously. "But Jill's complaining."

"If she didn't complain, her head would blow off from all the pressure," Mike muttered, a slight squeak slipping out of his lower intestine. The boy giggled, but Mike wasn't sure whether it was from what he had said or what he had done. The door closed again.

Jill was bound to complain. The Kramers were the most persnickety customers Mike had. They were regulars, coming in every Thursday night and occasionally on Tuesday, as well. Today was the old fart's birthday, possibly his three hundredth. Or three thousandth. As a younger man, Mr. Kramer had invested in the stock market with a razor-sharp mind, playing hardball with the big boys and amassing his fortune with fierce determination. His wife never lifted a finger—never had to. They had a servant for every menial task, including the daily washing and styling of Mrs. Kramer's waist-length mane of silver hair. It seemed such a shame they never had children. All that money and no one with whom to leave it.

Mike eventually arrived at this same thought each time he waited on the Kramers. Mr. Kramer's health was very poor, cancer having metastasized first in his lungs before invading his other vital organs. Five years ago, doctors had given him a grim prognosis: six months to a year. In many ways, it would have been much better had the doctors been correct. Instead, Mr. Kramer lingered on, his body failing one component at a time. The cancer had spread to his brain, and now his most formidable tool was proving more and more useless. His growing forgetfulness as well as his frequent inability to express himself often made him lash out in frustration, snapping at whomever may be nearby, growling and yapping like an angry stray dog. It was really very sad to see, the withered old man spraying spittle while he fumbled for the right term of belittlement. By their request, Mike had been serving them exclusively for almost two years now, every Thursday night as well as the occasional Tuesday. In that time, Mike had seen a dramatic difference in Mr. Kramer's overall appearance, his body weight dropping and dropping until he was merely a skeleton in liver-spotted, nearly translucent skin.

Tonight, Mr. Kramer hadn't even been able to finish his special chocolate dessert, discarding it after only a few feeble bites. To merely call it chocolate pie would be a supreme insult to Chef Henri, a faux French fag who pouted like a spoiled schoolgirl at any criticism of his self-professed culinary mastery. Mike had gladly cut off the portion that the old geezer had been nibbling at, leaving more than half the portion intact and ready for consumption by someone who might appreciate it. Mike had certainly appreciated it at the time, anyway. It was one of the perks of the job. He offset his living expenses by eating the delicious leftovers his customers opted to leave for the trash man. Trudy, his girlfriend, found the habit repulsive, and he didn't speak of it with her again after observing her initial reaction. He didn't understand; it just made good economic sense. He always trimmed off the portions that had touched the silverware of his customers. The food was too good to waste. Besides, his grocery budget stretched more than twice as far when he only had to provide himself with meals on his days off.

Trudy warned him that someday he would get worms.

Two fairly intoxicated patrons stumbled into the room, laughing raucously at something one or the other of them had said.

"Do you know what she said to me?" Voice #1, low and gravely.

"Un-unh. What'd she say?" Voice #2, high-pitched and slurred.

Liquid splashing against porcelain.

"She said she'd take two!"

Guffaws erupted into wheezing convulsions, and Mike imagined the two men peeing all over each other's shoes. The smile that momentarily flitted across his face was disrupted by a wave of nausea that made him want to wet his face with toilet water and lay on the cool tile floor. *Geez!* It was hot in here!

The hearty laughter receded as the men finished their business and returned to the dining area. Mike set the newspaper on the floor, unable to muster any enthusiasm for the wisdom of *Dear Abby*. A bit of the turmoil in his lower digestive tract released, allowing him to breathe a little more easily.

I hope to God I'm not getting the flu, Mike thought. *I've got finals all week long.*

Mike was majoring in advertising and marketing and was due to graduate the following month. He and Phil, a buddy from high school, were going to roll all of their precious possessions together and head for the Big Apple in Mike's little VW bug, trying their hands in the big leagues. Phil was an actor, determined not to be a struggling one. He was certain that all he had to do was get his foot in the right door and then—*POW!* Superstardom. First, a few months on a soap to build a fan base, then it was straight to prime time for a short but very successful sitcom run. From there, he would move on to the big screen, win more Academy Awards than anyone ever before him, and thus become a living legend—all before the age of twenty-five. True, Phil was a nice-enough looking guy, but his amateur dramatic readings at the local playhouse had been grandiose and pretentious, performing his leading role in last winter's production of *Cat on a Hot Tin Roof* with all the scenery-chewing ferocity William Shatner might bring to Shakespeare. Mike had been a dutiful friend, applauding at all the appropriate places, but the play had nearly lulled him into a coma. Subsequently, Phil's request for a critical appraisal of his performance had been satiated by lies, lies and more lies, each one making Phil's head just a little bigger than it had been before.

Mike would hit the ad houses and be snapped up immediately by a headhunter, given his choice of corner suites in a downtown high rise with a superlative view of Central Park below. His grade point average was a solid three point eight—not the best in his class, but nearly. He had already received offers for internships with several well-known partnerships, but none of them were in New York, and that was the only place Mike wanted to live. He had known it since he was six years old and sat rooted to the television, watching the lighted ball go down on Times Square during Dick Clark's New Year's Rockin' Eve.

Again, the bathroom door squeaked on its hinges. "Mike?" It was Jill.

"What in the hell are you doing in here?" Mike asked, unconsciously covering himself as if the partition wasn't sufficient. "This is the *men's* room, Jill!"

"Yeah, well, I'm supposed to be off in fifteen minutes. You need to get back out here and take your tables. The Pendletons are doing some new age parenting crap, letting their kids order their own meals, and I can't get a word out of the brats. As if that ain't bad enough, that Kramer guy just barfed all over my apron. I smell like vomit, and I've got a date picking me up after work."

Mike grunted with the next abdominal ripple, uncaring that Jill was hovering just inside the door.

133

"Well, Jesus, Mike!" Jill said awkwardly. "You could have just said that you needed another minute!" The door closed, and Mike slowly exhaled, cold chills running up his spine. His forehead glistened with tiny little beads of sweat. He feared that he might have to go to the emergency room. This could be gastroenteritis.

Mike knelt forward and put his head between his knees. He was very dizzy, the room tilting and swaying, the sound of the overhead vent magnified into the thunder of a cheering crowd. There was a commotion beyond the door, and the sound appeared to be coming from the end of a very long tunnel.

The bathroom door flew open again, banging hard against the wall. From Mike's slumped-over position, he could see Timmy's ridiculous blue tennis shoes fidgeting just outside the stall door.

"Hey, Mike! Oh, man! You've got to come quick!" Timmy said. His voice sounded slow, like it was playing at the wrong speed.

"Unh?" Mike asked, barely able to lift his head.

"Old lady Kramer just gave her husband his birthday present! He asked her to put him out of his misery!" Timmy was excited, the story coming forth in animated little bursts. *"Euthanasia,* dude!"

"Unh?" Mike repeated, feeling himself slowly sliding forward.

"He just dropped dead after dessert! She poisoned his whole damned plate!"

DANNY BOY

Stephanie Markham rose to the tips of her toes and strained her arm, attempting to reach the last bottle of her brand of laundry detergent tucked away high on the stratospheric top shelf of Aisle 18A. She hadn't even attempted to locate a store clerk.

McGruder's General Store was thick with customers this February evening. Once yearly, Carl McGruder, owner and proprietor of the only department store in the small village of Corgan's Bluff, pulled out all the stops with a seventeen-hour sale. Every item in the store was marked down a minimum of twenty-five percent. There were two-for-one's and three-for-two's and rebates and free samples. People poured into the store from the moment the doors slid open at 7:00AM until they closed at midnight. They came from

136

Corgan's Bluff, from the hills and canyons in the outlying areas, and even as far as Garrettsville, which was nearly sixty miles away. There were no nearby malls or other modern shopping areas. The closest mall was nearly two hundred miles north. This quaint concept was like science fiction to Stephanie, who had moved to Corgan's Bluff two months ago from a larger metropolitan area with her husband when his job transferred him.

McGruder always boosted his payroll for this extravaganza, but every year the store was severely out of proportion in its employee-to-customer ratio. Trying to find help was like playing a bizarre, live action Where's Waldo? game. What might appear to be the bright blue vest of customer service personnel would invariably turn out to be an optical illusion generated by the swirling colors of the thickly packed shoppers pushing past one another.

Stephanie had been warned to avoid McGruder's when the sale was in full swing. It would have been different when she was younger, single and able to joust elbows with the best of them. Her husband, Alan, would have enthusiastically applauded the savings, but since their little boy, Danny, had been born a year-and-a-half ago, simple undertakings like shopping, visiting her girlfriends or even going for a stroll had become much larger tasks. There was the car seat and the ongoing battle between Stephanie and

Danny as to who decided when its use was necessary. There was the E-Z collapse stroller that never collapsed even remotely as easily as the one in the television commercial. The diaper bag had to be loaded with enough changes to last any unforeseen diarrhea typhoon, baby powder, wipes, first aid supplies, baby food, formula (if Danny wasn't in the mood to breastfeed), pacifiers, a rattle...no matter how full the bag was, Stephanie always had the feeling she had forgotten something vitally important. She used to have a recurring dream in which social workers seized her son because she had the wrong brand of formula. But, alas, today was laundry day, and Stephanie had forgotten to buy detergent when she had come in three days earlier for her weekly sundries.

Stephanie used the tips of her fingers to grapple for the bottle. She made contact and for a second, a smile played at her lips. Then the effort of trying to rake the bottle a little closer had the opposite effect. It skittered back another inch. The smile dropped abruptly.

Stephanie, clenching her jaw with determination, clamped the fingers of her left hand onto the edge of the top shelf and tentatively moved her feet one at a time onto the bottom shelf. The maneuver rewarded her with two more inches of height, which was just enough to get her finger through the plastic handle of the detergent and pull it forward and into reach. Her smile was back, warm and triumphant. The detergent was hers, by God!

She turned to place the jug in her cart and froze with her arm suspended in midair. Something was different. She quickly turned around, thinking she may have gotten reversed somehow while up on the shelf, and this was the cart of another customer. She examined the contents. It carried her purse and keys, several packages of diapers, and a blouse she had had her eye on for several weeks.

Stephanie's eyes widened with horror, and her head jerked left and right, scouring the aisle for the precious cargo she was missing. "Oh my God," she gasped. "Where's my son?"

She spun around again, her eyes darting quickly up the aisle, down the aisle. Danny couldn't have gotten out of the cart by himself. He could barely walk, much less complete the acrobatic maneuver required to descend from the plastic child seat behind the cart's handle. She looked under the cart in case, God forbid, Danny had fallen out. He was not there.

Cold beads of sweat formed at the nape of Stephanie's neck and trickled down between her shoulder blades. Full-blown panic constricted her throat and filled her limbs with lead. She opened her mouth to scream, but no sound escaped. The thick volume of customers became a human quicksand, immobilizing her and pulling her under.

After what seemed an eternity, Stephanie was able to move, even if she hadn't yet found her voice. With eyes blazing, she began to push her way through the crowd of mostly elderly ladies, greeted by astonished gasps and surprising profanities. Her eyes darted from cart to cart, looking for any sign whatsoever of her little boy.

Scream, damn you! her brain instructed. Help! Help! Help!

But Stephanie could not. Her mouth formed words, but the only sound to come forth was that of her strangled sobbing.

The sea of bargain shoppers was swelling like high tide and she was drowning. Hot tears were flowing, blurring her vision. She was unable to discern individual features of these passersby, just flashes of color and sound. As she continued toward the front of the aisle, she thought she saw Danny, sitting in a cart, playing with his fingers. When she rushed forward, the illusion fell away, and she was face-to-face with a child she had never seen before. His mother instinctively pulled him to her, eyeing Stephanie with the unique mix of fear, distrust and menace only a mother's eyes can project.

Stephanie's ears were filled to overflowing with the chatter of all the people, the steady hum of the refrigerator units two aisles over, the buzz of the cash registers regurgitating receipts and a strange high-pitched whine that was punctuated with little hiccups. It occurred to her that this last sound was coming from deep within her, gaining volume as surely as if someone were turning a knob on the back of her head. The circle of shoppers around her had stopped and were staring with wide eyes, recoiling backward as if she intended to physically assault them.

Stephanie turned to her left and ran for the mouth of the aisle. Beyond it lay the bank of cash registers, buzzing and buzzing, all lanes open. The exit door was at the front of the store. It became Stephanie's sole purpose to get to that door. She had to make sure she saw any person who might try to leave the store with Danny tucked in the crook of his or her arm.

Suddenly, a very tall, thin man appeared, blocking the aisle. He wore some sort of uniform with dark blue pants, a light blue shirt and black tie. Through her tears, Stephanie could not discern much else about him. He was somewhere between twenty and fifty years of age, had enormous front teeth and thick glasses. The filter of her despair had rendered him into a cartoon image. A cartoon image who was in her way. His lanky arms stretched out to his left and right in an attempt to block Stephanie's progress and shepherd her toward him.

Stephanie had to reach that exit. Time had lost its meaning to her, and she had no idea how long Danny had been gone from the cart. He might have already been taken from the building. For that matter, he may already be in a car speeding far, far away from Corgan's Bluff.

In a smooth maneuver that was neither practiced nor expected, Stephanie lifted her right foot three feet off the ground and drove it with all her might down onto the lanky man's left foot. As soon as it connected, her left knee was in motion, swinging upward at a forty-five-degree angle, connecting solidly with the astonished man's groin. He made a shrill scream and started to drop like a stone, but Stephanie was already clawing and climbing over him, her focus still on the exit door. As he dropped, he made a convulsive twitching movement, protectively drawing his legs up into the fetal position and in the process, tangling Stephanie's legs with his own. She went down hard, hitting her head on the highly polished tile floor. Unconsciousness swallowed her whole.

Stephanie squinted her eyes, trying to adapt to the overhead light beaming down on her. She was lying on a couch with a cold rag pressed to her forehead. She wasn't sure where she was. She sat up abruptly, but two strong arms clamped firmly over hers and eased her back down. The arms were attached to a middle-aged balding man in dress slacks and a white button-down shirt that was too tight around his bulbous midsection. His long sleeves had been unbuttoned and were cuffed to his elbows. Around his collar hung a paisley tie which was loosened at the neck and tied unevenly, with the back hanging two inches below the front. His look of genuine concern comforted her.

"Easy, there, now you just lay still a minute, honey. You hit your head pretty good out there. I've called a doctor to check you over," the man said, rubbing his hands up and down her arms in a reassuring, paternal manner.

"What happened?" Stephanie asked, sending her right hand to investigate the source of the throb in her head. It emanated from a goose egg behind her hairline just above her right temple.

"Well, now, I was hopin' that you could tell me about that," he said, grinning warmly.

"I'm not sure," Stephanie said dazedly. She slowly maneuvered into a slightly more upright position. What had she been doing? Her mind was in a mosh pit, being hammered and pushed and pulled with sensory information. Whatever she had been doing, Stephanie was sure it was very important, maybe even a matter of life and death. The details were dancing in the distance, twinkling like animal eyes in a heavy pea soup fog.

The couch upon which she lay had seen a lot of use. It was dark brown simulated leather, with multiple cuts in its cushions and back. Most of these had been healed by furnace tape, although a few still gaped open, yellow stuffing protruding. The room was a small, fully enclosed cubicle. Behind her head was a door and beside that a large window which appeared to be an interior one. From Stephanie's position, she could see rows of florescent lights stretching across the ceiling that was beyond the window. There was an industrial metal desk across the room from the couch with bright orange bucket chairs facing it. Its surface was covered with green and white printouts, metal trays and many other varied office supplies. Sitting slumped into the large chair behind the desk was a young, lanky man, his eyes fixed suspiciously in Stephanie's direction. He was awfully familiar, but Stephanie's cognitive process was momentarily shattered, and she could not pull it all together.

"Do you know who you are?" the older man was gently asking.

She looked at him for a moment as if he were insane. What kind of question was that? Then, from somewhere, she realized that he was checking her orientation because of the blow to her head. "Of course."

He looked at her expectantly.

"Oh, you want a name. Stephanie. It's Stephanie," she said.

"Howzabout a last name?" He jotted something on a legal pad and waited.

Stephanie's eyebrows knitted together earnestly, reaching and straining. Everyone has a last name. How could someone not remember their own damned surname? "This is so stupid; I can't seem to..." Her voice trailed off and she shrugged with a weak smile.

"That's okay, honey. I'm sure it'll come right back. Just relax and stop trying so hard," he said, patting her arm.

"Where am I?" she asked.

"Why, you're in my office. I'm Carl McGruder. I'm the owner of this here store," he said with a smile.

Stephanie carefully pulled herself into a sitting position, swinging her legs down to touch the floor. A beige handbag rested on its side at her feet, presumably hers. "Store?" she asked, perplexed.

"Tell ya what," Carl said. "I'll tell you what I know, and maybe that'll jog ya."

"Okay."

Carl looked for a way to sugarcoat the incident as told to him by several store patrons and Lonnie, the lanky security guard who was still affixing Stephanie with suspicious eyes. "As best I understand, you were down in Aisle 18A, and you just kind of went nuts," he ended up saying. Eloquence and tact had never been strong points for Carl.

"Nuts?" she smiled, feeling a little mortified although unsure of why.

Lonnie authoritatively cleared his throat. Stephanie looked at him and wondered if this alleged security guard was old enough to vote. He had longish, greasy black hair hanging in strings around his face. His face was pitted and scarred with the ghosts of acne past and present. An especially angry red bump glowed on his chin, threatening to spore without provocation. He wore thick glasses with heavy black frames and his front teeth jutted out prominently from between his lips. When he spoke, his voice was as whiny and petulant as Stephanie would have expected. "What you done, Miss, is you assaulted an officer."

Stephanie laughed richly. She couldn't help herself. "An officer? Who?"

Lonnie's cheeks blazed red. "Me! Who the hell didja think I meant? Me!" With his pride clearly wounded, he swiveled halfway around and resumed sulking.

Rolling his eyes, Carl looked at Stephanie and smiled again. "Lonnie Akerman is one of our security guards here at McGruder's Department Store."

Stephanie tried to refocus. The name of the store was so familiar, like the tune of an old favorite song. "Okay, go on."

"Well, you were screaming and carrying on, but no one could tell what you were trying to say. Lonnie, here, heard the commotion and went to see if everything was alright. I guess you pulled out the ole kung fu on him and climbed right over him, quicker'n a cat can scale a tree."

"She caught me by surprise!" Lonnie yelled defensively. Nonetheless, he kept his eyes downcast, avoiding Carl's gaze.

"Anyway, you got all tangled up in Lonnie's legs as he was goin' down—"

Lonnie, his eyes bugging out, interrupted, "Jesus, Carl! You're makin' me sound like a dadburn foo-ool! It was taekwondo, man, taekwondo. I used her momentum to bring her down just like—"

"Lonnie. Give it a rest or I'm gonna send you to the parking lot to bring in some carts." Carl's voice was firm, and he glared unblinkingly at Lonnie. Lonnie could see Carl had every intention of following through, if necessary. He snapped his mouth shut, folded his arms across his chest and swiveled sideways, resuming his pout.

Carl returned his attention to Stephanie. "When Lonnie fell, you did too, and you hit your head on the floor. That pretty well brings us current. Your ID and your purse were in a cart partway up the aisle behind you. Your name is Markham. Stephanie Markham. Does that jog anything?" He handed her the purse, which she absently strapped over her shoulder.

Obviously, he had been trying to get her to remember on her own. Now he was attempting to spoon-feed her with pertinent information in hopes of an epiphany.

Stephanie scratched her head. Of course she was Stephanie Markham. Ever since she had gotten married. Before that, she had been Stephanie...Jarvis! That's right. Her mother's name was Beatrice and her father was Jacob. A smile started to spread across Stephanie's face. She had moved to town...Corgan's Bluff... just a few months ago. She moved because her husband, Alan, had gotten a new region to manage. He was in insurance.

Carl smiled, seeing the flickers of recognition in Stephanie's eyes. "Oh, good, good. Is it coming back?"

Stephanie nodded.

"We've got a doctor on the way to make sure you're okay, and we left a message for your husband, but he—"

Stephanie eyes widened with terror. Oh, God, she thought. Danny.

Carl's smile fell from his lips. "Ma'am? Are you alright?"

Suddenly, Stephanie leapt to her feet. The world beneath her seemed to be at a terrible incline, and she plopped back on the couch. "My God, my God, my God," she said, cradling her head in her hands. She got up again, more slowly this time. Tiny bursts of blackness played in her peripheral vision, but after a moment, it crept back, allowing her to think more clearly. How long has it been? she thought, stepping over to the large window overlooking the store's sales floor. People were everywhere, in every aisle, at every checkout lane. The cash registers buzzed and buzzed. "Someone kidnapped my son!"

"What?" Carl was on his feet immediately. "Are you telling me that someone has taken your son in my store?"

Stephanie nodded frantically, but she would not take her eyes away from the window. Danny might still be in the store. What could have happened?

Carl was already on the phone, calling the police. "We've got a missing kid down here at McGruder's. Send someone, pronto."

Lonnie had gotten up from his seat and circled the desk to stand by Stephanie. "What'd the little boy look like, ma'am?" He was an eager bloodhound begging for a scent.

"He's 19 months old, fuzzy brown hair, dimples....oh, he was wearing a powder blue snap-up jumpsuit. His name is Danny," she said. Suddenly, her eyes were drawn all the way left to Aisle 1. A willowy honey-blond woman was rounding the corner of the aisle, traversing the median that separated the checkout stands from the other perpendicular aisles. She pushed an empty shopping cart in front of her. Empty except for a small child in the safety seat. He wore a blue jumpsuit and had a fluff of brown hair leaping straight up from his head. He was red-faced, his mouth pulled open in a mighty bawl that was eerily silent from within the sanctuary of the office. Danny!

Stephanie didn't even remember going through the office door. She left Carl and Lonnie in a confused daze, her legs carrying her down the long aisle behind the registers. She sifted through the crowd at all costs, never losing sight of the top of that honey-blond head. She was vaguely aware of Carl and Lonnie following somewhere behind her.

At last, she was standing at the cart, looking down at the boy. Please, oh God, please, she thought.

It was Danny.

A fresh stream of tears dampened her cheeks. Her ears were joyously filled with the shrieking sobs emanating from the unhappy little fellow. Amazingly, the honey-blond woman had not yet noticed her. Just before Stephanie had reached the cart, the woman had been jostled by a heavyset teenage girl, and they were in the middle of exchanging choice words.

Stephanie reached into the cart and plucked the little boy up into her arms, cradling him to her breast. He calmed instantly, nestling into the warm crook of her arm. After hushing him and gingerly stroking his head, Stephanie's eyes darted back to the willowy woman. Her argument with the teenager had ended, and she was now staring at Stephanie.

Their eyes locked.

The woman's youthful, willowy appearance belied the hardness of her tight, drawn features. She was wearing a cut-off t-shirt that displayed her emaciated belly, threadbare blue jeans that were almost white, and yellow flip-flops that exposed her dirty feet. Her arms were wiry and muscular, with veins pulsing up and down them. Her eyes were almost black. Black eyes, burning a hole right through Stephanie. The woman's upper lip drew back, exposing an odd yellow grimace. One of her front teeth was missing.

Stephanie had no doubt this woman was unbalanced. Dangerously unbalanced. Who else would pluck an innocent child away from his mother in the middle of a store?

The woman started to reach out her claw-like hands. "What—" the woman began, but Stephanie wasn't about to stick around and wait for the rest of the sentence. If it came down to hand-to-hand combat, she was unsure of her odds. This woman looked like an animal.

Stephanie tightened her grip on Danny and whirled around and reversed course. The cart was between the two women and offered her only a minimal head start. Carl and Lonnie emerged from the crowd directly in front of Stephanie.

"Is that your boy?" Carl asked anxiously, as Lonnie proceeded toward the other woman. Stephanie nodded, her face pressed to the top of Danny's head. That was all Carl needed. He was only steps behind Lonnie, who had just reached the other woman.

Stephanie dared to look back. She had run far enough she could not hear the woman, but her mouth was moving

152

a mile a minute. Lonnie had his hands firmly on her shoulders and Carl was barking something at her, his finger jabbing the air in front of her face. She looked crazed. Her black eyes blazed with fury. Whatever she was saying was sending strings of drool dribbling down her chin. Then she started to violently throw herself forward, pushing Lonnie, and then pushing both Carl and Lonnie. Her arms were outstretched, clawing at the air, but her eyes were fixed on Stephanie. Above the buzz of the sale shoppers, Stephanie heard her unmistakable vow, "I'll kill you!"

Stephanie gasped and turned on her heel. She plowed through the people who stood between her and the exit. Nothing would stop her now. She saw the look in those eyes. She knew the woman meant business. She doubted Carl and Lonnie could hold her for long. Stephanie had once read some psychopaths exhibited superhuman strength while in the throws of rage. Her primary object was to get Danny the hell out of there.

At last, Stephanie reached the exit door. It slid open for her, but not quickly enough, so she pushed it along faster, causing the internal workings of the door's motor to groan in protest. She burst through and into the cold night air. The parking lot was packed. Frantically, Stephanie searched for her automobile, finding it two lanes to her left and several rows deep. An overhead light cast a ghostly pallor on the vehicle, spotlighting her exact location. A gentle snow was falling.

Stephanie fumbled with her purse which had mercifully remained on her shoulder. She found her keys and unlocked the driver's door. She depressed the automatic lock button on the inside panel of the door, freeing the locks from the remaining doors. Quickly, she opened the rear door and began to position Danny into the car seat. As if on cue, his wailing resumed followed by a flailing of unhappy little arms and legs.

"Danny! Stop it! We don't have time," Stephanie urged, gently holding his legs in place as she maneuvered the belts of the safety seat. Through the windows of the passenger side, she glanced up at the store's entrance.

The crazed woman was pushing her way out of the store.

Stephanie could see Carl and Lonnie just over the woman's shoulders. They both looked angry, frustrated the woman was gaining distance, staying beyond their grasp.

A strangled cry escaped Stephanie's lips as she locked the front of the car seat into place, despite Danny's escalating wails. She slid into the driver's seat and started the car. The engine roared to life. She geared into reverse and stomped on the gas pedal. Realizing almost instantly she was going to plow into the cars parked across the lane behind her, she slammed on the brake, stopping with only inches to spare. She jerked the gearshift into drive and cut the steering wheel hard and to the left. As her foot began to release its pressure from the brake, the woman threw herself onto the passenger side of the car.

Stephanie screamed. The woman was screaming, too, but it was unintelligible. She sounded like a baying wolf, dangerously close. Her hands were pounding the tempered glass, over and over, making the glass vibrate in its track. As she cursed, the spittle that was spraying from her mouth landed on the window in bubbly white oozing trails. Stephanie realized she hadn't relocked the doors just as the passenger door flew open.

Stephanie buried the accelerator. The car lurched forward and to the left, jarring the crazy woman's hold on the car. She tumbled backward into the parking lot. The swinging door slammed shut as it clipped the back end of a big white Cadillac parked in the next space.

Like a bullet from a gun, Stephanie rocketed up the paved tongue which served as the only entrance and exit to McGruder's General Store. As she neared its end, she slowed only as much as necessary to ascertain there were no oncoming vehicles on Main Street. She turned the car hard to the right and barreled off into the night. As she left, she could hear the faint approach of sirens as the police were nearing the scene.

Thank God, she thought. Let them deal with her.

Stephanie realized she had been holding her breath for some time. She allowed herself to exhale and replenish her lungs with fresh air. Danny, his cheeks shiny with tears, was screaming furiously in the backseat.

She reached the end of the city limits on Main Street. The streetlights stopped abruptly here, marking the perimeter of the little village. Beyond, Main Street became Route 313, winding out into the dark, rural countryside. Snow was falling harder, leaving a fine powder of white dust on the road. Stephanie and Alan's old farmhouse was five miles straight ahead. If she could make it there, everything would be okay.

Stephanie glanced nervously in the rearview mirror. She half expected to see a car closing in behind her. Instead, the road was dark and empty.

She looked at Danny who was still crying. "Danny boy," she said soothingly. "Mommy's here. Everything's alright. We just have to get home to Daddy, and everything will be all better. How's that sound, baby doll?"

Danny coughed and sobbed, having been aggravated by all the sudden action.

Stephanie's eyes alternated their focus. First, the road ahead, stretching out into the darkness. Snow was driving into the windshield. Next, the view in the mirror, still dark and empty. Then, Danny. She inspected what she could see in the rearview mirror. He didn't seem to be hurt. She could see his legs and arms squirming. All of his toes and fingers were still attached.

Danny!

Unintelligible ramblings of praise to God flowed from Stephanie's lips. Her baby was safe! Thank you, thank you, God!

The five-mile drive seemed to go on forever, but soon, her oversized mailbox, all decked out like a miniature farmhouse, appeared on the right side of the lane. The farmhouse stood on a hill, with a winding dirt drive that led beside the house and beyond to a ramshackle barn. Alan planned to tear the barn down this summer and replace it with a more modern garage.

The house was dark. Darkness fell earlier at this time of year, and Stephanie had lost all concept of time. She glanced at the digital display on her dashboard. It was 7:00PM. Alan would be home from work anytime.

Stephanie stopped the car at the side of the house. She extracted Danny, who had begun to settle, from the car seat and carried him up to the side porch. She cooed lovingly in

157

his ear and stroked the back of his head. They had bolted from the store so quickly Stephanie hadn't had enough time to find Danny's coat, much less put it on him. He was shivering from the cold.

Stephanie unlocked the door and carried Danny into the kitchen, flicking on the overhead light as she passed the switch. She wanted to squeeze him so tightly to herself it took conscious effort not to become overzealous and hurt him. His sobbing had stopped, and he was making little burbling sounds.

Stephanie pulled a chair away from the kitchen table and sat down. She eased Danny away from her and placed him on his back in her lap. He looked up at her with puffy, heavy blue eyes. He was sleepy.

Stephanie allowed herself to cry. She feared she would frighten Danny but could hold back no longer. She remembered the joy of being informed of her pregnancy. Some husbands were not nearly as supportive as Alan had been. He was a good husband and a good father. He had been elated. The nine months of her pregnancy seemed to last nine years. They shared as much of the experience as they physically could. Some of her more dour friends back in Portsmouth, Ohio, had filled her with horror stories of the pain of delivery. All she remembered was that magic moment when Danny had made his entrance into the world. He was the most beautiful thing she had ever seen.

The last year-and-a-half had been full of firsts and Stephanie was always filled with amazement and wonder that this little piece of her was so clever and talented. She supposed all mothers felt this way, but way deep down inside, she knew it was really true about her child.

She lifted him gently to her breast and carried him into the adjoining living room, pressing her nose into his soft, fuzzy hair and inhaling deeply. She loved the way the top of his head smelled.

Alan had bought a secondhand crib at a garage sale when they had moved into the house. He placed it in the living room so Danny could be close to Stephanie even when he napped during the day. Stephanie eased the baby down into it, carefully cupping her hand behind his head and lowering it onto the small pillow. He was already sleeping. She pulled a flannel blanket adorned with teddy bears around Danny and smiled down at him.

Her boy was safely at home.

As she gently traced the contours of Danny's face with her fingertips, she saw a beam of headlights pierce the darkness. A car was coming up the drive. Alan was home at last.

Stephanie kissed the top of Danny's head and reentered the kitchen, needing to see Alan, to feel his strong arms around her. Together, they would call the police and tell them what happened in the store. The woman should already be under arrest, but the police would need Stephanie's testimony.

Stephanie froze. Framed in the doorway to the porch was the wild-eyed woman, her honey-blond hair disheveled and a look of pure hatred on her face. Her arms were tensed and away from her sides, like a gunslinger from the Old West, poised for the draw. Her yellow teeth were fixed in a snarl.

Stephanie wanted to scream. She wanted to scream so loudly the sound would reverberate through the surrounding hills and be heard from one end of Corgan's Bluff to the other. Her mouth opened, but nothing came out.

From behind the woman came an authoritative voice, "Freeze! Police! You stay right there!"

Thank God! Stephanie thought. The police are right behind her. Of course, they are.

The woman didn't move, but her eyebrows knitted together in frustration. The policeman, a stout, barrel-chested man, appeared at the woman's elbow. He bent down closer to the woman's face and said gently, "You need to let us handle it from here. There's no need in getting yourself into any trouble." He turned his gaze to Stephanie. "Are you Stephanie Markham?"

"Yes," she said hesitantly.

"Ma'am, you are under arrest for the kidnapping of this child. You have the right—"

"NO!" Stephanie screamed, backing into the corner of the kitchen. Behind the officer, Carl and Lonnie from the department store were entering the kitchen. They looked at her with condemning eyes.

Alan came next, entering the kitchen with his briefcase in hand. He looked around, trying to comprehend all that was happening. In a booming voice, he said, "Just what the hell is going on here?"

The officer had taken Stephanie away in handcuffs. She had gotten hysterical and was lashing out at anyone within arm's reach. Another policeman, Sergeant Hitchings, had arrived on the scene and was taking statements. Carl, Lonnie, Alan and the honey-haired woman whose name was

Tina Charles, sat around the kitchen table. Tina was cradling the baby and holding him to her bosom.

"They won't hurt her, will they?" asked Alan. "She's not a criminal, she's just…"

"No, they won't hurt her," replied Sergeant Hitchings. "They need to get her calmed down, but then they'll turn her over to a doctor for psychiatric care."

"I can't believe this is happening. My son last week, my wife this week," murmured Alan, lowering his face into his hands. His eyes were lined with grief.

"What happened to your son?" the policeman asked.

"He was visiting his grandparents last week. There was a carbon monoxide leak in their heating system. He was gone…" Alan choked back a sob. "I've been a total wreck. I went back to work today for the first time since… Stephanie was being so strong. I thought it was amazing. I couldn't even look at his…things long enough to put them out of sight. Steph said we'd do it together when we were ready, and she went through the house covering all of it until then."

Sergeant Hitchings took details of the incident in the department store from Carl, Lonnie and Tina. Satisfied when he had enough, he stood to leave. Carl and Lonnie had already mumbled condolences to Alan and left.

"Wait a minute," said Tina in her sweet country twang, tugging at Sergeant Hitchings sleeve. "Do I have to press charges?"

"You don't want to?" asked the surprised sergeant.

"Well, can't we do something to get her help without puttin' her in jail?"

"I'm sure we can work something out that's to everyone's benefit," the sergeant replied.

Alan looked wonderingly at Tina. "Thank you so much. Why are you being so kind?"

"Looks to me like your wife's had enough hard knocks. I coulda killed her myself most of this evening, but instead, I'd rather take the high road. I think that's what Jesus would want me to do." She flashed her yellow smile at Alan.

"Come along, Mrs. Charles. I'll take you and your boy home," said Sergeant Hitchings, placing a hand on Tina's elbow.

"That's right," Tina cooed into the baby's ear as she and the sergeant headed for the door. "I bet your daddy's just about worried to pieces, ain't he, Danny Boy?"

THE BUENA VISTA MALLET CLUB

"Where did she go?" asked Millie Nelson, shielding her eyes from the harsh afternoon sunlight as she scanned the grassy field. She wore a flowered, pale blue sundress with elastic stretched tight around her ample midsection. Her wispy gray hair had turned to frizz atop her head, and she looked like a dandelion ready to send its seed airborne.

"She probably stopped to look at a frog," said Lizzie Shrout, shuffling her oversized feet in the emerald green blanket of grass. "She's always doing that." Lizzie had been straight as rail since birth, and neither babies nor old age had done anything to alter her posture.

"Well, I'll be old and dead by the time she gets back," groused Dottie Driscoll, swinging her mallet wildly at nothing in particular. She was a short-statured, short-

164

tempered woman wearing a smart pastel pink running suit specially designed for her by a New York City couturier who specialized in designs for the full-figured gal. Her fire-engine hair glinted like copper in the sun, held back by a pink sun visor which neatly matched her ensemble.

Millie ducked just in time to keep from being hit by the arcing mallet. "Watch that thing, Dottie! I won't have you knocking me down with it again this week." Last week, Dottie bopped Millie squarely on the head, discombobulating her completely and making her forget her secret family recipe for fried chicken for three whole days. If the recipe hadn't finally resurfaced, Millie intended to speak to her solicitor and file suit against her careless friend, citing crimes against humanity as her cause of action.

"*EMMY!*" boomed Dottie, her voice reverberating against the hills surrounding the Buena Vista Retirement Community. "*YOU'RE HOLDING UP THE GAME!*" Some game. None of the women in the Buena Vista Mallet Club actually understood the rules of croquet, much less how to keep score. They did, however, enjoy swinging the wooden mallets viciously at the helpless balls, launching them as far away as possible before they plummeted back to the earth like bombs from a warplane. They had dispensed with the stakes and wickets long ago. What fun was *that?* Lizzie

165

couldn't hit the broad side of a barn, and Dottie's specialty seemed to be shots of an airborne variety. Millie particularly liked to knock her opponents' balls as far away as possible. She had developed quite a nasty cackle over the years, something her opponents didn't appreciate in the least. Emmy DeLotell's area of expertise was the home run; it was the wrong sport but the same concept. She consistently plowed the ball out of bounds where it would come to rest in the most unlikely of places. They had once wasted an entire afternoon searching for a ball which had vanished forever down a drainage culvert.

The grassy meadow in which they now played dropped sharply at the south end to a narrow creek bed which burbled with sparkling clear water. Emmy had lowered her sturdy frame over the edge and down the steep, rocky path quite some time ago. There was nothing but birdsongs in response to Dottie's thunderous inquiry.

"You don't suppose she twisted her ankle, do you?" worried Lizzie. "She might be laying facedown in the creek."

"The good Lord wouldn't spare us from these insufferable games that easily," said Dottie, walking toward the edge of the meadow. Millie and Lizzie looked at each other and rolled their eyes, then followed along.

They had nearly reached the mouth of the narrow trail when Emmy came back over the edge. The women knew something was amiss because there was no sign of Emmy's croquet mallet. Besides that, her salt-and-pepper hair was disheveled, her glasses were crooked and there was mud streaked across her forehead.

"Oh, for heaven's sake, Emmy!" said Dottie. "Look at you! We were supposed to go for a nice tea after we finished. I'd be embarrassed to sit next to you!"

Emmy was a bit winded from her climb. She stopped and bent at the waist, putting her hands on her knees. Dottie was certain it was for dramatic effect, but she allowed the woman to complete her histrionics uninterrupted. After Emmy had collected her breath, she straightened and faced her friends.

"We have a problem, ladies," she said.

"A problem?" asked Lizzie.

"How so?" asked Millie.

"Oh, pooh!" said Dottie.

"Yes," said Emmy, nodding her head and straightening her glasses. "A problem, indeed. I ran into Mr. Herman Delaney at the bottom of the ravine. I'm fairly certain that he's dead."

"Oh, my," said Millie. "He *does* appear to be dead."

Millie prodded Delaney's lifeless body with the handle of her mallet. He merely slid to the side, his head lolling on his chest. His lips and tongue were swollen and blue, and his eyes seemed ready to eject from his skull. His legs had gone stiff, and when he rolled to the side, his knee stayed curiously bent, suspended slightly from the ground although the loose gravel underneath it had scattered.

Herman Delaney was also a member of the Buena Vista Retirement Community, as well as Chairman of the Board of Directors. He was a retired attorney who made his own fortune by investing wisely in the stock market—this, of course, was in addition to the millions and millions left to him in a family trust fund. His wife, Ella, preceded him in death ten years ago, and they had never been blessed with children. He was never in the best of health, but it was certainly a surprise to find him splayed out for the birds, looking so very ghastly.

"What should we do?" asked Lizzie, kneading her hands together in her loose-fitting dress. She had been mousy as a girl and was mousy as a woman. She relied on her friends' guidance in matters as simple as wardrobe; dealing with a dead man was definitely outside of her comfort zone.

"Call the police, of course," said Emmy. She turned to face Dottie, who was staring distastefully at the corpse. "Be a dear, Dot, and ring the police on your cell phone."

"I left it in the car," said Dottie, examining the gloss of her fingernails.

Emmy, Lizzie and Millie stared at Dottie expectantly.

"You want *me* to get it?" She threw her head back and laughed. "I'm sorry, dears, but I've already toppled onto my backside once getting down that mountain path. All of the gravel! I'll not do it again." As a reminder to her friends, she pivoted at the waist and showed them her soiled rear end.

"We have no choice then," said Millie, stooping to grab Herman Delaney's raised leg by the ankle. "We'll just have to haul him up."

"Millie!" the other three cried, wide-eyed with horror. Lizzie nearly passed out.

"You shouldn't move a dead man," said Emmy, shooing Millie's hands away from Herman's leg after coaxing her to lower it back to its previous somewhat-suspended position.

"I don't think we're going to *hurt* him," said Millie, hands on her hips.

Emmy was about to say something else, but the conversation was mercifully cut short by the sound of approaching sirens. They were coming from above, right across the peaceful green meadow which had been home to their croquet club for years. An ambulance and a police car simultaneously nosed up to the edge of drop-off. Sheriff Roger Newton, a short and stout man in his fifties, emerged from the squad car and looked down at the women, shaking his head.

"Emmy DeLotell," he said. "I should've known you'd be involved."

"Oh, look dear!" called Millie from several yards behind the others. "I've found your ball!" She held the prized object high above her head for all to see.

Several hours later, the Buena Vista Mallet Club gathered in Emmy's bright yellow kitchen, drinking steaming cups of tea around her spotless Formica table. They had all been widowed for years and had no responsibilities beyond those of tending to themselves. They often congregated in the kitchens of the various members— except Dottie's kitchen, for she was too fussy with her possessions to tolerate interlopers. She nearly had a stroke when Millie had eaten a piece of cheesecake on one of her Franklin Mint collectibles.

"I don't know why Roger has to give me such a hard way to go," groused Emmy.

"It's because you stick your nose in his business all the time, dear," reminded Lizzie.

"He finds your credentials questionable," added Millie.

"He's an ass," said Dottie.

"Oh, he is *not!*" said Emmy, taking a thoughtful sip of her tea. For over twenty years, she had been the office manager for Skip Parker, a private detective in Cleveland. He had more or less forced Emmy into early retirement by taking his own; three years prior, his heart had given out on the sixteenth hole during his weekly golf game. Once the agency closed its doors, Emmy decided she was too old to learn a new position for another company. Although she had never handled any of Skip's cases herself, she always found them interesting, and her natural curiosity caused her to cross paths with Sheriff Roger Newton several times in the past.

"Roger received an anonymous telephone tip about Herman's body. That's why he showed up when he did," said Emmy.

"So, what did he say happened?" asked Lizzie.

"Poison, would you believe," said Emmy.

"How exciting!" said Millie.

"Not for Herman Delaney," said Dottie.

"They've arrested his niece, Diane Crankshaw," said Emmy. "Roger said it was all open and shut."

"*Ooo!* That's very efficient sounding, isn't it?" asked Lizzie.

"I didn't know Mr. Delaney had any family," said Millie.

"Neither did I," said Emmy. "Roger says that Herman's sister died in childbirth. The baby—Diane—was given up for adoption. The Crankshaws raised her as their own until Diane recently uncovered paperwork detailing the adoption."

"What about her birth father? Why didn't he raise her?" asked Lizzie.

Dottie snorted. "Isn't that just like a man? Word to the wise: If you want to be rid of a man, give him something to be responsible for. He'll be out the door like lightning."

"You're shameful!" gasped Lizzie.

Dottie shook her head. *"Truthful."*

"So had the niece been in town for long?" asked Millie, adding spoonful after spoonful of sugar to her tea.

"About a month, I gather," said Emmy.

"Why does Roger think she killed her uncle?" asked Lizzie.

"She was his sole beneficiary," said Emmy. She stood from the table and crossed the small kitchen, retrieving a pan of chocolate chip cookies from the oven. "Roger said she wouldn't say a word until her lawyer arrived, but as of yet, they haven't been able to reach him." She eased the cookies off the sheet with a spatula and arranged them on a cooling rack.

"Well, it sounds open and shut to me," said Dottie.

"Really?" mused Emmy. "Not me. The only thing the girl stood to gain was time. The money was coming to her as soon as her uncle passed, and he was already in poor health. The risk hardly seems worth it."

Millie had hefted her bulk from the table and ambled across to the counter, greedy fingers sneaking toward the cookies. Emmy smacked her hand away before they made contact.

"Ow!" Millie pulled her hand to her mouth and shot Emmy an astonished glance. "What was that for?"

"These cookies aren't for us," said Emmy.

"Who are they for?" asked Millie.

"I was thinking that poor dear must be awfully hungry waiting for her attorney to arrive," said Emmy.

"Oh, dear," said Lizzie. "Here she goes again."

Emmy waited until she saw Roger Newton and his deputy leave the small station before she waddled in with her gift for the prisoner. Zelma Clark manned the switchboard and front desk, but mostly she chatted on the telephone with her friends, as she was doing now. She paused in her conversation long enough to wave Emmy through to the rear of the building where the single holding cell was located.

Diane Crankshaw wasn't at all what Emmy had expected. She was a hard-looking bleached blonde in her mid-twenties with suspicious eyes and a determined set to her jaw.

"What do you want?" Diane asked.

Emmy was startled by her abruptness. "Why, I thought you might like something to eat."

Diane eyed the foil-wrapped plate thoroughly before seizing it through the bars. She pulled the aluminum foil back and started wolfing down chocolate chip cookies. After the third one, she paused, realizing Emmy was still standing expectantly on the other side. "Are you just going to stand there all day?" she asked.

Emmy smiled patiently. "I thought you might like to talk to someone. I live in Buena Vista a few blocks over from where your uncle lived."

"You a cop or something?"

Emmy laughed. "Heavens, no! Do I look like a police officer?"

"If you think being friends with my uncle makes you a friend of mine, you're mistaken," Diane said, spraying cookie dust through the air as she spoke.

"I didn't say we were friends, just neighbors," said Emmy. "I guess you weren't close, then?"

"I didn't even know he existed until recently," said Diane, bitterly. "When I think of the way I was raised compared to the way things *could* have been."

"Did the Crankshaws mistreat you?"

"I should say! You should have seen the fit I had to throw to get my own car when I was sixteen. All that effort, and I still only got a *Chevrolet*. Then I find out that my *real* family—Uncle Herman, that is—could've easily afforded to buy me a different car for each day of the week. How do you think that makes me feel?"

Emmy deliberated over her response. The girl was completely spoiled, and Emmy suspected the Crankshaws had spent more than their fair share of evenings wondering where they had gone wrong. Emmy wanted to appear sympathetic in order to draw information from the girl, but it was difficult to keep herself from reaching through the bars and smacking some common courtesy into her.

"That's very difficult, dear," she finally managed.

"And *finally,* the old geezer kicks over, leaving me his entire fortune, and *I'm* the one arrested for killing him," Diane said. "Unbelievable."

"It most certainly is," said Emmy. "I understand that your uncle was poisoned."

Diane nodded. "Arsenic in his banana bread."

"I assume the police think you had the opportunity to poison it?"

"Well, I made the bread and didn't eat any of it, so I guess it doesn't look good."

"Why didn't you eat any?" asked Emmy.

Diane screwed up her face. "Banana bread? *Yuck!*"

Emmy was just finishing her dinner dishes when the other three members of the Buena Vista Mallet Club arrived. Normally, they played Yahtzee on Tuesdays, but Emmy's heart wasn't really in it. She kept thinking of the ill-tempered Crankshaw girl, sleeping on the hard cot at the sheriff's station.

"So, did you learn anything from the niece?" asked Dottie.

"I certainly did," said Emmy. "I learned that she has no manners whatsoever. Not a single word of thanks for bringing the cookies down."

"But do you think she killed her uncle?" asked Lizzie.

"There are only three dice in the box," muttered Millie, rummaging through the open container of Yahtzee. "Why are there only three dice in the box?"

"It still doesn't make sense to me. Why would she risk her entire future for things she would inherit soon enough?" asked Emmy.

"People are impatient," said Dottie. "It's all in the here and now."

"There's a big difference between being impatient and being stupid," said Emmy.

"I only see two scorecards," said Millie, still fussing with the contents of the game. "There are four of us. This will never do."

"Well, I guess that puts an end to your investigation," said Dottie, sipping from a glass of iced tea.

"Au contraire, my dear," said Emmy.

"Oh, dear," sighed Dottie.

"What are you going to do next?" asked Lizzie excitedly. Lizzie was always prone to get swept up in the excitement of the moment.

"What is at the center of every successful household?" asked Emmy.

"A furnace?" mused Millie, looking up from the contents of the Yahtzee box.

"No," said Emmy. "A woman."

"Isn't that a lovely thought," said Lizzie dreamily. Lizzie was also prone to mooning over romantic ideology.

"It's the *truth*," said Dottie. "When my Albert was alive, he was completely lost when I wasn't around. But how does this apply to Herman Delaney? He's been a widower for quite some time."

"Abigail Pritchett," said Emmy, smiling with satisfaction. She studied each of her friends' faces and could hear the flies buzzing behind their vacant eyes. "His *maid*. If anyone knew what was going on in that house, she did. I think it's time we invited Abigail out to play croquet."

"Good. Maybe she can loan us a couple of dice, too," said Millie, putting the lid back on the game and shoving it aside with a sigh.

In a small town like Buena Vista, Ohio, people know each other well. If one receives a sudden invitation to join the Buena Vista Mallet Club for a round of croquet, there is most certainly an underlying purpose. Abigail Pritchett appeared on the green (as the ladies called their meadow) at eight o'clock sharp Wednesday morning. She knew all of the other women well enough to greet at the market, but no more than that. She had received Emmy's telephoned invite with the proper mixture of suspicion and curiosity. She looked lost behind the wheel of the SUV which she guided with ferocity into the clubhouse parking lot. She was a thin-lipped woman with dark chestnut hair, fastened at the base of her neck in a ponytail. Millie thought the style was rather juvenile for a woman in her forties, but she graciously elected to keep her opinion to herself.

"We're so glad you could join us, dear," said Emmy, placing a hand on Abigail's elbow and giving it a little squeeze.

"Well, thanks for inviting me, I guess," said Abigail, still unsure and feeling every bit the outsider. "I've never once played croquet, though, so I pity whoever has me on their team. Are there teams?"

Lizzie shrugged. "Sometimes. We don't really play, either. It's an excuse to get out and stretch our legs." She was watching Abigail intently, as if at any moment the secrets of life might come tumbling forth from her lips. Emmy nudged her discreetly to break her moronic stare.

"FORE!" shrieked Millie, swinging her mallet downward toward the hapless ball. She misjudged the radius of her swing and drove the mallet straight into the ground. The impact traveled up her arms and rattled her false teeth. Abigail distanced herself from Millie as she kept a careful eye on the mallet.

They plodded along for nearly an hour, mallets swinging and balls flying. As they entered the meadow in which their play had been interrupted the previous afternoon, Emmy said, "It was just over that ridge that I found poor Mr. Delaney."

"Hmm," said Abigail, lightly tapping her ball so that it puttered a few feet ahead.

"Not like *that*, Abigail," said Millie, sidling up to her own ball. "You're hitting like a girl. You've got to put your whole body into the swing—like this." She brought her mallet around and sent the striped ball flying over the lip of the ridge, her mallet sailing through the air after it.

"Except you hold onto your mallet," whispered Lizzie to Abigail.

"So, do you think the niece did it?" asked Dottie bluntly, tired of jockeying for position in the conversation.

Abigail looked at her sharply and made a face like she had been force-fed a sour lemon. "Oh, that horrid girl! I'm sure she did. There wasn't a thing in this world that was good enough for her! To think of the way that Herman opened his house up to her! Such an ingrate. Couldn't even bother to pick up a few items for me at the store when she was already there. Said it wasn't her job to do the shopping. You can bet she would have been all for it if shopping meant new things for her. She treated me less than human."

"I don't see my ball!" shouted Millie from the edge of the grassy ridge.

"Why don't we cool down at the house," suggested Abigail. "I'm allowed to stay there for the time being, and there's a big Olympic-size pool just sitting empty. It's too hot to go on."

Herman Delaney's property at Buena Vista was like none of the other lots in the retirement community. His house was a mini-mansion, located on acres of green lawn cut in a checkerboard pattern. His lot overlooked the rest of the community, its elevation suggestive of a pedestal from which Delaney could oversee his people. All of the women were familiar with the place, but none of them had ever actually been inside the house.

Abigail led them into the foyer through the main entrance, casually tossing her purse in a straight-backed Victorian monstrosity that looked like a throne. The Buena Vista Mallet Club entered in a tightly packed huddle, clutching each other's arms as if they were afraid to touch anything. Lizzie's eyes were wide as a child's at Christmas. Millie *'ooh-ed'* and *'aah-ed'* appreciatively at everything in sight. Dottie ran a mental tally, deciding her own prized possessions were more valuable than the assortment of trinkets Delaney had amassed. Emmy carefully studied each detail, remembering her dead boss's sage advice, "Clues turn up in the damned stupidest places."

"How long was Mr. Delaney retired?" asked Emmy.

"About five years," said Abigail. "Shortly after I started working for him. He sold his remaining interest in the firm to his partner, Al O'Grady."

"I'll bet Mr. O'Grady is devastated," said Emmy, absently running a finger across the dusty surface of an end table. Apparently, Abigail Pritchett didn't feel it necessary to continue functioning as a housekeeper since the lord of the manor was dead.

"I should say!" said Abigail. "If that little trollop hadn't breezed into town, Hermie would never have changed his will."

"I assume Mr. O'Grady had been mentioned in the prior version?" asked Emmy.

Abigail nodded. "With no heirs, Herman planned to return his personal equity to the partnership he had helped to found. Mr. O'Grady wouldn't have *directly* benefited from the donation, but the increased capital would have allowed him to expand in other directions, hiring attorneys to handle very specialized areas of the law. I expect it would have eventually made Mr. O'Grady a very wealthy man."

The conversation ended with a thud as Millie got her feet tangled in a pile of shoes behind the clawfoot sofa. *"Ooooo!"* she squealed as she dropped to the ground in a confused mass.

"Oh, for heaven's sake, Millie!" said Dottie, helping the portly woman to her feet. "Would you watch where you're going?"

Lizzie snickered in the background. "You've put a runner in your stocking," she giggled.

"I'm not wearing stockings!" groused Millie, dusting herself off.

"Well, I think the niece did it," said Millie, folding her arms across her chest. Millie, Emmy, Dottie and Lizzie were collected around a glass-topped table eating deli sandwiches from the Buena Vista clubhouse. Men of various white-collar positions, some retired, shuttled around the greens of the golf course in little motorized carts, laughing broadly at jokes they had heard before and would hear again. The women did not partake in golf, mainly because they had been asked by management to refrain from doing so. They had attempted it upon the early formation of their club, but their fellow golfers seemed to object to their rather liberal interpretation of the game's rules. Millie gouged countless pits into the flawless green, while Dottie smashed the windshield of a BMW with a club flung in a fit of temper over where they were going for lunch. As a result, the staff stayed on alert even if the women were merely on the premises to dine.

"She sounds perfectly dreadful," added Dottie.

"Spoiled," nodded Lizzie.

Emmy took a thoughtful sip of her iced tea and shook her head. "It's too easy."

"How do you figure?" asked Millie. "She made the poisoned food and refrained from partaking."

"If Roger Newton arrested her, that's good enough for me," said Dottie.

Emmy folded her hands to form a teepee in front of her nose. "Well, if all that's true, then there's no harm in what I plan to do."

Millie looked at her suspiciously. "Emmy DeLotell. I can hear the wheels of your mind clicking from clear over here. What are you plotting?"

"Just a couple of phone calls," Emmy said, the corners of her mouth trailing up mischievously.

The next afternoon, Emmy's plan hit its first snag by way of foul weather. Dark clouds rolled in from the lake and angry thunder reverberated in the air. Rain fell in sheets rather than droplets, and a few minutes outdoors guaranteed a drenching to the bones. Emmy sighed and plodded across the meadow, the water running off her yellow rain slicker, and matching rubber boots left squishy footprints behind. Lightning forked overhead, and Emmy flinched. There was no turning back now.

She hoped the other girls had taken their positions. Emmy had given Dottie the least responsibility once she had seen the inclement weather; Dottie couldn't much be relied upon in the rain. She was supposed to stand watch and phone Roger Newton when she saw the vehicle approach, as it surely would. Unfortunately, Dottie's reliability was directly related to the likelihood her hairstyle might become besmirched, so Emmy had asked Lizzie to act as backup, observing the rutted path which provided the only access to the backside of the meadow where Herman Delaney's body had been found.

Millie had the pole position, already planted near the ravine where she could observe the scene from a distance. She was armed with her favorite mallet, and clearly relished the opportunity to use it as a weapon in a purposeful manner.

Emmy stood near the exact spot where she had earlier discovered Mr. Herman Delaney. She kicked around at the loose gravel proliferating the ground, waiting for the telltale sounds of someone approaching. As the rain pattered down, she had time to reflect. Emmy was an excellent judge of character. Rightfully, she prided herself on it. If coerced, the others would also be forced to grudgingly admit it was true. And Emmy's inner voice was telling her the foul-tempered girl sitting in the holding cell at the sheriff's office wasn't responsible for the murder of her uncle. If she had hated him so badly, why had she spent an entire month with him? Wouldn't she have at least verbally unloaded on him long before now? Why wait an entire month if her intention was to kill him all along? Diane Crankshaw certainly didn't seem capable of ingratiating herself to anyone, so Emmy could hardly picture her wheedling her way into the old man's good graces and, consequently, his will. All this before feeding him a breakfast of poison? It didn't make sense.

With nothing to lose and the sneaking suspicion that she was right, Emmy had placed phone calls to two individuals, saying the same thing in each. "I am The One Who Knows Too Much. I know what you've done, and I've got proof. I will be at the scene of Mr. Delaney's murder tomorrow at noon. If you don't want the police to see what I have, you'll come." She figured the innocent party would consider the call a crank and would thusly disregard it. The real murderer would suspect blackmail and would surely be flushed out.

Lightning split the afternoon sky and thunder echoed underfoot. Emmy could feel the clammy wetness underneath her slicker, but she positively refused to catch a cold. The church bazaar was just next week, and she didn't have time to be sick. She *did* wish the murderer would hurry along, though.

As if on cue, Emmy heard the rumble of an engine, winding around the grassy dunes on the far side of the creek. She shielded her eyes and watched the small blue Jeep rise over the crest of a hill and enter the clearing. The rain was too heavy to see the driver's face, no matter how hard Emmy squinted. She didn't recognize the vehicle. She turned sideways and checked her handbag for the walkie-talkie she had "borrowed" from clubhouse security. She and each of the other women were carrying one. They were all on the same frequency, and Emmy could discern the faint sound of Lizzie humming distractedly in the background.

She depressed the button on the side of her walkie-talkie and said, "Get Roger!" When she released the button, all she received in response was the second verse of the tune Lizzie was humming.

Oh, the twit! thought Emmy. *She's got the button stuck, and none of us can hear each other!*

The Jeep stopped, its brakes squealing in protest. A middle-aged man in a pinstriped suit stepped out from the driver's side, deftly twisting an umbrella out the door before emerging underneath it. He was round-headed, rosy-cheeked and bald, with kindly eyes squinting from behind circular lenses perched on his nose. He stepped up to the edge of the creek and called across to Emmy, "I say there!"

Emmy's eyes narrowed and she took a cautious stance. "Yes?"

"Are you The One Who Knows Too Much?" he asked.

Emmy's head turned from side to side, looking for her backup. By now, Roger Newton should have appeared, flashing his badge and his gun before hauling this man away. In the meanwhile, she decided to stall.

"And you're Al O'Grady?" she asked.

He smiled most charmingly and nodded. "Why, of course, my dear! I figured you already knew that. You did call *me*, didn't you?"

Emmy cocked her head and studied the man. He seemed awfully aloof for a murderer. "So why did you do it?" she asked.

O'Grady's smile fell, and he said, "Wha—?" before all hell broke loose.

Another engine roared in the distance, approaching quickly across the rugged terrain. Both Emmy and O'Grady looked around, and Emmy crowed, "You'll get yours now, Mr. Murderer!"

Just then, Millie descended from the narrow path above, her mallet swinging in a crazed rotation above her head.

From her open mouth spilled such an ear-splitting wail that birds from nearby trees took flight in protest. When she hit the apex of the high note, she let the mallet sail, swooping end over end toward a stunned O'Grady. He watched stupidly as the club zeroed in and hit him right between the eyes, splitting the frames of his circular little glasses and knocking him cold.

"Well done!" clapped Emmy, momentarily forgetting the misery of the rain.

Millie had lost her balance after releasing the mallet and had skidded to the bottom of the trail on her backside. "That Lizzie is going to be the death of us someday," she grumbled. "Daydreaming about butterflies, I'd bet."

"Well, it doesn't even matter now, because you've saved the day!" said Emmy. "I expect that's Roger Newton coming now to collect this riffraff."

"I don't see how," said Millie. "Lizzie's still humming on the two-way."

"Maybe Dottie's bringing the Cadillac through," suggested Emmy.

Millie laughed and rolled her eyes. "Are you kidding? She won't drive that thing over a speed bump, much less ground like this. Oh, dear! I think I've got mud up my knickers."

The approaching vehicle loomed into sight, but it belonged to neither Dottie Driscoll nor Roger Newton. It was a large SUV with a tiny, dark-haired woman at the wheel. Abigail Pritchett emerged from the vehicle, a steady grip on the gun in her hand that was pointed at Emmy and occasionally Millie, who seemed less threatening in her seated position. The creek was between them, but Emmy knew that it wasn't enough of a head start to outrun a bullet.

"I don't know why you couldn't just leave well enough alone," said Abigail, pressing her thin lips into a tight line.

Emmy cleared her throat. "I couldn't leave that poor girl locked in a cell for a crime she didn't commit."

"That 'poor girl?'" Abigail laughed. "That 'poor girl' had Herman eating out of the palm of her hand! It was positively revolting!"

"You were on quite familiar terms with your employer, weren't you?" asked Emily. Millie eyed Abigail as an angry dog might, suppressing the urge to growl aloud.

Abigail ignored the question. She waggled the gun at Emmy. "So, you say you've got proof. Let's have it."

"The proof is that you're here," said Emmy. "Well, and this." She pulled a handheld tape recorder from her handbag.

"You're a ridiculous old woman," Abigail said. "I'll take it off of your dead body."

"Would you at least do me the courtesy of telling me why?" asked Emmy. She had taped this much; she figured she may as well go for the full confession.

"I was in love with Herman. I put years into making him love me, too. He was just about to propose when that damned girl came to stay. Suddenly, Hermie didn't have enough time for me. He was trying to make up for all of the time he had lost with his niece. When he actually changed his will in favor of her, I knew that he was never going to be mine," she said.

"So, this was all to punish Diane?" asked Emmy.

"She deserves to spend the rest of her life in prison," said Abigail. "She was going to get everything I had coming to me."

"All right, Miss Pritchett. Put the gun down."

It was a male voice, coming from the meadow at the top of the trail. Emmy looked up and was relieved to see Roger Newton, his own revolver locked onto Abigail. At the same time, another engine roared from across the creek, and Dottie fairly burst onto the scene in her Cadillac, bumping the frame and jostling forward, blowing her horn as if in a parade. It proved that Millie wasn't always correct where Dottie and her Cadillac were concerned.

"Ow!" Lizzie shrieked, dropping her mallet suddenly. "It bit me!"

"What? Let me see that," said Millie, taking Lizzie's hand and inspecting it. "It's just a splinter. Dot, do you have a tweezers?"

"Probably. Let me check," said Dottie, rummaging in her ever-present makeup case. "Aha! Here you go. What's holding up Emmy? We seem to spend half of our lives standing around waiting for her."

"She had to finish up with Sheriff Newton," said Lizzie, suckling at her wounded finger. Millie swatted it away from Lizzie's mouth and began digging rather thoroughly for the fragment of wood, ignoring Lizzie's assorted cries of pain and protest.

Emmy suddenly appeared at the far end of the path, hurrying down toward her friends. She had a large, floppy hat on her head that she didn't trust to remain put as she crossed the field; she kept a hand clamped firmly to its crown.

"I've just had the most satisfactory morning," she said, picking up her mallet from where the women had left it for her. She made a spectacle of flexing this way and that—preheating her muscles, as she liked to call it.

"So, Diane Crankshaw is free?" asked Dottie.

Emmy nodded and smiled. "And you wouldn't believe her change in disposition. She came to me this morning and apologized for being so vulgar at our first meeting. As it turns out, her adoptive parents provided her with all of life's material essentials, but emotionally, they had no time for her. When they adopted her, it seemed like a novel idea, but the novelty wore off quickly. She's spent her life in a state of utter loneliness, and she was actually quite thrilled at the prospect of finding a blood relation. She had no aspirations for Herman Delaney's fortune, only his love and companionship. When he was suddenly murdered, she felt as if she had been abandoned again, alone in the world with no one to turn to. You can believe that Abigail Pritchett was no friend to her."

"Didn't the girl suspect Abigail? I mean, wouldn't she be the only other one likely able to poison Herman's food?" asked Millie.

"Exactly," said Emmy. "But she had no proof. She couldn't even figure out a motive. You see, Abigail Pritchett was far more in love with Herman Delaney than he was with her. According to Diane, he had never even spoken of their relationship. Diane didn't want to make any wild accusations to the police until she had spoken to her lawyer."

"Just like a man," said Dottie, swinging her mallet broadly, catching the corner of her ball and sending it spiraling into the woods at the edge of the meadow. "Has a woman stalking him, and he doesn't even know she's there."

"Poor Mr. O'Grady," said Emmy. "I figured he would consider my telephone call a prank and ignore it, but I guess he found it amusing. He wanted to know who had called him with such a cryptic message. He's also the one who called Roger Newton and had him meet us out in the meadow just in case it was more than a prank. Roger was very gracious in his words to me after I had given my statement."

"Really?" asked Lizzie. "What did he say?"

"Well, the words aren't important, it's the sentiment," said Emmy. Roger had told her that she was damn lucky she hadn't gotten shot playing Nancy Drew and that the sheriff's department thanked her for her contribution but would appreciate it all the more if she would just stay home in the future. Emmy felt that in the spirit of victory, she was free to interpret those words however she saw fit.

"You talk as if you knew it was Abigail Pritchett the whole time," said Dottie.

"I did," smiled Emmy.

"Oh really, then," said Dottie, with a smirk. "Then why even bother calling Mr. O'Grady?"

"Well," said Emmy. "I had never even spoken to the man, so it seemed reckless to preclude him. But I knew it was Pritchett, all right."

"How?" challenged Millie, her eyebrows arching together in a way that they simply shouldn't. The expression conveyed no more than bovine intelligence.

"There was no way the woman was a maid," said Emmy, wrinkling her nose in distaste. "Did you see the state of that house?"

A HALF-MILLION REASONS TO DIE

Jason Rowe stared at the small kitchen table, fingertips of his right hand drumming rhythmically against its yellowed Formica top, fingertips of his left finding locks of his own sandy hair to twist and knot. The muscles at the base of his neck were wound tight, causing a tension headache so severe it filled his skull and threatened to propel his eyes from their deep, dark sockets. He had stared for hours at the papers scattered across the table, making piles first this way, then that. Their order didn't affect the outcome; the Rowes were flat busted.

Gillian stood at the sink washing breakfast dishes, radiant in her simplicity. She and Jason had married five years ago that summer. She looked even younger now than she did on that day, captivating an assemblage of friends and family as she floated seraphically down the aisle toward her adoring young groom. Her rounded face, with its smooth skin and ice-blue eyes in startling contrast to her shoulder-length, jet black hair, contained a smile which would render most men helplessly subservient. Of her exquisite beauty she seemed unaware, although it could have easily been weaponized to acquire the finer things in life which she currently could not afford. It didn't matter. She had Jason, and he made her complete.

The tiny apartment, although spotlessly clean, was stained with age, yellowing surfaces and threadbare carpets exhausted by tenants who had come and gone before the Rowes had grown to think of it as their own. It was a single unit, tucked behind Anna's Bouquets—an afterthought added to supplement the income of the struggling florist. What it lacked in features it made up for in privacy, its exclusive entrance accessible only through the brick patio which was fenced off from the alley beyond. Thick shrubbery and full trees gave the illusion of the Garden of Eden, Jason and Gillian the only man and woman on God's earth.

As Jason rearranged the stacks of bills yet again, he realized they were caught in a downward spiral which would probably cost them this haven as well, or at least the majority of its modern conveniences, such as electricity and natural gas. They hadn't had a telephone for months now, the account falling into arrears before the service had finally been disconnected.

"Trouble?" asked Gillian, turning to offer him one of her magnificent smiles.

Jason scowled at the paperwork mess, then smiled weakly back at his wife. He started to say something, to defend their financial position, but he knew he would only be avoiding the inevitable. The smile slipped from his lips, and he nodded gravely, placing his elbows on the table and burying his face in his hands.

Gillian was beside him in a second, easing onto his lap and draping her slender arms around his neck. She pulled his face to her breast, cooing nonsense into his ear while she caressed the tousled locks which danced feverishly atop his head. Jason surprised himself by sobbing wretchedly, hot tears streaming down his face. His arm circled her waist, and he held her tightly, as if his very life depended on it. He had wanted to provide Gillian with such good things, to make her so happy and now it was as if he were her child, needing her more desperately than she could ever need him.

"Shhh," she whispered in his ear. "It's all right."

Jason shook his head and swept the bills from the table with his free hand. "I've let you down," he repeated time and again, his voice muffled against the faded cloth of her pale blue sundress.

"*Shhh,*" she said, stroking his hair. "I'll get a better job."

Jason was on his feet immediately, carefully setting Gillian upright on hers before pacing the small kitchen. "No. *I* should be the one finding a better job, not you. You're going to school."

Five years ago, graduation from high school had seemed like freedom to both of them. No more homework, studies or tests. Neither of them had a desire to attend college. Gillian took a job as a waitress at Hal's Family Diner, the only one of its kind in the small village of Plydon, and Jason worked in commissioned sales of this type or that, sometimes retail, sometimes insurance, sometimes door-to-door. As the years passed, Gillian came to detest her work but went in like religion, knowing how difficult it was to find hourly wages in the little town. One spring, she applied for financial aid and received enough grants to attend the small community college in nearby Branford as a part-time student. In three more years, she would receive her degree in social sciences, not that there was much call for that particular qualification in Plydon. Jason changed positions multiple times since they had married, sales jobs as easy to find as the thick mushrooms which pervaded their small patio garden. He always started well and finished poorly,

200

his enthusiasm beaten down and decimated before he finally quit or was fired. He had just been released from Wholesale Foods because his quotas weren't in line with the company's projections. How excited could he be peddling new varieties of processed chicken and canned sauces?

As Jason paced the kitchen, Gillian collected the strewn mail and slid into his chair, flipping through the stack of bills with interest. She had always left the household budget to Jason, not minding if he occasionally spent too much on beer when he went sailing or hunting with his buddy, Clemens Brown. A man was entitled to *some* of life's simple pleasures, after all. But the hopelessness in Jason's eyes scared her; she had never seen such a look on his face. He had never held back from Gillian, always telling the truth no matter how difficult or unsettling it might be. It wasn't just because he loved her with all of his soul; he was simply that type of man, honest and unassuming in his goodness. Now, her eyes absorbed the figures representing their debts, her brain crunching the numbers with a skill Jason would have found surprising. Indeed, they were in deep trouble.

After sorting the bills her own way, she found an unopened envelope tucked near the bottom of the pile. It was from National Life of Maine, a company for which Jason had sold insurance a few years back. Gillian held the envelope up and asked, "What's this?"

Jason stepped over and took the envelope, looking at it as if for the first time. Finally, he said, "It's nothing. It's just a policy I can't renew." He tossed it to the far edge of the table where it teetered before falling to the floor.

There was a sharp rapping on the flimsy screen door followed by, "Hell-*ooooooo?* Anybody home?" The door popped open, and Clemens stuck his head into the kitchen.

Jason crossed to the sink at the first sound, offering his back to his friend while blotting his face and making himself presentable. "Hey, buddy!" he called over his shoulder, the lighthearted words falling like dead birds from the sky.

"You ready?" asked Clemens, easing his body through the narrow crack of the door to stand in the room. He winked playfully at Gillian, who nodded and smiled in greeting. Clemens was lanky and tall, his dark hair shaved nearly to the scalp. His summer tan had not yet faded, and he wore bright orange shorts, rubber flip-flops and a blue Hawaiian shirt flowing loosely around his upper torso. The three had known each other since grade school.

Jason turned and looked at Clemens, his mind blank.

"Fishing?" reminded Clemens.

"Oh," said Jason, looking at his feet. "I don't know, Clem. Maybe not today."

Gillian stood and crossed to Jason's side, hooking an arm through his elbow. "Nonsense," she said. "You go on. Have a good time."

Jason looked at her questioningly, wondering what he had ever done to deserve a wife as understanding as Gillian. In that moment, he fell in love with her all over again and made a solemn promise to himself that he would find some way out of this mess. He would not stand by and watch her lose what few possessions she had. A day on the boat with Clemens was exactly what he needed. Fresh air and sunshine and time for self-examination. He would find an answer. He simply *had* to.

When Jason returned, Gillian was nestled amongst the lumpy springs of their ancient olive sleeper sofa, purring softly in her slumber. He shook her gently, whispering, "Gilly? Honey, wake up."

As her sleepy eyes found his, she once again saw the bright fire which she loved about them, and she knew that somehow Jason had found a way. She sat upright immediately, leaning forward as Jason took her hands into his own and knelt before her. On the floor beside him was the envelope he had tossed aside that morning, the renewal notice from National Life. She looked at it briefly before returning her gaze to Jason. She raised her eyebrows in anticipation, waiting patiently for him to begin.

He smiled and lifted the envelope from the stained carpet. "This is the answer to all of our prayers," he said.

Her eyes narrowed, realization dawning. "We're going to defraud the insurance company?" she asked.

Jason's smile faltered slightly, and he wondered if he had made a mistake. In his mind, there was a vast difference between stealing from an individual and stealing from a faceless corporation. In part, he felt entitled to the money, paying premiums month after month for a policy that would only reciprocate if he suddenly dropped dead. It didn't seem any fairer than the current state of their finances. He wouldn't have even taken the damned thing out if he hadn't been working for the company at the time and collecting commission on his own sale.

Gillian took the envelope, which had now been opened, and extracted the invoice. "How much?" she asked.

Jason felt his confidence renewed. Gillian was interested; he could see it in her expression. "The premium's only—"

"Not the premium," she interrupted. "What would the policy pay?"

"$500,000," he said, and she gasped.

Gillian stared at the invoice and slowly began shaking her head. "We can't. We don't have criminal minds. There's no plan we could conceive which hasn't been attempted before."

Jason eased onto the couch beside her, still holding her hands. "Faking a death wouldn't be that difficult. As I sat on the boat today with Clem, I realized how easy it would be to slip over the side, to disappear into the ocean."

She looked at him, startled. "You thought about killing yourself?"

"Never," he said immediately. "But the ocean is enormous, and people are lost at sea all the time. It would be next to impossible to find a single body that had been pulled down by the undertow and eaten by whatever might feed from it."

"There'd be an investigation," Gillian said.

"Of course, there would," said Jason. "And I'm sure it would be months before you saw a dime, but if you only had to deal with your expenses and not mine—it would be tight, but I think you could make it work. You would probably qualify for some kind of federal aid until the money came through."

"But how long would you be gone?" asked Gillian, and he knew then that she was with him, only wanting to be prepared for what was to come next.

"That's where I believe most people screw up," he said. "They come back too soon. I think I should be gone no less than two years."

"No," she said, shaking her head. "I can't be away from you that long."

Jason lifted his hands and caressed the smooth skin of her face. "I'll be back before you graduate."

"No."

"It's the answer we've been looking for," he insisted.

"*No.*"

"I will take the money we have and renew this policy immediately. Someday when you least suspect it—although soon—someone will come to inform you of my tragic death at sea. You have to mourn me as if I *were* dead, but no more than that. Claim examiners will be watching you, probably even private detectives. If you overdo or underdo, they'll know. After you've collected the money and enough time has passed, I'll call you and we'll meet, but I can't be in contact with you beforehand. Every time we communicate, we would be opening ourselves up to discovery."

Gillian's eyes welled with tears of resignation, and she said, "I'll do it just right. There won't be any playacting involved. I will mourn for you every day that you're gone."

When the moment came, it was Clemens who delivered the news. He and Jason had been fishing off the coast, having a pretty miserable go of it, when Clemens had gone down to the galley to get more beer. When he returned to the boat's deck, Jason was gone, his lucky hat riding the gentle swells of the ocean. Clemens had spoken with the police already, so there was no need for Gillian to deal with them. Clemens was devastated. He felt horribly responsible and cried for the loss of his best friend. It was easy for Gillian to mourn with him. She didn't know how she would spend the next two years without her husband.

Prepared for disbelief and intense scrutiny, Gillian had been quite relieved when the transaction with National Life of Maine had gone almost effortlessly. She had the money sooner than expected, and suddenly she was in the black again, all of her delinquent bills brought current, her telephone service restored, all of her needs covered—the sole exception being her need for companionship.

The first month, she had cried every night, her pillow sloppy and wet against her face as she watched the digits change on her bedside clock. She missed the sound of Jason's voice, the feel of his shape next to hers in the bed. She wandered through her days, shuttling between classes and work like a zombie, only to return to an empty apartment each night. The funeral had been unbearable, Jason's ridiculous family treating her like dirt while they carried on and on about the son they had never visited, never cared for. She despised them for their hypocrisy and was glad that eventually, once Jason returned, these people would be out of their lives forever. Gillian had no family of her own, having been orphaned as a teenager and raised as a ward of the state. There would be no one to miss her when she was gone—with the possible exception of Clemens, who was such a dear, sweet man.

Clemens took the tragedy of Jason's 'death' so personally he found reasons to frequently stop in and check on Gillian, the least he could do for his best friend's widow. He encouraged Gillian to find someplace else to live, a place not saturated with memories, but she always shook her head, a hopeless romantic in Clemens's eyes. Of course, Gillian had not disclosed to Clemens nor anyone else the vast amount of money she had been paid under the life insurance policy. Jason said it would be important for her to continue on as before, not flaunting her newfound wealth, and Gillian herself wanted to keep as much of the money intact so she and Jason could decide together how it was best spent.

But she felt badly for Clemens, seeing the pain in his eyes, knowing he could never know the truth about Jason's 'death.' She knew he had assigned himself as her protector, and she took solace in the familiarity of his presence. Jason and Clemens had been best friends since they were small boys. Gillian had known Clemens almost as long as she had known Jason, and she found conversation with him smooth and comfortable.

After six months, Gillian not only looked forward to Clemens's visits but also looked for reasons to invite him over. The apartment wasn't so dismal when Clemens was there, eating with her across the Formica table, watching television with her while it stormed outside, spending hours talking about his dreams for the future as well as her own. Hers, of course, were pure fiction, and she felt revulsion for herself as she spun her lies.

It was at Plydon's annual Fourth-of-July fireworks when things between them changed. Families huddled thickly in the small-town square, *oohing* and *aahing* at the magnificent, multicolored spectacles of light dancing overhead. Children laughed and ran through the crowd, playing tag between the still forms frozen gazing skyward in wonder. An unexpected sonic reverberation shook the ground as a new pattern unfolded above, and Gillian found herself in Clemens's arms, her eyes locked on his face, absorbing the simple joy reflected there. His gentle, sweet lips found hers.

Astonished, Gillian backed away, her eyes wide with horror. Her hand fluttered up to touch her lips, feeling the warmth that still made them tingle, and she fled into the crowd, leaving Clemens to stare after her in an uncomprehending daze.

Gillian ran to the apartment and locked herself inside, sitting in the dark room and hating herself. She had only been there for a few moments went a gentle knock sounded on the door.

"Gillian?" Of course, it was Clemens.

"Please go away," she said, her voice pleading miserably.

There was silence from the other side of the door, but Gillian knew Clemens still stood there, trying to understand what had just happened. It was so unfair of her to do this to him, and yet she didn't trust herself to open the door, to look into his eyes. She hadn't even suspected the desire she felt for him until that night and yet, there it was, pulling and twisting at her heart. With fierce concentration, she closed her eyes tightly and pictured Jason, his tousled hair, his lopsided grin.

"Gillian?"

She didn't even trust her voice now. She sat silent, staring at the dark outline of the door.

"I'm sorry," he said, his voice cracking in despair. "It was too soon. Too soon." And then he was gone. His words were ironic to Gillian, because for her it was almost too late. Clemens had somehow sneaked into her heart, taking hold in a way she hadn't expected. She couldn't be overtly cruel to him. As far as he knew, Gillian was a young widow who would eventually find herself wanting love and companionship. He had every reason to believe that she might choose him for that role. A growing part of her wanted to do that very thing.

Gillian was relieved when at their next encounter it was as if nothing had ever happened. Conversation she feared would become brittle and forced was as engaging as ever, and the subject was not raised again for many months. Still, when Gillian looked into Clemens's eyes, she could tell he remembered their kiss clearly but was reluctant to ever bring it up for fear she might permanently dash the hopes he held for them. She decided it was a safe place to be and felt that as long as *she* didn't bring it up, neither would he, and she continued to see him on an increasingly frequent basis.

Nearly a year-and-a-half had passed since Jason's supposed death, and Gillian was finding it hard to picture him in her mind. Individual features came easily, but the entirety of the picture was lost, and while it disturbed her greatly, she also found it lessened her guilt in the way she felt toward Clemens.

By then, Clemens had surprised her again, revealing himself to be a shrewd businessman with a technically trained mind—quite different from his laid-back private persona. Clemens had quietly built Plydon's first internet company, providing a service many of the town's residents didn't understand. Councilmen wished him luck and scoffed under their collective breaths, never believing for a moment that the idea would prosper in a town so small.

Months later, they were begging for a piece of the action—any piece.

Gillian watched curiously as Clemens became more and more successful. It didn't spoil him in any way, quite the opposite, in fact. Where he had been relaxed, exuberant and playful before, he was only more so now. He still dreamed of great accomplishments, but unlike Jason, he seemed to actually develop plans to achieve them. The mechanics of his mind were mesmerizing, and Gillian couldn't help but be a little in awe of him. He showered Gillian with small gifts to which he attached no strings, yet each one served as a reminder of how cruel she was being, holding him at arm's length.

Finally, it was more than she could bear. One winter evening, as snow fell gently from the clouds, Gillian went to Clemens's house, her feet following unconscious instruction. Once she arrived, she stood on the porch, staring blankly at the heavy oaken door, wondering why she had come and yet knowing the whole while. As if preternaturally aware of her presence, the door opened, and Clemens was there, framed in the golden light cast from the warmth of his living room. He reached out and she took his hand, allowing him to lead her inside.

For two days afterward, Gillian cried herself to sleep. She hated herself for betraying Jason and hated Clemens for being so kind and gentle, so hypnotically compelling as if he were an addictive chemical. She promised herself it would never happen again, but she knew even then she was lying.

As Plydon was so very small, talk of Clemens's and Gillian's blossoming romance spread through the village quickly. Gillian expected to be treated like a jezebel, forced to face the scornful glares of the town's elders, subjected to hushed whispering at the marketplace. Instead, she found her neighbors were deliriously *happy* for her, finding Clemens a perfect replacement for the husband she had lost nearly two years prior. Unbeknownst to Gillian or Clemens, the townsfolk often debated how long it would be before the two were wed. After all, it *must* be their destiny.

And the day finally came when Clemens *did* propose marriage, before a blazing fire in the parlor of his spacious house. Gillian felt more torn than ever before. In Clemens's eyes, she saw something close to terror, afraid she might again reject him, and if so, he would have nothing left to live for because this would be the most profound rejection of all.

Gillian smiled sweetly and promised him an answer within three days. She left immediately, racing back to her dingy little apartment where she again sat in the dark, contemplating her thoughts. She wanted to be with Clemens more than anything else in the world. She had lived for months now with the fear the phone would ring at any moment; Jason calling to announce his imminent return. Her memories of him were faded and bittersweet, and she knew she couldn't go back to the way it had been. Jason was a dreamer, not a doer. He was a player, not a thinker. Their marriage and all it had entailed seemed pale and sophomoric next to the inner adventure which Clemens had begun for her. Legally, she would have no problem marrying Clemens as Jason was dead in the eyes of the world. The money, or most of it anyway, was tucked safely away in the basement, away from the prying eyes of her neighbors who surely would have known about it the minute she deposited it with Plydon Community Savings. The claim had been disbursed in the offices of National Life of Maine located a hundred miles away in Portland, so she had been spared the spontaneous gossip which can occur after the simplest of transactions in a town so small. The money was rightfully hers, as she was Jason's sole beneficiary. The only problem remaining was Jason was *not*, in fact, dead.

Gillian deliberated in dark rooms for all three of the days during which she had requested patience of Clemens, sleeping very little and agonizing over what to do. Jason had been violently jealous as a young man in high school, and Gillian had no doubt his fury would only be intensified by the knowledge the man who had stolen her heart from him was none other than his own best friend. The more she deliberated over this, the more afraid she became, fearing for Clemens's safety, because a dead man had a certain amount of exemption from prosecution.

It was when the phone rang, shrill and loud against the silence of her darkened living room, and Gillian realized what she must do. It rang three times, then four, then five. She picked up the receiver slowly and placed the cold plastic surface to her ear.

"It's time," he whispered, soft and low, and Gillian found her head involuntarily nodding. It had been a little over two years since she had heard Jason's voice, and it was an odd sensation, almost as if a stranger were calling to announce a dreaded appointment. His inflection was foreign and unfamiliar to her now, a mysterious man trying to transport

her back to a place in the past which she could not revisit—
would not.

"Yes," she breathed.

"I'll be over shortly." The line went dead in her ear, and
Gillian replaced the receiver. She felt strangely anxious,
eager to dispense with the ugliness before her as quickly as
possible. She went into hers and Jason's bedroom and knelt
by the bed, her arm reaching underneath the bed frame.
When she found what she was looking for, she went first to
the kitchen, opening the door so that only the screen was
in place, then into the adjoining living room. She pulled a
tattered recliner to the center of the room and sat in it,
facing the short hall which led to the kitchen and the open
doorway beyond. She was hidden in the shadows of the
room, leaving the lights off as she had for the past three
days. She knew what she had to do but couldn't bear to see
the look on Jason's face, or see the event unfold as it must.

The stock of the rifle managed to find light somewhere in
the murky shadows, glinting its promise of cool death as it
lay across Gillian's lap.

When footfalls sounded in the alley, Gillian raised the rifle clumsily in the direction of the door. She had never fired one before, but at such close range, she doubted she would miss her mark.

She hesitated only briefly when she saw the outline at the screen, the head and shoulders of the man coming to remove her from what had become the happiest days of her life. The report from the rifle was deafening, but the privacy which Gillian and Jason had once treasured now acted as reassurance the discharge had not been overheard by passersby.

The figure stopped cold, then slumped to the ground, feet striking against the doorframe in its clumsy descent. As much as Gillian didn't want to see the aftermath, she couldn't leave Jason on the patio to be discovered by some random passerby. She forced herself into numbness and crossed the dark room, again hesitating only briefly before stepping through the screen door and out onto the patio.

Moonlight trickled through the branches of the trees overhead, little fingers of light painting everything with a delicate silver cast. The shot had been lower than Gillian expected, and she gasped when she heard the burbling sounds of speech trying to emerge from the wounded and dying man. She clasped her hands to her ears, not wishing to hear Jason as he condemned her with his final breath.

As the clouds parted, the moonlight intensified slightly, and Gillian's eyes adjusted. Again, she gasped, and a horrific cry came from deep within. Clemens lay on his back, bleeding from his stomach, staring at her with frightened eyes as he fought admirably against the inescapable.

Gillian dropped to her knees, touched his face, and held his head in her lap. He looked at her with the strangest expression, not one of surprise but rather reluctant acceptance.

"*Shh*," she whispered, rocking slightly, knowing he was too far gone for medical assistance.

He managed a wincing smile and gestured for her to draw near. His voice was but a burbling whisper, emerging from his ravaged interior. "As much as I love you, Gillian, and I think you love me, too, I knew you could never forgive me."

Gillian looked at him, her tears falling like rain on his upturned face. "Sweet Clem," she said. "It's *me* who can't be forgiven."

Clemens weakly shook his head. "I have loved you longer than you will ever know. That is why I did such a horrible thing. Fate would never allow me such an ill-gained victory. I—I needed to know tonight whether you would have me, but I didn't expect you would, even if you weren't fully conscious of the reason why." He then choked, his throat thick and wet.

"What are you saying?" she asked.

Clemens's voice was so low Gillian had to lean forward to understand. "That day in the boat—I was so lonely—so jealous—I only pushed a little...

THE NEW CAR

It started with the car, and it ended with the car.

My name is Harlan Woodridge. I'm thirty-six years old and live in the Ohio town of Klein, population 50,000 or so. We're not exactly small but not exactly big, either. It's a nice, safe little Midwest town where children ride their bicycles in the streets and door-to-door delivery from a milkman is still an option, albeit one less exercised with each passing year. I grew up here, the byproduct of Ethel and Burgess Woodridge. My father worked hard and long at the Brickton Shoelace Factory, paid standard wages which were low even in those days for such a grueling job. He plodded along until his retirement at age sixty-five and currently occupies a well-padded recliner in the inner sanctum of the old homestead—the TV room. My mother

221

has always been a homebody, presenting meals at the appropriate times and buzzing about in the background with endless busy work. She was quiet when Dad's friends infrequently came over, smiling politely and nodding her head subserviently. I often wondered if she was happy. It wasn't as if they argued or my father physically abused my mother, but there was a sort of psychological voodoo going on there that I never have been able to fully comprehend. Occasionally, there would be an unprecedented sparkle deep in my mother's eyes, and I knew that wherever she had gone inside, it was a much better place than where she was now. Ah, but she always came back.

This story isn't so much about them, however. Only in the sense that to know about me, it seems relevant you should know something about from where I came. I had determined at fifteen that I wanted something more out of life than what my parents had. Not that unusual, really. It is all parents' desire that their children's accomplishments succeed their own, right? Well, I guess so. My parents were unenthusiastically supportive, and I knew if I were to actually make it through college, I was on my own. I began working that summer and haven't stopped since. I didn't finish college, although I was able to begin easily enough between the money I had saved and the grants I had been awarded. Of course, that first year was all I managed before life pulled one of its nasty little tricks, as effective as a one-ton cow lying across a bend in the railroad tracks. Derailment is inevitable.

Mary Jo McAllister's legs were unavoidable. They swung hypnotically as she sat at her desk, drawing my eyes away from Mr. Rochester, the nasally voice of American History 101. She had auburn hair which spiraled down to her shoulders in loose, careless waves. She had a wicked grin which she cast my way frequently, knowing full well what the shape of her calves was doing to me. We began dating early in the semester, and by the time finals rolled around, she was pregnant. My grades didn't have a chance to suffer by that time, thank God, but there was no doubt the road I thought I was taking had dead-ended onto a one-way street. At nineteen, I had a new wife, a baby on the way and no time to consider continuing education. I had no skills, unemployment in Klein was high, and we were going to need mucho dinero, *pronto*, my friend. I started at the shoelace factory in the fall and worked there for far longer than I care to admit.

Those years turned me into a very practical, nose-to-the-grindstone sort of fellow. No luxuries, just necessities. I plodded along, making sure we had everything we needed as best I could. Not that Mary Jo didn't hold up her end of the bargain. She went to work in an office downtown, typing letters and memos for a fat ambulance-chasing lawyer named Arthur Barrister—no kidding. Little Jonathan was born healthy, happy and relatively bright, I think, even if I might be predisposed to say so.

In marriage, Mary Jo and I turned out to be amazingly compatible. We never had the luxury of falling in love, but we seemed to fit together well. We were polite to each other and played our respective parts appropriately, but occasionally I saw a faraway look in her eyes, just like that of my mother, and I knew she was off to a better place, one in which I played no part. Still, we never argued—at least not until the car, but I'll get to that.

When Jonathan turned eight, Mary Jo and I thought it would be a sensible birthday gift to buy a computer for the boy, although the expense made my pulse race. With the computerization of the world expanding exponentially, it seemed the proper thing to do as an investment in our son's future. He thought some of the games were really cool, but lost interest in a remarkably short period of time, even for him. I, however, found the device to be fascinating, and in six months knew enough to be dangerous.

It was this happenstance hobby which propelled me out of the shoelace factory, and for months, I fought the urge to kiss the damn thing every time I saw it. I didn't realize how many people are intimidated by computers, but believe me, it's a staggering lot. They suspect that pressing the wrong key at the wrong moment will end all life as we know it. I began installing parts in computers for cash (under the table, of course) and soon, I was made a legitimate offer by Gordon Pridemore, the brother-in-law of my old pal, Bert Parnell.

Mr. Pridemore was the president of First Deposit National Bank on Main Street. It wasn't a branch office, but the real deal—six stories of executive offices in a brick-fronted building with a full-service banking center on the first floor. He had an in-house staff of computer programmers, but no one to run around and fix the little things that happen when a user tries to make his computer do something it was never designed to do. So, I took the job, and Mary Jo and I celebrated my new earnings by spending them nearly as quickly as I made them. Money is funny that way—the more you earn, the more you spend.

But part of that money was spent buying a larger house, and we were happy about that. I was home more now because my new job was only forty hours a week where the shoelace factory had required sixty. It was good to be around my son as he stumbled through adolescence.

When Jonathan turned sixteen this past fall, he came to me one afternoon with a course catalog from Ohio State University and said, "Dad, I think I can finish high school a year early. I've been studying really hard, and I've got the marks. Ohio State is a good school, and I want to start. Mr. Prescott says I need your permission. What do you think?"

I thought a lot of things, but mostly I was proud. He *had* worked hard, and his grade cards had consistently shown it. I also knew he wanted something more than what his old man had. I certainly couldn't fault him for that. I was determined to provide him with the encouragement I had always felt was lacking from my own parents. Mary Jo was pleased as well, and we sent him to college the next year.

A strange thing happened then. With Jonathan away at college, the tuition paid in full by academic scholarship, Mary Jo and I suddenly experienced what felt like a windfall of cash. Interest rates dropped, and we were able to refinance our house for a significantly lower monthly payment. Our cars, both purchased from a used car lot over five years before, were paid in full the same month. Just as most parents were beginning to financially feel the pinch of college-age children, ours was on his own and out of our hair.

It was shortly after then that I saw it on the road.

She was a beauty, a 1999 anniversary edition Ford Mustang GT convertible, candy-apple red with black leather seats and a 5-speed manual transmission. A guy about my age was at the wheel, a look of contentment on his face like none I'd ever seen before. He and I were built similarly although I had more hair. He pulled over to the curb in front of the bank, and a shapely blonde delicately eased herself into the passenger seat. He smiled a high wattage smile, and off they went, king and queen of the universe.

I wanted the car.

Not that *specific* car. It was already more than a year old. I wanted to buy a brand spanking new, right-out-of-the-box Mustang. Mine would be black, with a hood scoop, and although it wasn't as popular, I'd opt for upholstered seats over leather, because I hate the way leather sticks to skin in the summer sun. I had never had a new car before, nor had Mary Jo. Usually, when we bought a used car, Mary Jo would get it first, and I would take her hand-me-downs. I had never considered such a luxury before, and I doubt I ever will again. But when I saw that Mustang drive away, squealing its tires as it rounded Second Street, I knew I had to have one.

Mary Jo would be a problem. She would point out its impracticality, and I frankly didn't have the courage to fly the idea past her first. She would say I must be going through my second childhood or some other psychoanalytical crap. If what I was doing fit that definition then so be it, but all I knew was I wanted that car.

I went to Lenny's Ford on Wyland Court and tried to keep myself from appearing too overeager. A round salesman named Charley Porter met me at the door, a smile painted in broad strokes across his face. He offered a giant hairy paw to shake while in the other, a Philly steak sandwich oozed clear juice down his meaty arm. We exchanged introductions, and I got out of the handshake as quickly as possible.

"What can I do you for?" he asked, his tongue picking at bits of sandwich stuck in his upper palate.

"I'm just looking," I said disinterestedly. But salesmen are intuitive little bastards, aren't they? Porter watched me make a beeline for the line of Mustangs featured at the front of the lot. No matter how nonchalant I may have sounded, my body language was screaming, *'Sucker!'*

They had a total of ten Mustangs in all, some of them GTs, some of them not. None of them were black, although several had hood scoops. At first, my heart sank. I saw the sticker price and had misjudged the cost of the car by about $8,000. The only new Mustang I could afford was all window dressing with an anemic V-6 shamefully hidden under the hood. I must have looked like a disappointed kid at Christmas when I turned around, a fact not lost on Porter.

"We've got new Focuses starting at—"

I shook my head and made a sour face. What kind of substitute was a *Focus* for a *Mustang?* None, that's what. I wasn't buying the car because I *needed* it. I was buying it because I *wanted* it. If you're set on filet mignon, a McDonald's Happy Meal doesn't quite cut it, now does it?

"I'm guessing that cost is a factor," he said. I nodded dumbly and followed him over to the non-GTs where he began to itemize the car's fine, fine features. Now I *did* feel like a disappointed kid at Christmas, the one who dreamed all winter of a walkie-talkie spy set that, once received, only had a transmitting radius of about three feet.

I made polite conversation, hemmed and hawed appropriately, then dragged my broken heart toward my ten-year-old Buick. The one with the faded blue paint and half of its front grille busted where one of the punk kids in the neighborhood had skateboarded into it. The one with the sagging canopy and the ripped upholstery. The one with the engine that sputtered on right turns before finding its purpose again.

"Mr. Woodridge?" Porter startled me when he spoke; I was so lost in my own self-pity that I hadn't realized he was following me.

"Yes?"

"I do have one 2000 model left in the back that you might want to see."

"But it's a *2000*," I griped.

"Yes, but it's never left the lot—well, other than test drives, you know. I have too many 2001 models to display right now, so I pulled this one into the back until I have room to bring it out again. She's a real bea-yoot, and she's priced to sell."

"*How* priced to sell?" I asked.

When he told me, my tongue went numb. I could do it. It would be a little tight, but I could pull it off. But surely the car was chartreuse or hot pink. Did they still make four-cylinder Mustangs? *Something* had to be wrong with it.

But I followed him to the garage at the back of the lot, my mouth dry and full of my hopeful heart. A quick surge of adrenaline coursed through my veins as the tail end of the car appeared. It was black. I could see the shiny chrome "GT" insignia.

"What's wrong with it?" I asked.

"Nothing! Nothing at all!" Charley said, a little too quickly, and for a moment I thought of that old story about the monkey's paw, the one that granted wishes but only after devastating personal consequence was delivered upon the wisher. "Well, there's *one* thing—"

"Yes?"

"The car was specially ordered by a retired schoolteacher over in Borden—he passed away before the car came in. He had had the front end modified, and while I *personally* think it's a very attractive addition, it seems to put some customers off."

"Modified? How so?" I pictured sixteen headlights on the front grille or a birdfeeder as a hood ornament—or worse yet, a stuffed bird.

Charley shrugged and popped the last bite of his greasy sandwich into his mouth. "Guy thought it looked better with a scoop on the hood. Apparently, Ford agrees, because the 2001 GT models have one."

I quickly walked around to the front of the car and there it was, the icing on the cake, the bow on the package, the very cherry on top. The car was *exactly* what I was looking for. Peering through the windshield, I saw charcoal gray bucket seats—*cloth.*

"I'll take it," I said, and Charley Porter nearly choked as he swallowed.

"Don't you even want to take it for a test run?" he asked.

"Oh! Of course," I said. "But I want it." If there had been any possibility of negotiating the price further to my advantage, I had just kissed it goodbye. That was okay. This was the car, and I would have it.

A few moments later, I was tooling down the street in the sleek machine, its engine thrumming powerfully, its steering tight and responsive, its suspension surprisingly smooth for a sports car. As I drove, I began to laugh uncontrollably, a hysterical giggle which was borne of equal parts excitement and satisfaction. It poured forth from between my lips, and anyone looking would have thought I had lost my mind. And people *were* looking; it was a *Mustang*, for heaven's sake! I took the car back to the dealership, and Porter had trouble keeping up with me as I raced into the sales office to complete the paperwork.

"You did *what?*" Mary Jo's face had taken on a crimson edge which crept upward and even seemed to tint her mousy brown hair. She glared at me with her hands on her thick hips, her once sleek legs locked in a gunfighter's stance.

"She's *something*, Mary Jo," I enthused. "Just wait until you *see* her!"

"How could you do such a thing without talking to me?" she demanded. "I would never presume to spend *your* money for you."

"I know, honey, but—"

"No 'honeys,' no 'buts,'" she said. "The car is going back."

"*What?* I can't return it! They wouldn't accept it!" I protested. "Even if they did, they would charge us a ton of money for their trouble."

I was lying through my teeth, but she didn't know any better. In Ohio, you have three days to cancel a contract. It didn't matter. There was no way I was going to return the car. I was currently in the mental process of selecting an appropriate name for her. I hadn't been this enthusiastic about naming our own son!

Mary Jo's lips pressed firmly together, and I thought for just a moment she was going to call my bluff and phone Lenny's Ford, demanding to speak to the manager about what her incompetent husband had just done. After emitting a disgusted sigh, she turned and stormed out of the room.

She didn't speak to me for two weeks.

I was washing the car when Mary Jo finally came around. Out of the blue, she came out with a tall glass of lemonade and got my attention by bumping me with her elbow.

"You look hot," she said.

I nodded as sweat dripped from the tip of my nose. I tossed the sponge I was holding into a bucket of warm, sudsy water. "Am I forgiven?" I ventured.

"No." She walked around the car, giving it her first really good look. It wasn't an entirely favorable look, but she didn't immediately start picking it apart, either. I considered it a good sign. "The least you could do is take me for a ride in the damned thing."

My grin couldn't have been any wider. "Let me take a shower, and we'll take her out."

Her nose wrinkled in that funny way that tells me she thinks I'm being silly. "A *shower?*"

"I'm all sweaty. I don't want to get the upholstery messed up. I'll be back in a flash." I ran toward the house before she had a chance to protest.

I used the button on the key fob to unlock the doors as I always did. I didn't want to use the key itself because I was afraid I might scratch the vulnerable area around the lock. I opened the passenger door and guided Mary Jo into the contoured bucket seat.

"It sure smells new," she said, and I wasn't sure if it was a compliment or not. She swung her legs into the car, and I watched in horror as the soles of her shoes scraped along the grille which covered the speaker in the door, leaving twin white ribbons behind. A strangled gasp seized my throat, and I was on my knees in a flash, rubbing at the tracks.

"What's the matter with you?" Mary Jo asked, impatience creeping into her voice.

"You can't just toss yourself into the car any old way, Mary Jo. Look what you've done," I said, pointing at the speaker. The tracks faded easily enough as I rubbed them. "Thank God. I don't think there's any damage done."

"Oh, for heaven's sake!" snapped Mary Jo, and I knew I was on the verge of losing her again; if I didn't act quickly, she would never want anything to do with the car.

"I'm sorry," I said, trying to sound duly penitent. "I know I'm being a ninny."

"You sure are."

"Bygones?"

She snorted and folded her arms across her chest. I leaned in and fastened her seatbelt, giving her a peck on the forehead before I carefully closed her door. I walked-skipped-ran to the driver's side and slid behind the leather-covered steering wheel, caressing it lovingly before carefully inserting the key into the ignition. I always made sure the key lined up with the slot *exactly* before inserting it because I didn't want to scratch the black plastic guard which surrounded the ignition. When I twisted the key, the engine caught and revved smoothly. I glanced out of the corner of my eye at Mary Jo, and she was studying the car's interior, determined to appear indifferent.

I backed slowly out of the driveway after checking thoroughly for passing cars. I put the car in drive and smiled at Mary Jo. "Let's see what Diana can do."

"Diana?"

"Well—sure," I said. "A car's got to have a name, doesn't she?"

"No-o-o."

"Sure, she does."

"What did you call your Buick?" she challenged.

"That doesn't count," I said.

"Why not?"

"It wasn't a *real* car. Not like this." I found myself caressing the steering wheel again. I had finally chosen Diana with respect to the mythical goddess of the hunt. It seemed appropriate. A car had come along behind me and honked its impatience. It was a small Hyundai. I pulled forward, waving my apologies into the rearview mirror, both for my inattentiveness and for the misfortune of the poor soul forced to drive such a thing.

We drove aimlessly through the streets of Klein, and for a moment I pretended I was that happy man with the blonde in his car. I *was* the happy man, but Mary Jo couldn't quite bring herself to enjoy the experience.

"Can't this thing go any faster?" she finally asked as I manipulated a safe and steady turn from Main to Second at five miles per hour.

"Oh, sure! Diana can hit a hundred miles per hour in no time flat."

"You've driven this thing that fast?"

"Quit calling her a thing."

Mary Jo sighed. "Fine. Have you?"

"No, but I've read all of the performance reviews in *Hot Rod Monthly*."

"*Hot Rod Monthly?* A man your age doesn't read *Hot Rod Monthly*. What's the matter? Are you going through your second childhood?"

And there it was, just as I suspected. Why is it that a man is accused of recurring infancy merely because he can finally afford some of the things he always wanted as a teenager?

"Let's go to Harold's," I suggested, successfully changing the subject. Harold's was Mary Jo's favorite—a somewhat expensive seafood restaurant on the east side of town. If there was one thing that Mary Jo had come to excel at after all these years, it was eating. Not that she was *huge*, but she certainly had gained a significant amount of weight since we had gotten married.

Her face lit up for the first time in two weeks with a surprised smile. *"Really?* If I knew this was what it would take to get you to Harold's, I would've gotten mad at you a long time ago. Do you think I'm dressed all right?"

I smiled and said, "You look fantastic, dear—but could you please keep your feet on the floor mat?"

We ate until we could eat no more. We each ordered a dinner sampler, with lobster, shrimp, fish, clams, crab, hushpuppies and coleslaw. I ate most of mine, and for what I didn't eat, Mary Jo requested a carryout box.

"What for?" I asked as the waitress headed back to the kitchen.

"Duh," she said, rolling her eyes. "The leftovers."

"They won't get eaten," I said. "They never do. Even if they're reheated, they'll just get soggy and gross."

"Nonsense. I could grind up that crab, add some dressing and have a nice sandwich spread."

I shook my head. "But you won't. They'll just go to waste. They always do."

"Always? What always? We hardly ever go out to eat, much less bring leftovers home."

"I don't want you to take them home," I said.

She arched her eyebrows and stared at me. "Why wouldn't you want me to take them home?"

I paused. If I told her the real reason, she would be furious, and I would undo whatever goodwill I had fostered over the meal. Still, the thought made me shudder involuntarily. I couldn't allow it. I just couldn't.

"Diana will smell like seafood for days to come," I finally said. Her spine stiffened, and her cheeks burst into red roses immediately. "I mean, with the hot sun and—"

The waitress had returned to the table with my change and the carryout box. Mary Jo stood and walked past the waitress as she tried to hand her the box.

"She's changed her mind," I whispered to the befuddled waitress before chasing Mary Jo out to the parking lot.

I bought myself another two weeks' silence for that one. I could see the contempt in Mary Jo's eyes every time she looked at the car.

Diana was a big hit at the bank. All the guys wanted to drive her—like I'd really *let* them—and all the gals wanted a ride around the block. Most of them encouraged me to drive faster, but I didn't see any reason to be reckless. I'd be paying for the car for the next five years, and it had to last.

I wasn't altogether surprised when Gordon Pridemore himself stopped by my cubicle one afternoon to ask for a transportation favor.

"My Cadillac is in the shop—nothing major, of course," he said, trying to retain his presidential dignity by subtly reminding me his car had cost more than mine. That was fine. His car was a big, square tank, luxurious for sure, but in a grandfatherly sort of way. Diana was fast and sleek and—

I get carried away sometimes.

"Do you think you could drop me at the dealership on your way home tonight?" he finished. I could see the eager look in his eyes, the nervous way he licked his lips, the way his hands twittered at his side. I had the ultimate veto over this powerful man, and the feeling was magnificent.

"Of course, Mr. Pridemore," I said. "I'd be happy to."

A quick, satisfied nod, and he was gone.

I sat back in my chair and reveled in his obvious envy. At the time, it didn't occur to me Gordon Pridemore could have easily afforded a handful of new Mustangs if he wanted them. There have been several key points in my life where my thinking has gotten muddled where Diana is concerned. She is such a beautiful creature.

When the time came, I met the old man in the front lobby. He seemed eager to get underway, as I would well imagine he would be.

"Thank you so much, Harlan," he said, smiling politely. "I won't forget it."

"Thank you, sir," I said automatically.

"I do have one more favor to ask," he said.

"Certainly, sir."

"My wife's car broke down this afternoon, and I wondered if we might swing by and pick her up—if it's not too much trouble. She's a few blocks before Crown Caddy, so it really wouldn't be far out of the way."

"Certainly, sir," I said. "No problem-o."

"Thank you, son. I won't forget it."

241

We walked companionably to where Diana slept in the lot, the sun shimmering off her glossy black exterior. I watched Mr. Pridemore eye her appreciably as he walked around the rear of the car to the passenger side. I unlocked the doors with the remote, and we got in.

I found what I considered to be appropriate music on the Mach 460 stereo and adjusted the volume accordingly. Mr. Pridemore looked blissfully content as we drove along the city streets, weaving our way steadily toward our destination. Diana's engine purred happily as I guided her along.

"Where am I going?" I asked.

"Dryden. 300 block," he said crisply, and I headed in that direction. "Do you always drive so slowly?"

"Carefully, sir," I said. "Carefully."

He cleared his throat and mumbled something else, but I didn't catch it. I couldn't keep the smile from my face. Mr. Pridemore was impressed. I could tell. Furthermore, he showed the proper respect for Diana—his feet never left the floor mat. He would remember me when salary reviews came along, I was sure of it. And if Diana had cost a bit more than I could comfortably afford, an increase would certainly be timely.

It was as I contemplated this perfect day that things fell into a rapid, irreversible decline. We arrived at the 300 block of Dryden Avenue, and I was waiting for further instruction from Mr. Pridemore about where we were to pick up his wife. Before he had a chance to say anything, I spotted her on the right-hand side of the road, standing at the curb. Regina Pridemore had been to the bank plenty of times, and there was no mistaking her. She was unusually tall, well over six feet, with silver hair that shimmered as if it were actually spun from the ore. Two realizations descended on me with the weight of an anvil, and I could barely keep from gasping aloud in horror.

Regina Pridemore was standing outside a veterinarian's office.

Regina Pridemore had a filthy, hairy little dog in her arms.

She waved at the car, and it wasn't until later that it occurred to me Mr. Pridemore must have thought enough of Diana to mention her to his wife; Mrs. Pridemore obviously recognized her on sight. There was no time for such foolish pride. I had a real situation on my hands. I did something I had never done before.

I depressed the gas pedal a quarter of an inch closer to the floorboard.

My heart raced as Diana's speedometer stabilized at forty. We passed a dazed and confused Mrs. Pridemore, the filthy beast in her arms yapping the whole while. Mr.

243

Pridemore did a double take as he watched his wife grow smaller in the back glass.

"That was my wife, Harlan," he said. "Didn't you see her?"

"Yes, sir—I did, sir."

"I don't understand."

"It's the—the dog, sir. I'm sorry, sir, but I can't have that filthy, peeing beast in my car, not in my Diana. I just *can't*, sir. I hope you understand. I'll drop you off to pick up your Cadillac, and you can come back and get them, okay? It's only a few blocks. You said so yourself."

Mr. Pridemore's bottom lip snapped upward, driving his upper one down into a scowl. "That so-called 'filthy, peeing beast' is our dear pet, Mimi. She has been with my family for fourteen years. She has never *once* had a problem with incontinence. She has been a friend to my children and another child to my wife and myself. I find what you are saying to be inexcusably offensive."

"I'm sorry you feel that way, sir," I said. I didn't know anything else to contribute. Sometimes you have to make a stand for what's important, and I couldn't allow that animal in Diana. There was probably pet hair all through the Pridemore home. I wondered if Mr. Pridemore was depositing little bits of fur in the deep crevices of the bucket seats, the areas that were the hardest to reach with the vacuum.

It was the longest eight blocks I've ever driven. I allowed Diana to settle back to a safer speed of twenty-five, and we suffered in uncomfortable silence for the remainder of the trip. As I deposited Mr. Pridemore at the service entrance to Crown Caddy, he turned and leaned slightly into the car.

"Thank you for the ride," he said stiffly. "I won't forget it."

A wave of chills like melting ice cream oozed down my spine. There was no questioning his intention.

All of this happened on a Thursday.

By Friday morning, my position as the computer guy at the bank had been eliminated.

I was numb as I drove home. I knew what Mary Jo would say. She would want me to get rid of Diana, and without a job, I didn't know how I was going to keep her anyway. All I needed was a little time to figure things out. Fortunately, she was at work and had no idea I was arriving at the house so early. I tucked Diana into her customary spot in the garage and got out, careful not to bump the door against the garage wall.

I went upstairs and crawled into bed, shoes and all. My nerves were tied in knots, and my future was in the toilet. Klein wasn't well known for its employment opportunities. Would I be able to get my job back at Brickton Shoelace? Even if I did, it wouldn't pay enough to sustain our current standard of living. I was *so* screwed.

Amazingly enough, I dropped off into a deep, dreamless sleep. Maybe the answers to my problems would come to me in a dream.

I awakened with a start at seven o'clock in the evening. The summer sun had dipped far enough into the western horizon to cast a warm beam through the window and across my head as it lay on the pillow. I wondered where Mary Jo was. She should've been home by then.

I got out of bed and went downstairs. "Mary Jo?"

No answer. It was just as well. I still didn't know what I was going to tell her about losing my job.

I spotted a note in Mary Jo's neat script leaning against the telephone on the stand in the front hall. "Went shopping for new clothes for Jonathan. Didn't think you'd want to go. Be back soon. MJ"

Great. Another expense.

What could I possibly tell her? At least it was Friday, and I had the whole weekend to come up with something plausible. I could leave as if I were going to work on Monday morning and pound the pavement, looking for a new job. Maybe I would luck out. Maybe I would find a position that paid even more than the one I had previously held.

And maybe donkeys would sprout wings and fly to the moon.

I needed to relax. I decided to give Diana a bath, give her some quality time. I got a plastic bucket from the laundry room and filled it with warm water, adding a measured amount of soap. I went upstairs into our bathroom and got the softest towels I could find. Mary Jo said they were reserved for our special guests, and that's exactly how I felt about Diana. Then, I headed back to the garage to pull Diana out. My heart nearly stopped when I opened the door which connected the garage to the house.

The garage was empty.

I set the bucket down with an abruptness that sloshed soapy water onto my legs. Someone had come and stolen Diana while I slept. I *knew* this was going to happen. All of the neighbors were jealous. I had seen it in their envious eyes every time I drove around the block. Although the car was insured, I found no comfort in that. Who knew what monstrosities were being done to Diana by her abductor? If I got her back, she would surely show signs of violation. Bile rose to the back of my throat, staining my taste buds, and I felt a little light-headed, too.

And then I heard the familiar thrum of her engine through the garage door. I made a beeline for the button that would raise the door and jumped when the door started up on its track before I had depressed it.

The first thing I saw was Mary Jo's Pontiac parked on the right side of the driveway. I looked up, and in came Diana with Mary Jo behind the wheel. The mixture of relief and fury left me wide-eyed and speechless at the mouth of the garage. Mary Jo smiled and waved and eased Diana to a halt before cutting the engine.

I sprung from the garage like a madman, and I think Mary Jo suspected I was coming out to help her with her packages. I went right by the driver's door, scrutinizing the glossy black metal for dings, dents or scratches.

Mary Jo got out of the car and stood with her hands on her hips, watching me intently. "I went to get Jonathan's clothes and decided to give the new car a whirl since I haven't even driven it yet."

I said nothing, still intent on my appraisal of Diana. She appeared to have returned unscathed. Despite the fact we had traded cars often enough in the past, I couldn't believe that Mary Jo had taken Diana without asking first. The rational part of me, infinitesimal as it was, told me to bite my tongue and say nothing. This was the first interest Mary Jo had taken in Diana since the dinner fiasco.

"What are you doing?" she asked, following me around the car.

"Nothing," I said absently, inspecting the wheel wells.

"I didn't hurt your damned car!" she screamed, slamming her handbag against the driver's door.

When she moved her bag aside, there was a jagged scratch in Diana's lovely veneer.

My vision blurred red, and I can't clearly remember the exact sequence of what followed next. I don't remember rounding the front of the car, nor do I remember my fingers closing around Mary Jo's throat. The next thing I knew, I was stooped over her prone body on the blacktop, her lifeless eyes bulging from bluish-red flesh, her tongue swollen and extended through her parted lips.

When the bank repossessed Diana, they had no trouble selling her for the balance of the loan. The scratch on the door was merely on the surface and buffed right out, leaving no evidence of where Mary Jo's purse had struck it.

Although my financial needs aren't a concern here and the meals are regular if not good, I will be paying dearly for Diana for the rest of my life.

A TERMINAL CASE

"I'm leaving, darling," said Milton, pulling on a worn tweed jacket.

His wife, Anita, sat at a large antique mahogany desk, pecking away at the keyboard of their computer. Her long fingernails clicked in rapid bursts of speed; her attention focused completely on the monitor in front of her face.

"Darling," repeated Milton.

Anita brushed an errant strand of auburn hair out of her face. "What?" she demanded.

"I'm leaving for work," said Milton, adjusting his unfashionably thin tie before covering his balding head with a well-worn fedora.

Anita snorted and returned her attention to the computer terminal.

251

"Would you like me to bring something home for dinner?" he asked, picking up his bulky leather attaché and slinging it clumsily over his shoulder. "Janet's off tonight."

Anita's fingers continued to peck away. Occasionally, her right hand would flash out like lightning, seeking the mouse, clicking away rapidly before rejoining the left on the keyboard.

Milton stood in silence for a moment, looking like a pathetic schoolboy who patiently awaited acknowledgement from his teacher. When it became clear Anita was not going to respond, he cleared his throat gently at first, then again more loudly.

"What do you want?" asked Anita sharply. "Can't you see I'm busy?"

"Sorry, dear," said Milton, shifting from one foot to the other. "I just wondered if you might like me to bring supper when I return tonight."

"Well, you damn well better," said Anita, momentarily surrendering her attention. "I sure as hell ain't whipping up a smorgasbord."

"Do you have a preference?" asked Milton. Anita was already lost in the computer screen. Milton sighed quietly, picking his keys up from the sofa table. "I'll call you before I head home. You can tell me what you want then."

Anita didn't look up. She was riveted to the computer. Milton silently crept from the room and left the house, locking the heavy wooden door behind him.

As soon as the latch clicked, Anita's annoyed gaze fixed on the door. How in the world had she gotten herself into this mess? She had never been in love with this man. She was, however, very much in love with his money.

Milton Theodore Stempel III was a scientist by profession, a multi-millionaire by inheritance. He was forty-two years old and aging poorly, with the personality of a tree stump and looks to match. By comparison, Anita was thirty-four, vivacious and curvaceous, green-eyed and auburn-haired. She had no wealthy family who would someday shower her with a magnificent dowry—quite the opposite, in fact. Anita Nelson had been orphaned at the age of five, with no living relatives to claim her or save her from the state institutions and foster homes in which she had grown, and there had been many of them. Anita tended to make trouble wherever she went, and inevitably ended up back in the custody of the state. At the age of eighteen, she had taken a job at Burger Buster, up to her lovely arms in grease and animal parts on a daily basis.

It was at Burger Buster that she had met Milton two years ago. Milton was not the sort of man Anita usually dated. His hair was thin, his glasses were thick, his pencils safely protected by a plastic sleeve in the breast pocket of his ill-fitting dress shirt. Anita usually went for bodybuilders, troublemakers and thrill seekers. There was something about Milton that made Anita pause, however. Not that she found him attractive. Good Lord, no! But there was the unmistakable scent of cash surrounding the man. It certainly wasn't the clothes he wore or the car he drove— a boxy, mud brown Volvo. In retrospect, Anita wasn't sure what it was, but the man smelled of money so old the dinosaurs may well have used it to play poker.

When Milton had come in that Friday night two years ago, he hadn't ordered his usual pickle and mustard sandwich. Instead, he had laid his head on the table, crying like a child.

"What's wrong, Milton?" Anita had asked, working authentic-sounding concern into her voice. It was always about maximizing the tip.

"My parents," Milton had finally managed. "They're dead."

"What?" Her hand flew up to cover her mouth as her eyes widened.

Milton had nodded emphatically, as if to assure Anita that his parents were, in fact, quite dead. "They were mauled by lions while touring Africa."

And so, Anita had consoled Milton, flirted with him, teased him, and eventually asked him out for coffee. Milton was shy and inexperienced, unsure how to respond to this newfound attention. For a short while, Anita feared the man was gay, and she had been barking up the wrong tree the whole time. However, she had finally worn him down, experiencing the single most awkward physical encounter of her life.

During their dates, Anita had learned the particulars about Milton's wealthy family, the Stempels. His mother and father had been grand explorers, traveling the globe and experiencing different cultures firsthand. Anita found the notion exciting (minus the lion attack, of course), but Milton had always found his parents to be eccentric. How two such free-spirited creatures could produce offspring so completely different was unimaginable to Anita.

Anita had never possessed any more money than it had taken to keep a roof over her head and food on her table—sometimes not even that much. What lay before her was a passport to a new lifestyle, even if Milton Theodore Stempel III didn't currently live in a manner befitting his personal wealth. Anita would provide guidance, getting him out of his cracker box apartment and into a suitable house. If Milton wouldn't spend his money, Anita would do it for him.

They had married after a short courtship, and Anita had set her plan in motion immediately. She had been eyeing the Patterson estate on Preston Ridge for some time. The sprawling manor had been on the market for months, empty and just waiting for new owners to move in. It had three levels and a basement, large rooms with high ceilings, and all of its antique mahogany furnishings were included in the purchase price. Anita had convinced Milton with very little difficulty to make the acquisition. He was so eager to please her; it made her plans all the easier to execute.

What Anita hadn't counted on was her own growing impatience with Milton. The man was truly a maladroit, immersed in beakers and lab rats, test cases and control groups. He lived and breathed science, babbling enthusiastically about elaborate scientific theorems which skipped right over Anita's head. There was no doubt the man was a genius, but who really cared about subatomic structures and nucleotides? Anita surely did not.

After about six months, Anita's own personality shifted dramatically. No more would she pay rapt attention to the scientific ramblings of her wealthy husband. No more would she hide behind schoolgirl giggles at his inane attempts at humor. It was so difficult to fake enthusiasm for a man who more and more made her skin crawl. She had originally hoped it wouldn't be so bad, consolation coming in the form of pretty packages and expensive gifts. She had pictured confining Milton to specific areas of the house and having the run of the rest, but Milton had refused to stay put, always wandering in during Anita's favorite television programs to talk about his latest laboratory experiments. As if she cared. By their first-year anniversary, Anita had dropped all pretense of civility toward the man.

Anita's original scheme had involved a divorce around the two-year mark, helping herself to half of Milton's family fortune in the settlement, but an obstacle had been thrown in just prior to the wedding. Hayden Brock, long-time attorney for the Stempels, had come by Milton's old apartment with a document for Anita to sign.

"What's this?" she had asked, her pleasant smile faltering.

"It's a prenuptial agreement," the silver-haired lawyer had said, his eyes studying Anita's face. "It's fairly standard when there's this much money involved."

Anita had turned a wounded gaze to Milton. "Is this what you want?" she had asked, her voice trembling.

"It's the first I've heard of it. Hayden, do we really have to mess with this nonsense?" Milton had asked.

"I'm afraid so, folks. In the event of your engagement, the requirement of a prenup is a stipulation of your parents' will," Hayden had said, laying the documents out neatly on

Milton's cluttered workspace. He turned to face Anita, his eyes cold and perceptive. "They just wanted to make sure some shark wouldn't come along and try to take the family money."

Milton had laughed while Anita held her breath. "Not my Anita. She would never do anything like that."

"Of course not!" Anita had said, laughing half-heartedly and wincing slightly as Milton pulled her close.

Hayden's pause was almost imperceptible. "Nevertheless, there's nothing we can do about it but sign the appropriate paperwork." He had slid the first form toward Anita and offered a pen.

"Should I have a lawyer read this?" Anita had asked, taking the pen and stalling while she tried to formulate a way around this little snafu.

"You can if you want to, but it's pretty basic stuff. If you leave, you get what you brought with you and not one thing more. Is there a problem, Miss Nelson?" The lawyer had nearly licked his lips at the prospect of making Anita squirm.

"None whatsoever," she had replied, signing her name with a flourish. "There's no need worrying about what will never come to pass." She had planted a sloppy wet kiss on Milton's mouth. When she had finished, Milton's ears were bright red and his expression was pure bliss, but the attorney had not been fooled. His disapproving gaze would have been hard to mistake.

And with that, Anita had signed away her opportunity to divorce Milton, provided she wanted to retain her financial stature—and she very much wanted to retain her financial stature.

In the meanwhile, Anita had insisted upon hiring help to maintain the grand old house. "Everyone else in this neighborhood has staff. I want a maid, too," she had said petulantly.

Any other man might have pointed out that Anita had plenty of free time on her hands since she had quit her job immediately after the wedding, but Milton had merely been concerned that his treasured wife was unhappy. "Start interviewing at your leisure, dear. You're here more often than I, so you should hire someone with whom you are comfortable."

"Obviously," Anita had said, rolling her eyes. "I want a maid who cooks, too. I've been cooking my whole damn life. It's time to let someone else do it."

"Whatever you think is best."

"But I don't want a live-in," added Anita. "I'm not comfortable with the thought of someone thinking of my house as her own."

"However you want it to be, dear."

Janet Norris, a slight woman in her mid-thirties, had been hired shortly afterward. She came in every morning to fix breakfast and left shortly after dinner each night, taking Wednesdays off. She was a mousy woman, hard-working and easily intimidated. Anita remembered her type from high school, the type who faded into the wallpaper during school dances, afraid to express her own opinion about anything. Anita figured that Janet would give her another outlet through which she could vent her frustrations. Antagonizing her would be terribly fun, after all.

From that point, Anita's day was entirely free from responsibility. She generally slept until eleven, then took a long, hot soak in the Jacuzzi before heading out to fill the trunk of her car with packages from the mall—not the crappy mall at Midtown, either. Anita preferred to do her shopping at the Pinnacle Square Mall, where the customers drove Lexuses and BMWs and the price of a single sweater could challenge a middle-class budget.

Still, shopping had gotten boring after a while. Anita longed to travel, but Milton would never leave his work long enough for that. Restlessness was setting in.

One day about three weeks earlier, Milton had come home bearing gifts. Anita was wary as he trundled back to the car to bring in box after box. The last gift he had spontaneously purchased was a collection of fossils embedded in a hunk of petrified wood, presumably to place on the mantel as a conversation piece. Anita had been horrified and ordered Milton to keep the hideous thing either in his workspace or down in the basement.

Milton had carried the final box in before stopping to wipe the perspiration from his brow.

"What is it?" Anita had asked suspiciously.

"It's a PC," Milton had said proudly.

"A what?"

"A computer, dear. I thought you might enjoy—"

"A computer? What in the world do I need with a computer?"

"Well, I thought you might enjoy surfing the internet. You wouldn't believe the amount of reference material available. It's simply staggering!" Milton had continued babbling, praising the technology as Anita stared skeptically.

Finally, she had said, "Do what you want. I might look at it later."

Milton had assembled the computer, monitor, printer and scanner in no time, and soon, he was offering operational advice and demonstrating the equipment's many features.

Anita was unimpressed. She could understand how a scientist might find a computer invaluable, but she didn't see any reason she might use it.

"There are also online communities," Milton had said, wrapping up his tutorial.

"Online communities? What, a bunch of eggheads trading recipes for anthrax?"

"Not at all, dear. They have online communities for every type of interest. Sports, entertainment—why, they even have communities to help single people meet each other. Quite a different spin on computer dating, wouldn't you say?"

Anita's interest level had heightened. "You're kidding, right? People actually meet each other on the internet?"

"Oh, sure. It's like having an electronic pen pal, and the best part is, you don't have to wait for the postman to deliver."

The thing most sorely lacking in Anita's life was romance. She wanted the wealth and prestige that came with being Mrs. Milton Theodore Stempel III, but she also wanted heat and passion. These were things that Milton would never be able to provide.

"Isn't that kind of dangerous?" she had asked. "You wouldn't have any idea who you were dealing with."

Milton had chuckled. "That's half the point, dear. Anonymity. They have no more idea about you than you do about them."

Anonymity. What a wonderful concept! Anita had never had many friends, mostly due to her lack of social graces. She was perceived as bossy (which she was), phony (which she also was) and manipulative (which she was again). The only person she had ever fooled was poor, sad Milton. The computer afforded her the opportunity to become someone else, someone whose facial expressions wouldn't give everything away.

Anita had spent the next several days acquainting herself with the device, learning how to access the internet and participate in chat rooms. The computer quickly became a window into another world, where she could be anyone she wanted to be; single, teenaged, sex-starved—she could be male or female, for heaven's sake! There were plenty of kinky people out there, she had quickly discovered, but soon she focused on public chat rooms geared toward lonely people of her own age group. There was nothing overtly sexual about the conversations. Mostly, they were the types of exchanges common between good friends, but since Anita had never had any good friends, she couldn't be entirely certain. Her screen name was MZZ KITTY, and she never divulged any real details of her own life. She became so protective of this alternate persona that she shielded the screen from Milton's eyes anytime he neared the desk. It wasn't that Anita's activity was incriminating, but it was like having someone stand over your shoulder while you read your mail. It was personal, dammit! Furthermore, half the fun of MZZ KITTY was the fact that she had never even heard of Milton Theodore Stempel III.

On this particular afternoon, Anita had been conversing with several of her regular chat partners when Milton had interrupted her. Now, as his Volvo buzzed away toward his research center downtown, Anita returned her attention to the computer terminal and her friends, PITA LOVIN RITA, LITL BLAKE and DIAMOND CLEO.

PITA LOVIN RITA:	U STILL THERE, KITTY?
MZZ KITTY:	MEOW
PITA LOVIN RITA:	WHAT DO U THINK?
DIAMOND CLEO:	I THINK U R MAKING IT UP
PITA LOVIN RITA:	I DIDN'T ASK U

Anita had to scroll back through the conversation to see what she had missed. Apparently, PITA LOVIN RITA had heard about a friend who was stalked by someone she had met in a chat room.

MZZ KITTY:	IF SHE'S DUMB ENOUGH TO GIVE HER ADDRESS...
LITL BLAKE:	AMEN!

264

PITA LOVIN RITA: I KNOW I WOULDN'T, BUT SHE
                     WAS LONELY:-(

Anita was only just learning the abbreviations and various symbols associated with internet chatting. She had to think for a minute before remembering that this represented a sad face.

Suddenly, a chime sounded brightly through the computer's speakers. A small square popped up, declaring a private instant message was available for MZZ KITTY. This is new, Anita thought. She had heard the terminology but had never actually received one. Her internet friends conversed as a group. This message was from a user named BIRDMAN. MZZ KITTY didn't know any BIRDMAN.

BIRDMAN: CAN I ASK U A QUESTION?
MZZ KITTY: AS LONG AS U R NOT SELLING
                     SUMTHING
BIRDMAN: NO SALE. IS IT TRUE THAT
                     CURIOSITY KILLED MZZ KITTY?

Anita read and then reread the last line. Had she just been threatened? She didn't know how to reply or if she even should.

The clever little chime sounded again.

| BIRDMAN: | GOD! THAT SOUNDED PSYCHO. WISH THERE WAS AN "UNDO" BUTTON ON THESE DAMNED INSTANT MESSAGE THINGS. I WAS TRYING TO BE CLEVER. |

Anita relaxed a little but wondered who in the hell BIRDMAN was and what he wanted. Cautiously, she typed her response.

MZZ KITTY:	CLEVER ABOUT WHAT?
BIRDMAN:	OK. ALREADY PUT MY FOOT IN IT. MIGHT AS WELL GO FOR BROKE. I'VE BEEN IN THE PUBLIC CHAT ROOMS WITH U SEVERAL TIMES. I'VE NEVER JOINED IN, JUST WATCHED. U R SO FUNNY. I LOVE TO READ YOUR CONVERSATIONS. I HOPE U R NOT OFFENDED. AS I TYPE, IT SEEMS KIND OF CREEPY AND SICK.
MZZ KITTY:	Y DON'T U JOIN IN?

There was no response for some time, and Anita began to think that BIRDMAN had turned chicken. Anita was suspicious of this stranger, but remained intrigued, nevertheless. She was a smart woman. She wouldn't fall victim to some internet prowler.

The chime sounded again.

BIRDMAN: I NEVER KNOW WHAT TO SAY. I WANT TO B FUNNY BUT AM NOT. (SEE FIRST QUESTION FOR PROOF)

MZZ KITTY: LOL :-)

Anita happily entered the abbreviation for "Laugh Out Loud" and as an afterthought, followed it by a smiley face. She had only recently learned the abbreviation and used it at every opportunity. The smiley face was inspired by PITA LOVIN RITA's earlier use of the opposite symbol.

MZZ KITTY: BUT SEE, THAT WAS FUNNY!

BIRDMAN: IF U SAY SO

MZZ KITTY and BIRDMAN continued for the next half hour, exchanging quips, and asking little questions about each other. Anita found the mysterious messenger to be less suspicious and more intriguing with each passing line of text.

Anita awoke from her afternoon nap with a mischievous smile on her face. She had dreamed about BIRDMAN again. It didn't matter that she had never laid eyes on the man. Her imagination was filling in all the blanks. He was tall, dark, mysterious—every cliché imaginable, but as provocative as one of the men on the covers of those trashy romance novels. Despite his earlier claims of being unfunny, Anita found him very witty and quite charming.

MZZ KITTY and BIRDMAN had developed a routine of chatting nightly at 7:00. They had been doing it for two weeks now, and Anita found herself looking forward to it more than any other event of the day. They had recently discovered they only lived thirty miles apart. It was amazing how two people so geographically close had found each other on a network that spanned the entire globe.

Realizing it was 6:45, Anita descended the stairs bouncing on her toes, nearly floating to the bottom. Milton had gone to work hours ago and was working on a big experiment. He expected to be late, and Anita realized she would have more time than usual to chat with BIRDMAN.

Her smile left her face as she rounded the corner to the study. Janet Norris sat on the padded window seat, her feet pulled up and a notebook propped on her knees. Pens and pencils stuck out randomly from within her mousy brown hair which was coiled atop her head. The girl was deep in thought.

Anita cleared her throat, and Janet jumped. "Just what are you doing?" Anita asked, her hands on her hips.

"I'm sorry, ma'am," the girl squeaked. "I had done everything on the list. All I was waiting for was to serve you dinner before I was on my way. I've had so little time to do my writing—"

"So, you thought it was just fine and dandy for you to take up your hobby while you were on my clock?"

Janet tucked her notebook into a well-used book bag with trembling fingers. "I'm sorry, ma'am. I didn't think you'd mind since I had done everything on the list."

Anita sighed exaggeratedly. "Let's be clear, Janet. When you are working for me, you are working for me—not writing your little stories. The list is what I need done before you leave. If you complete the list, you can grab the vacuum cleaner and sweep something. You could get busy in the garden. I had bulbs delivered. They need to be planted immediately."

Janet's eyes had drooped to the floor, and she cowered in the presence of her employer. "Um, okay. I didn't know I was to do gardening."

"Oh, for heaven's sake, Janet! Must you complain about every little thing? Milton and I are paying you good money for your services. Another girl I interviewed at the time we hired you had no problem with gardening or anything else we might need. Maybe I should pull my file and see if she's still looking for a job," threatened Anita.

"Oh no, ma'am! Please!" pleaded Janet. "I didn't mean to make noise. It's just that I've never done any planting before. I'm afraid I don't know how."

"What's to know? You dig a hole, throw the bulb to the bottom, cover it, water it, voila! You're done," said Anita.

"What if I ruin them?" Janet's tremulous tone suggested that she didn't wish to be caught in the wrath of Anita Stempel should the plants die.

"Just go!" Anita shooed Janet away impatiently. It was 6:57. Time to get online.

MZZ KITTY: GOOD NEWS. RAT MAN WON'T BE HOME FOR QUITE A WHILE. WE CAN TALK LONGER.

MZZ KITTY and BIRDMAN had already discussed their respective spouses. Both were married and both were bored. BIRDMAN had discussed the inevitably of his divorce. MZZ KITTY wasn't quite that committed yet.

BIRDMAN: I THINK IT'S TIME WE MEET.

Anita's fingers froze. PITA LOVIN RITA's story about her friend's internet stalker floated to the forefront of Anita's mind. Still, she was very tempted. Part of her wanted to know what BIRDMAN looked like, while the other part was afraid that her perfect illusion would be shattered beyond repair.

BIRDMAN: U STILL THERE?

MZZ KITTY: SORRY. I DON'T KNOW IF WE SHOULD MEET.

BIRDMAN: I UNDERSTAND. U DON'T REALLY KNOW ME FROM ADAM. TELL U WHAT. HOW BOUT I GIVE U INFORMATION ABOUT ME? U CAN CHECK ME OUT AND I'LL NEVER KNOW IT WAS U. THEN WE CAN MEET IF U WANT.

MZZ KITTY:	WHAT KIND OF INFO?
BIRDMAN:	MY NAME IS BOB DRANSDALE. I'M A RIDING INSTRUCTOR AT THE COUNTRY CLUB.

Anita made careful notes, capturing the information on a steno pad she kept by the keyboard.

That night, she tossed and turned, wondering what she should do next. Milton had come home close to midnight and was now snoring soundly beside her. He had attempted to engage her affection, but she had begged off with a headache.

Anita's mind invariably wandered back to the steno book. Bob Dransdale. She could slip over to the country club tomorrow afternoon and see what he was like. She liked the thought of him on a horse. The image was so virile and exciting. Anita couldn't even imagine Milton on a horse.

Still, what if he was an ogre? What if he had double chins? What if he turned out to be worse than Milton?

By morning, Anita had decided what to do. She realized she was falling in love with the fantasy of her internet pen pal. She needed to know if Bob Dransdale measured up. By his vocation, he wouldn't be a wealthy man. That was the biggest disappointment in the scenario. Anita tried not to think about it much, but it was such a big factor. She may have never loved Milton, but she had certainly adapted to having his bank accounts at her disposal.

Anita drove her BMW convertible down State Route 10. With the top down and the warm summer air blowing through her hair, she drove toward the country club at a pace which would best be described as pensive. None of the other country club wives had cars as nice, but it truly didn't seem to matter. Try as she might, Anita was never able to impress that lot. The Stempels had been long-standing club members for generations, but Anita had only been allowed in by virtue of her marriage to Milton. She was an outsider, and they wouldn't let her forget it easily.

Ultimately, it didn't matter all that much to Anita, either. She could come and go as she pleased, do whatever suited her fancy and leave whenever she wanted. She didn't have to cozy up to the other women, forcing false attentiveness and fluttery little laughs. It was a relief, in fact.

Anita parked her car and headed directly to the rear of the large property. The stables were there, and Anita nearly ran in anticipation of finally seeing what BIRDMAN looked like. She slowed as she saw a group of three middle-aged women being guided out of the stable on sturdy, gentle horses. The man pulling the reins was undoubtedly Bob Dransdale. Anita stepped behind a large oak tree, not wanting to be seen. Other stablemen carried on about their business, but they didn't seem to notice Anita's presence.

Bob was ruggedly handsome, six foot three, two hundred twenty-five pounds, and a mane of jet-black hair that spilled slightly over his shoulders. Anita's heart beat faster as the man turned and swung up nimbly into his saddle. She licked her lips as she watched him smile and encourage one of his students to move forward. He was every bit as attractive as Anita had hoped he might be—even more so. Should she run to him? Should she announce who she was?

For God's sake, woman! Get a hold of yourself! You're at the country club!

It was with true regret that Anita watched the group ride slowly out into the field. She then returned to her car, never bothering to go into the club itself. She had seen what she had come to see.

The next few nights, Anita dreamed of BIRDMAN, but now his romance novel image had been replaced by the face and body of Bob Dransdale. Although they had chatted in the interim, Anita had not yet told BIRDMAN she had come to see him. If she told him she'd seen him and she approved, he would surely want to meet immediately. Where could they meet? If she wasn't careful, everyone in town would be talking about her affair, and as deep as Milton kept his head buried in the sand, even he would inevitably find out.

Anita felt trapped, unable to relinquish her claim on Milton's money yet longing fiercely for the touch of her online companion. If only Milton would have an accident on the way to work, a drunken driver careening into his Volvo. Oh! Or maybe an accident at work, chemicals exploding when introduced to each other in the wrong proportions—but it would never happen. Milton was far too careful in the laboratory for that.

The next afternoon, BIRDMAN asked the inevitable.

BIRDMAN:	SO, HAVE U CHECKED ME OUT?
MZZ KITTY:	YES.
BIRDMAN:	WHEN SHALL WE MEET?
MZZ KITTY:	IT'S NOT AS SIMPLE AS THAT. THERE'S A LOT AT STAKE.
BIRDMAN:	LIKE MY HEART.
MZZ KITTY:	DON'T GET ALL GOOEY. I'M TALKING CASH.
BIRDMAN:	I SEE.
MZZ KITTY:	NO U DON'T. LOTS OF CASH. IT WOULD BE SO MUCH EASIER IF MY HUSBAND HAD A HEART ATTACK.

There was no response for some time, and Anita feared that she might have scared her paramour away. When she re-read the lines, she saw the coldness of her words, yet they were truthful. There was no shame in being truthful.

BIRDMAN: HAVE U EVER THOUGHT OF HELPING HIM ALONG?

Anita's breath caught in her chest. Was she reading correctly? Did BIRDMAN just propose murder?

MZZ KITTY: WHAT DO U SUGGEST?
BIRDMAN: I SUGGEST WE MEET.
MZZ KITTY: NO! NOT YET. HOW COULD WE HELP HIM ALONG?

There it was in electronic letters. She had officially opened the can of worms. There was no retrieving the question.

BIRDMAN: ANY NUMBER OF WAYS. POISON, A GUN, A KNIFE, STRANGU-LATION...WHICH DO U PREFER?

| MZZ KITTY: | I'D PREFER IT IF HE HAD A HEART ATTACK. I DON'T WANT TO SPEND THE REST OF MY LIFE IN JAIL. |
| BIRDMAN: | I'VE GOT AN IDEA, BUT U HAVE TO TELL ME WHO U R. I CAN'T HELP U IF I DON'T KNOW. |

Anita hesitated. She was now to the point of no return. If she answered him, she would have committed herself completely to the grisly plan, whatever it might be. The dream of a future with Bob Dransdale by her side and Milton Stempel's money in her pocket was powerful motivation.

| MZZ KITTY: | ANITA STEMPEL. MY HUSBAND IS MILTON. |
| BIRDMAN: | WELL, ANITA, GLAD TO MEET U. HERE'S WHAT'S NEXT. I'M GOING TO SEND U A PACKAGE OF TULIP BULBS. BUT WHAT'S INSIDE WILL BE SOMETHING FOR U TO SHARE WITH MILTON. THREE DROPS IN A BEVERAGE. IT'S SLOW ACTING AND |

IMITATES THE SYMPTOMS OF A LETHAL HEART ATTACK. HE WILL HAVE BEEN AWAY FROM THE PLACE HE INGESTS THE TONIC FOR HOURS BY THE TIME IT TAKES EFFECT. GIVES U TIME TO DESTROY ANY EVIDENCE.

They signed off shortly afterward. Anita couldn't believe she was even considering the plan, but the aftermath would be pure nirvana. The thought of growing old with Milton was repugnant, and the thought of being held in Bob Dransdale's arms was hypnotic. Even then, Anita knew which choice she would make.

Two days later, as Anita was checking up on Janet, she spotted the girl prying open a box of tulip bulbs that had arrived in that afternoon's mail.

"What are you doing?" Anita shrieked, crossing the room and seizing the package.

"I'm sorry, ma'am. I had some extra time and thought I'd do some gardening, like you suggested. I saw these in the mail today, and—"

"And you opened my mail? That's inexcusable, Janet, absolutely inexcusable!" Anita clutched the package to her breast like it was her own child.

Janet's face deepened red, and she fumbled with her apology. "It didn't occur to me that—I mean, I never thought you'd mind if—oh! I'm so sorry, Mrs. Stempel. It will never happen again!"

"You're damn right it won't! You're fired!"

"Oh, please, ma'am! I was truly only trying to be helpful! Please don't fire me!" Tears had formed in Janet's big brown eyes.

Anita made her grovel for several more minutes before finally letting her off the hook. "All right then, Janet. I'll give you this one last chance. But you had better understand that what comes to the house addressed to me is for my eyes only. Are we clear?"

"Oh, yes, ma'am. Thank you, ma'am." Janet nearly bowed out of the room, dabbing at her eyes as she went.

The nosy fool! If she had opened the parcel, she would have known it didn't contain tulip bulbs. If the police were at all suspicious after Milton passed away, Janet would have been able to tell them about the mysterious vial which

279

arrived in the mail for Mrs. Stempel, masquerading itself as flowers. Anita's pulse raced, and her temples throbbed with each heartbeat. She was so close to her goal, yet one innocent observation by a third party could have caused the whole plan to capsize.

At 7:00 that evening, Anita signed on to the internet. Milton had called to say he was in the middle of a laborious project and would be later than usual getting home. That was fine with Anita. She didn't want him to walk in while she plotted his murder onscreen.

BIRDMAN:	DID U GET MY PRESENT?
MZZ KITTY:	I DID.
BIRDMAN:	WHEN R U GOING TO DO IT?
MZZ KITTY:	SOON. HE GOES TO A CONVENTION ON THE EAST COAST NEXT WEEK. I'M DOING IT RIGHT BEFORE HE LEAVES FOR THE AIRPORT.

BIRDMAN:	BRILLIANT! HE'LL BE HUN-DREDS OF MILES AWAY WHEN THE MEDICINE DOES ITS MAGIC.
MZZ KITTY:	THEN WE CAN MEET?
BIRDMAN:	NOT RIGHT AWAY. IT WOULD LOOK SUSPICIOUS.

Anita knew that he was right, but her longing for Bob Dransdale was intense. Still, to have come this far, what harm would there be in waiting a month or two more?

MZZ KITTY:	U R RIGHT.
BIRDMAN:	NEXT WEEK IS STILL A WAY'S OFF. I'M WORRIED FOR U. WHAT IF HE FINDS THE VIAL? HE'S A SCIENTIST. HE'LL KNOW WHAT IT'S FOR.
MZZ KITTY:	HE WON'T FIND IT, I'M CERTAIN.
BIRDMAN:	DO U HAVE A GUN?
MZZ KITTY:	WHATEVER FOR?
BIRDMAN:	IF HE THINKS U R TRYING TO KILL HIM, HE MIGHT TURN VIOLENT.

Anita laughed at the thought. Milton was the least threatening man she had ever met, and she had met quite a few in her day.

| MZZ KITTY: | THAT'S RIDICULOUS. |
| BIRDMAN: | JUST THINKING OF YOUR SAFETY, DARLING. |

The days went by in slow motion, long afternoons stretching into longer evenings. It didn't help that BIRDMAN was unavailable for chat three consecutive nights. He had a pressing family emergency and had to leave town. Anita spent her days criticizing Janet's efforts around the house and her evenings listening to Milton theorize and hypothesize endlessly, about what she did not know—the words all ran together.

Nights were surprising. Anita's wonderful dreams about Bob Dransdale had been supplanted by nightmares of Milton trying to kill her. In each dream, Anita had left the vial of poison on her desk by her computer terminal. Milton's reaction was different in every iteration but equally horrifying. Sometimes he strangled her. Sometimes he stabbed her. Sometimes he shot her. Once he even doused her with gasoline and lit a match. She had woken up screaming with the smell of burning flesh in her nostrils.

The benevolent Milton Theodore Stempel III had become an evil night stalker, seeking revenge in the most brutal ways.

After the fourth night of horrid dreams, Anita wandered into Milton's study. He had never declared the room off-limits or shown any privacy concerns whatsoever. It was merely one of the areas to which Anita had tried to relegate the man. He collected little bits of this and that, wartime memorabilia, antique documents, and so forth. What Anita was interested in was his weapons collection. He didn't have many pieces, just a few small handguns, several knives and a magnificent samurai sword. It was from the handguns that Anita made her selection, a small pearl-handled piece that could easily be concealed in her pocket. Milton kept the ammunition locked in a separate cabinet, but Anita had no trouble locating the key. She would feel much safer with the small pistol at her side.

Finally, the day had arrived. Milton had been fussing for hours, dragging his feet about what to pack in his suitcase. He hated to fly, and this flight would be a particularly lengthy one.

"I don't know why they can't all just fly here," he groused.

"Oh, for heaven's sake, Milton! You've flown a hundred times before. Don't be such a baby," said Anita.

283

"Wouldn't you like me to run down to the village and pick you up some dinner? Janet's out tonight, and you'll be by yourself."

"Quit stalling. I've got a frozen dinner in the freezer. I'm fine. You need to get yourself together. I'll tell you what," said Anita, her voice sweeter than it had been in quite some time. "I'm going to get you something to settle your stomach. You'll feel so much better. All right?"

"Of course, darling. Anything you say."

Anita's smile broadened as she traveled down the hall. Her work was almost done. She went downstairs and retrieved the blue vial from the depths of her desk. The liquid inside was completely clear. Anita fixed an Alka-Seltzer and carefully placed three drops from the vial into the fizzy mixture. It blended seamlessly with the tonic.

She carried the glass upstairs as if it contained nitroglycerin. She didn't want any of the liquid to spill out and onto the carpet. It would contain traces of the poison, and that kind of evidence could not be left behind. She would have to pay close attention to Milton, as well. If he spilled any of the liquid, she would need to see exactly where.

She needn't have worried. Milton downed the Alka-Seltzer in one shot and belched perfunctorily.

"Thank you, dear," he said, returning to his suitcase to fasten the straps. "I'm sorry to leave you alone like this. Are you sure you won't go with me?"

"And listen to a roomful of scientists go on and on? I'd rather be dead," said Anita.

Milton smiled and kissed Anita wetly on the cheek. "I'll see you in a few days."

The next time I see you, you'll be dead, thought Anita.

At 7:00, Anita signed on to her computer.

BIRDMAN:	WELL?
MZZ KITTY:	IT'S DONE. ALL WE HAVE TO DO IS WAIT.
BIRDMAN:	R U SCARED?
MZZ KITTY:	EXCITED!!!

And Anita truly was excited. She knew there'd be talk around the village of how Anita didn't deserve the vast Stempel fortune, but she could live with that. She could nearly feel Bob Dransdale's big arms around her, holding her tight.

After signing off with BIRDMAN, Anita collected a small paper bag from the corner of the desk. She and BIRDMAN had discussed what she should do with the contents of the bag. It contained the vial and drinking glass which Milton had used. Anita grabbed her car keys and trotted out to her BMW. It was after 10:00. Traffic would be nearly non-existent on Old Mill Road.

As Anita drove slowly along the gravel road, she remained alert for the headlights of oncoming cars. She hadn't seen any for miles when she approached the section of road which skirted the quarry. The black waters of the quarry were very murky and very deep. Finding the bag in there would be like finding a needle in a haystack. She pulled off to the side and hurried out of the car, anxious to be done with the whole affair. She drew her arm back and threw straight and hard, sending the bag in a high arc that ended far away from the edge of the water. As soon as she heard the gratifying plunk, Anita raced back to her car and started the engine. She saw the faint pinpricks of headlights on the horizon and put her car in gear, pulling back out onto the roadway. She wanted to be back up to normal speed when she passed the other car.

Adrenaline was pounding again, and Anita almost expected the other car to be a police cruiser, but as the headlights finally drew upon her, she realized it was only an old beat-up farm truck. She laughed like a crazy woman, her hair whipping wildly in the night air. The coolness felt good against her bare arms, and with the top of the convertible down, she felt as though she were flying. Flying like a BIRDMAN.

The house seemed large and foreboding as she idled up the winding drive to park beside the mansion. It was the only drawback to a residence of this design. Anita hadn't thought to leave lights on throughout the house, and goosebumps raced along her arms as she ascended the veranda stairs. Wind rustled the bushes around the portico, sounding like animals scrambling through the branches. Anita fumbled with the lock and then let herself in.

She could hear the steady ticking of the grandfather clock in the library. It resounded through the silence with exaggerated volume, setting Anita's nerves on edge. Milton should have reacted to the poison by now. He should be laying cold and dead on a slab in some coroner's office.

Anita wondered if she would appear appropriately upset when the police officers came to tell her the bad news. She figured they could come at any time. She would have to be prepared.

287

It was then that she heard a noise upstairs. It was a distinct thudding, like something heavy dropping from a shelf. Anita froze. She stood at the bottom of the stairs, peering up. A faint light shone from the end of the hall, casting its diminishing luminescence against the back wall. Anita had almost convinced herself she had imagined the sound when she saw a shadow move distinctly through the spillage of light.

Panic seized Anita's throat, constricting her airflow and stifling her voice box. There was someone in the house with her! She felt in the pocket of her sweater and was relieved to find the gun still there. She tiptoed to the telephone in the foyer and dialed 911.

"Please, there's someone in my house. Send the police immediately!" She banged the phone down without bothering to give her address. She had read about the sophisticated equipment of 911 operators. If the call weren't originating from a cell phone, they could pinpoint the exact location within seconds.

With the gun emboldening her, Anita quietly ascended the long stairway to the second floor. She held the gun out front, leaving little room for debate as to her intentions. She felt violated. Someone had dared to breach the security of her private residence, and they would have to pay for it.

Once she reached the landing on the second floor, she could hear the steady rise and fall of her own breathing. She could see the shadow more clearly from here. It was moving back and forth within hers and Milton's bedroom. Obviously searching for my jewelry or other valuables, thought Anita, her fury mounting. Of all the jewelry she had squeezed out of Milton, there was one garnet ring buried amongst it that was absolutely irreplaceable. It was a ring that had belonged to her birth mother, and it was all she had left of her.

She couldn't wait for the police any longer. The prowler might have already found the garnet and stuffed it into his trouser pockets. She crossed the hallway and pushed the door open, keeping the gun extended in front of her.

"Don't move or I'll pull the trigger!" she shouted.

The intruder froze by the dresser, his back toward her. He began to turn slowly.

Anita continued, "If you make any funny moves, I'll—"

Anita heard a loud snap from behind her in the hallway. A sharp pain registered between her shoulder blades as she began to lose muscular control. Her arm grew heavy, the gun sagging at her side. As her knees grew wobbly and her legs grew weak, she realized the intruder was Milton. He was observing her casually as she dropped to the carpet.

The investigating police officer was a short, round man named Taggert. He looked tired with dark bags folded into crescent moons under his eyes. He was substantially overweight, and his dark pants and yellowish dress shirt strained at various seams. His partner, an angular woman named Rogers, took notes with definitive strokes, her bony fingers holding a Bic ballpoint tightly in her grip. The ambulance had just left, taking Anita's body away. Others circulated through the house, doing their jobs as unobtrusively as possible.

"Terrible tragedy, Mr. Stempel, just terrible. I'm sorry to ask, but the facts always tend to be more accurate if we gather them as quickly as possible after—well, you know. We responded to Mrs. Stempel's 911 call. She obviously wasn't expecting you to be here. If you would be so kind, start at the beginning and tell me what you know," said Taggert, his voice gently coaxing.

Milton cleared his throat and dabbed at his eyes. His voice quavered with despair. "I was supposed to be at a science convention in New York for the next few days.

Although the subject matter was intriguing, I am deathly afraid of flying. I've done it before, but I think I hate it worse with each trip. I simply couldn't make myself get on the plane."

"Didn't your wife normally accompany you to these events?" asked Taggert.

"No," he said quietly. "She didn't care for conventions. She said it was just a bunch of boring old scientists going on and on about things in which she had no interest."

"So, you came home?"

"Yes, eventually," said Milton. "I have to admit, I was embarrassed by my own cowardice. I knew Anita would be disappointed in me, so I went to my laboratory downtown for a while."

"I've confirmed that with the folks down at the lab," interjected Rogers.

"When did you arrive at home?" asked Taggert.

"I'd say it was close to ten-thirty. To tell you the truth, I wasn't paying much attention to the time. Anita's car was gone, so I figured she had gone out to see friends. I carried my suitcase up to our room and started putting my things away. It was while I was doing this that Anita came in, her gun drawn. She must have thought I was a burglar," said Milton, his voice breaking on the last word.

"How do you figure into this, Miss—Norris, is it?" asked Taggert, consulting notes he had made earlier. He turned to face the woman seated in a rocking chair, her knees pulled up to her chin, her eyes red and swollen.

Janet was barely intelligible, her words coming out in fragments punctuated by gut-wrenching sobs. Taggert conferred with one of the other men in the room, a kindly-faced doctor who administered a sedative to the woman. After several moments, her hysterics had subsided enough that she was able to respond.

"I'm the maid, but I was off-duty today," Janet said. "I came back because I had left my book bag. I attend the university part-time. I have a composition due in English tomorrow morning, and I left my things here."

"Okay, Miss Norris," said Taggert. "What happened when you arrived?"

"It was unusually quiet in the house. Usually, Mrs. Stempel would have the television on or maybe the stereo, but it was completely quiet. It was unsettling. After a moment, I saw a shadow on the wall at the head of the stairs. I couldn't tell who it was, but I could see the outline of the gun she was holding very clearly. I thought someone had broken in to kill Mrs. Stempel."

"How did you happen to have your own gun?" asked Taggert.

"I have a permit," said Janet. "My father made me start carrying one when I moved out on my own. We're from the country, out where you can leave your doors unlocked and not worry about a thing. He's convinced the city is filled with stalkers and rapists, even a small town like this. Oh, I wish I'd never listened to him!" Her tears overcame the sedative for a moment before she regained control.

"So, you shot her?" asked Taggert gently. "Why didn't you ask her to stop where she was, identify herself?"

"I didn't think there was time. Her gun was drawn, and I could see Mr. Stempel over her shoulder, directly in her line of fire. I was afraid if I hesitated, she would have shot Mr. Stempel. It wasn't until after she fell that I realized it was Mrs. Stempel holding the gun. Oh, how can I live with this? I've killed another human being!" The sedative was useless by this point, and Janet returned to the quivering mass of jelly she had been when Taggert had begun questioning her.

Taggert mumbled something to Rogers and sent her on her way. He asked Milton to accompany him out into the hall.

"If we need any more information, Mr. Stempel, we'll call, but I think we're about done here. I'm going to have Dr. Adams take a look at Miss Norris, maybe leave her with something to settle her down."

"She won't be arrested, will she?" asked Milton. "She's such a frail girl. She's so upset about what has already happened. I think being arrested might seriously push her over the edge."

"Oh, no, I doubt if the prosecutor will want to press charges. It's pretty obvious that this was a tragic accident. I'm very sorry for your loss, Mr. Stempel," said Taggert, offering his hand. Milton shook it absently before wandering back into the bedroom. Poor man, thought Taggert. Completely devastated.

Dr. Adams wrote a prescription for Janet to help her get some rest, leaving a sample behind until the prescription could be filled. Everyone else eventually returned to the places from where they had come. Milton had offered one of the guest rooms to Janet, as the medication would make driving an automobile an unwise choice. She had retired while Taggert had collected his men.

Now that the big house was empty, Milton kicked his shoes off and wandered down to the study. He glanced at the desktop and placed his hand on the cool metal frame of the computer terminal.

"Coast's clear!" he shouted.

Janet bounded down the stairs and threw herself into Milton's arms. "I can't believe it actually worked!" she cried.

"She would have never given me a divorce, you know," said Milton.

"I know. She would never have given up the money," said Janet.

"And how do I know that you're not after my money?" asked Milton playfully.

Janet sighed and pulled him closer. "Because you just do. Besides, the money we're going to make from our own talents will make your family fortune look like chump change." Milton had suggested that he and Janet collaborate on a book of revolutionary scientific theorems, with Milton supplying the technical expertise and Janet supplying the turn of phrase. She worked magic with the written word, capable of taking a list of ingredients found on the back of toilet bowl cleaner and making it read like poetry. The combination of their talents would be powerful, indeed.

"Oh, darling," said Milton. "I never knew how love felt until you started working here. I can't believe I ever mistook what I had with Anita for love."

"That's all part of the past. We'll have to wait a respectable amount of time before we can start seeing each other socially, but in the meanwhile, I'll be here like normal to do the housework and keep you company. It won't seem inappropriate at all," said Janet.

"And we can retire BIRDMAN?" said Milton.

"We can retire BIRDMAN," confirmed Janet. "I think he did his job quite well, considering that he was both you and I."

The poison had been clear because it had been tap water. Milton had played on Anita's insecurities to make her fear him and start carrying the gun. Even if she hadn't pulled it out, Janet would have shot her anyway, and together they would have placed the gun in Anita's cold dead hand. The rest of the story would have played out the same. There were a few elements which could have muddied up the works, such as if Anita had actually spoken to Bob Dransdale the afternoon she had gone out to the country club, but Milton had determined it was an acceptable risk. Anita had commented on various occasions that the women at the country club were gossip mongers, and it was doubtful that she would have blatantly exposed her intent to Bob Dransdale while she was on their turf. That was part of the reason Milton had selected Bob in the first place— that and his brooding good looks. Overall, Anita had taken her cues well, and there was no sense in worrying what might have gone wrong now. Milton and Janet would be happy together for the rest of their lives.

Their love was a terminal case.

A 70s CHRISTMAS STORY

The box appeared beside Dad's chair mid-November, plain brown and inconspicuous, secured by plastic ties like the ones used to bundle the newspapers I delivered daily. I was only ten—well almost, and my curiosity was—I want to say voracious, but it's probably more apt to say out-of-control. I found new and inventive ways to quiz Mom about what might be in the box, and her always-ready and all-too-clever responses only served to confirm what I already suspected.

The box was for me!

This was a big year. On December 17th, I would be hitting the double digits—ten, to be precise—and this was also the year I had discovered music. Not just the old fuddy-duddy stuff Mom and Dad played on the car radio or our ancient General Electric "portable" record player with the glowing tubes, but music I, along with my older sister, Gina, had discovered on our local rock and roll station. The gift I wanted most was my very own portable music system, known at the time as a boombox. Kids today would laugh—those things were freaking heavy and had a battery life of about thirty-five minutes, requiring eight "D" batteries, which weren't exactly cheap. It was also something that would fit very nicely into that nondescript box.

My family always went to the grocery on Friday nights. It was the last Friday before Christmas, and I was desperate to know what was inside that container. My mind went into overdrive trying to devise a feasible plan, when a circumstance was handed to me, almost as if by God Himself. You see, this was also the year *Wonder Woman*, starring Lynda Carter, premiered on ABC. I was completely smitten after the pilot, but during its first season, the show never aired at a regular time. It was used to fill in gaps in the programming schedule and always performed well. Whether this was due to the support of ladies who appreciated a strong female role model or because of a bunch of eager young fellas like myself—well, and their fathers—is a topic for another time. The point is, I never missed an episode, and one was scheduled for that Friday night. DVRs and VCRs weren't an option in 1977, so it had to be viewed live or risk missing it altogether. I begged the parents to let me stay home while they went out to dinner and to the grocery with my brother and sister. I promised to stay inside, and answer neither the telephone nor any knocks at the locked front door.

I was already spying that box out of the corner of my eye when they agreed.

Once they had gone, I gave them all of ten minutes—to make sure Mom hadn't forgotten her list or Dad his wallet. I was too smart to get caught like that. I knew from my paper route that the ends of the plastic bands securing the box were glued together, and once that glue was breached, there would be no reattaching them. I took great care to ease both bands centimeter by centimeter until they were no longer holding the box shut. I had a moment of panic when it occurred to me that if the box itself were sealed with tape, my investigation was over—I would have had no way to hide where I had cut my way in. But Mom had already investigated the contents, and the only things keeping the box together were those plastic bands, and now they were on the floor, the box flaps beginning to open on their own! I pried them open carefully, noting the exact positioning of all the packing material as I removed it, piece by piece.

And there it was!

My beloved boombox! The brand was Yorx, and it was even better than I'd ever imagined! Not only did it have an AM/FM radio, but also an eight-track player and a cassette player! Joy of joys! But that wasn't all—it wasn't the usual one-speaker jobbie most of my friends had. It was actual true-blue stereo!

I knew this was my mother's doing...she always went that extra mile.

I rounded up a couple of those old fuddy-duddy eight tracks and cassette tapes, carefully got the player out of its box and spent the next twenty minutes or so in a state of bliss I'll never know again.

But it was getting late, and it was time to carefully repack everything before Dad's car pulled back into the drive. I took great care to ensure that everything that came out of that box went back in, and in the reverse order from which it had come out. Everything was going according to plan. I eased the first plastic band back over one end of the box and got it into place. I almost had the second one in place when the unthinkable happened.

The glue on the band broke.

It sprung away from the box like a live wire.

Cheezits! I was busted!

Panic seized my throat as I considered my options. I tried pulling the strap's loose ends underneath the box and attempted to secure them with Scotch tape, but it wouldn't hold, and Mom would have noticed the bulky tape. Scratch that. I tried again, using only the weight of the box to keep the ends tucked beneath the box. Eyeballing it from across the room, I thought it might just pass muster. When Mom eventually moved the box, she might just believe the glue had only just then come undone...

I was awakened that night with Mom standing over me, furious. She hadn't noticed the box until shortly after she sent us to bed, but once she did, the jig was up. She told me this was the last straw. I was a notorious Christmas snooper, but I'd gone too far this time. First thing in the morning, she was shipping the stereo back to Spiegel, where she had ordered it from their catalog. I was devastated. I cried, begged, and made promises I could never keep, but that box disappeared from beside Dad's chair first thing in the morning, just as Mom had guaranteed.

On Christmas morning, I dreaded seeing the inevitable hole under the tree where my present should be while my brother and sister delighted in whatever spoils they discovered. As I followed them into the room, I was stunned to see my beloved Yorx stereo sitting amongst a handful of Blondie, ABBA, and Olivia Newton-John eight-tracks and cassettes.

Mom took me aside, kneeling to my height as tears of wonder and joy ran down my face. She put a finger under my chin and forced me to look directly into her eyes. "Do you know why your Christmas snooping makes me so angry?" she asked.

I shook my head, snuffling and wiping my eyes. I honestly didn't understand.

"Because for us," she indicated to herself and my father. "The joy of Christmas is seeing the reaction in each of your faces as you discover your gifts. When you snoop, you're taking our Christmas away from us. It isn't really fair." She stood and smiled, patting my face before sending me over to the Christmas tree.

A light bulb flared brightly in my head. I hadn't even considered her perspective. I felt so incredibly stupid and inconsiderate. I was utterly ashamed of myself. I made a promise then and there that I most definitely could keep.

And I never snooped again.

NOT EVEN FOR A MILLION DOLLARS

Donald sat on the park bench alone, listlessly scattering breadcrumbs to the pigeons gathering at his feet in anticipation. Was it Monday? Wednesday? Friday? All the days ran together after retirement. If he had known how utterly boring his life would become, he would have probably stayed longer, maybe even forever—or at least until they forced him out. He had a sense of purpose back then, a reason to get out of bed in the morning.

Now, he had nothing.

Who could have predicted Nancy's fatal aneurysm not even three weeks after they had celebrated together at his retirement party? They had been married for forty-one years, and he couldn't even remember a time before she was in his life. Every day since had been unbearably long.

They were both only children and had no children of their own, save for a procession of four-legged canines and felines who had provided companionship throughout the years. The last, a chihuahua called Bobbie, had passed away peacefully one night shortly after Nancy was gone, and Donald believed with every fiber of his being that the dog had died of a broken heart. That stupid little yapping dog adored Nancy but only tolerated him. Death had been preferable to spending one more day without her.

That was five years ago. Eighteen hundred and twenty-five lo-o-ng days.

They had met in a bowling alley in 1953. Donald had just returned from serving in Korea, and Nancy worked for the local newspaper. He was taken with her bright-eyed intelligence, and she thought he was impossibly good-looking. She began showing up conveniently on Tuesdays and Thursdays, Donald's regular league nights. She was ten years his junior, but only their families seemed concerned by that. They bypassed all the wagging tongues by eloping on a warm summer evening, the beginning of a union marked by highs, lows and everything in between.

Bowling remained a staple throughout their marriage. Their social set was comprised of the members of the mixed leagues in which they participated. Their own team was an evolving roster of co-workers from the paper where Nancy was employed and the bottling plant where Donald spent his days, but they were always constant members. After Nancy died, his teammates had encouraged him to continue with his leagues, insisting it was good for him to get out of the apartment. It had only served to remind him of the tremendous void in his life, and he began to grow resentful of anyone else who filled her empty spot on the team.

And then Roy had his stroke, and Geraldine had a massive coronary within months of each other.

It seemed that Donald's teammates were dropping like flies. Roy wasn't a real surprise; he was overweight and smoked like a freight train, but Geraldine was only forty-seven. She was a single mother of four and had just welcomed her first granddaughter into the world. Why had God taken someone with so much life ahead and left Donald behind with nothing and no one? It had shaken him to his very core, and he had quit what little of the team remained. He couldn't risk friends any longer; the price was simply too high.

He stared at the pigeons as they waited impatiently for more breadcrumbs. Did they even recognize him? Or was he just one of a countless number of strangers who performed this daily ritual? The weight of his own insignificance brought tears unbidden to his eyes, clouding his vision. He was startled when the pigeons abruptly took flight, disrupted by a young boy with strawberry blonde spiky hair and freckled cheeks who climbed right up onto the park bench beside him. He couldn't have been more than four or five, and his eyes twinkled brightly.

"Can I feed them, Grampa?" he asked eagerly.

Donald struggled for a response, stammering as a young woman came running up the path, completely winded.

"Max!" she gasped. "I've told you not to run ahead like that!"

She turned toward Donald and smiled apologetically. "I'm so sorry. He calls all old—older men Grampa." Her cheeks were bright with embarrassment. She reached for her son, but he pulled away, still intently focused on Donald. The pigeons had slowly begun to regroup at their feet.

He waved her concerns away. "It's all right, Miss—"

"Abbie," she said, extending a hand, and he shook it gently.

"Donald," he said, indicating himself. "I don't believe I've seen you and your son in the park before."

She shook her head. "We're new to the neighborhood. Just moved into that big old brownstone on the corner." She pointed to the very building where Donald and Nancy had spent most of their years together.

He smiled. "Well, welcome, neighbor. I'm on the 3rd floor." He handed Max the container of breadcrumbs and encouraged him to toss a few to the gathering flock. "Just a little at a time. There, just like that."

The little boy's face shone brightly as the birds ventured closer, taking his offerings. He giggled. "They're very hungry, Grampa."

Abbie buried her face in her hands. "I'm so sorry," she said again. "His best friend at preschool lives with his grandparents, and I can't seem to break Max of the habit. He doesn't have any grandparents of his own. It's always been just me and Max."

Donald smiled up at her. "It's okay. I've been called worse."

"Come on, Max," said Abbie, successfully snagging her son's hand this time. "We've taken up enough of this nice gentleman's time."

Max pulled away once more and leaned over to hug Donald. "Thank you, Grampa." Then he jumped down from the bench and took his mother's hand. Abbie smiled and waved, before guiding Max in the direction from which they'd come.

After a few steps, she paused, turning back. "Would you like to have lunch with us, Donald? Nothing fancy, just tomato soup, but I do make a mean grilled cheese."

Donald was touched by her kindness and was surprised to hear himself readily agree. He gathered his things and returned to the brownstone with his new friends.

Donald could never have foreseen what was yet to come.

He would teach this boy how to drive a standard transmission. He would be in the front row when Max graduated as valedictorian of his high school senior class. He would pretend he had something in his eye as he helped Max move into his freshman dorm. He would walk this young woman down the aisle and give her away to a ridiculously funny man named Wally who she would soon meet in a bowling alley, of all places. He would become both a father figure and a grandfather to a family into which he had been invited, and these would be the faces that saw him through his final days before he was finally reunited with his dear wife, Nancy. It was an eleventh-hour miracle that began with a simple act of kindness, something he would have never believed possible as he struggled to make himself get out of bed that morning.

And it was a mean grilled cheese. He wouldn't have traded it for anything, not even for a million dollars.

BEST LAID PLANS

"I don't think I can fit one more thing in the car, but I swear we're forgetting something," Traci said, wiping sweat from her forehead before pressing the button to close the hatchback of our Hyundai Santa Fe. Her face was deeply flushed, and it was only 7:00AM. She had pulled her thick, chestnut hair into a knot on top of her head to allow whatever faint breeze might pass access to the back of her neck. A heat wave had rolled across the Ohio Valley pushing temperatures into the mid-90s with smothering humidity and little-to-no air circulation whatsoever.

"You say that every time," I said, double-checking my own personal belongings as I locked the front door of our house. Keys? Wallet? Glasses? Prescription caddy? *Check!*

"And I'm always right," said Traci.

And she almost always was. A big fan of checklists, Traci had started the one for this trip months ago and had exhaustively pored over it with increasing frequency as the date of departure approached. No item remained unchecked, but nothing ever displaced the nagging feeling of forgetting something vitally important.

"Start the car!" Nicki bellowed from the back seat. "I'm dying back here!" She had already filled the other seat with necessities for the long trip ahead: laptop bag, iPhone and charging cable, assorted snacks, a small cooler loaded with soda and water, and a collection of dolls whose various hairstyle and fashion choices would be updated throughout the entirety of the trip and fully documented in vivid photographs taken on her iPhone at countless rest stops and other locations along the way. At 18, Nicki no longer played with dolls but aspired to become a doll designer.

"All right, all right!" I said, wincing as the bare skin on the back of my legs made contact with the hot leather seat. It was a momentary discomfort I could deal with—long pants were completely out of the question. I pushed the button to start the ignition and was greeted with a blast of hellfire straight to the face. I turned to Traci as she pulled the passenger door closed behind her and added, "We can buy anything we've forgotten. There are Walmarts everywhere."

311

"Yeah, yeah," she said, doing a quick inventory of her own personal belongings before we headed out. Glasses? iPad? Diet Pepsi? *Check!* "Okay, let's do this thing."

I backed out of the drive, slipped the car into "Drive" and eased out of the neighborhood.

The trip was already all wrong, but we were determined to make a go of it, no matter what.

❦

Traci and I had been in the same class in our small school system from first grade forward. I still have the awkward group portrait of the class with us standing uncomfortably side by side on the top row of bleacher seats. Our classmates were festively adorned in the latest Brady Bunch fashion, stripes and plaids as far as the eye could see. The teacher, Mrs. Piatt, stood stern guard over her charges under a headful of tightly wound grey curls. She was either unwilling or unable to smile. Most of the children looked distracted or frightened. We just looked annoyed at being positioned within cootie range of one another.

Garry had moved into our school system in the seventh grade, and after a bumpy start—few new kids have it easy changing schools and being forced to make new friends— he integrated into our circle for the duration. After graduation, we continued to hang out throughout the summer and into the fall. We felt more like family than friends. We rarely disagreed, always laughed at the same stupid shit, and genuinely enjoyed each other's company. Garry's girlfriends (and the occasional wife) might come and go, but we were constant.

Lack of decent employment opportunities led me and Traci north to Columbus, while Garry stayed and started a family, eventually having two daughters and a son. Having decided that children just weren't our thing, we were the best aunt and uncle to Garry's children we could possibly be. We always spent birthdays and holidays together, as well as the occasional vacation. We loved those little boogers like they were our own.

As the years went by, we came to realize the only thing we truly regretted was that we hadn't had a child of our own. The proverbial biological clock was persistent in both our cars, and as Garry's kids reached their teens, our daughter, Nicole, was born.

A warm Saturday evening the previous October found Garry, Traci and I sitting in three of four chairs arranged in a semi-circle around a small, circular table on the wood-planked porch that ran the width of Garry's two-story country house in Minford. Indian summer had pushed temperatures back up into the high 70s after a chilly start to the month. As we did every four to six weeks, we were sharing a relaxing weekend, laughing and trading stories, our cheeks a bit flushed from beer and whiskey. Nicki was inside with Garry's stepdaughter, Regan, huddled around their phones and laughing raucously over who-knows-what. They had been thick as thieves since Garry first introduced us to Regan's mother, Susan, and her kids, several years ago. His stepson, Alex, was upstairs engaged in mortal combat against various internet nemeses.

Garry's house sat on several acres of property with neighbors only barely visible in the periphery. In front of the house, a burbling creek wound parallel to the narrow asphalt ribbon that claimed to be a road. Thick woods bordered the property at the rear and across the street in front. Traffic noise was non-existent, with only the gentle susurration of night insects doing their thing and our own frequent outbursts of laughter to disrupt the tranquility. We sat in the soft glow of light cast through the living room window, the porch light purposely left off to help keep said insects at bay.

Susan stepped out onto the porch, her arms laden with fresh beers and a can of Mountain Dew for me as a chaser for my whiskey. "Give me a hand, here, babe," she said to Garry as she struggled to close the front door. "I'm about to drop everything."

Garry relieved her of half her load and snuck in for a quick kiss. "Have you ever seen anyone more beautiful?" he said to us with a grin and a wink as he sat back down.

Although they had been married for nearly five years, their relationship was still in the honeymoon stage. Frequent compliments, cutesy nicknames and loads of kissy-face were always on full display. Traci and I, who had known each other since the age of 6, were a bit more subdued.

Susan settled into the empty chair. "So, what did I miss?" she asked, her eyes bright under dark bangs. Susan was a real find. She accepted us as family, no questions asked. She tolerated our frequent one-sided trips down memory lane as opposed to resenting our past history with her new husband. This hadn't always been the case. Some of Garry's past loves had been downright hostile toward us, their displeasure at our intrusion apparent despite Garry's assurances to the contrary.

"We were just talking about our trip to Gatlinburg," said Garry. "What was that—like ten years ago?"

"Fifteen," said Traci. "Longest car ride with a toddler I ever care to endure." She rolled her eyes at the memory.

"It would have been a whole lot shorter if your husband would have let me take the lead. How far past that missed turn did we go before we realized we were lost?" Garry scowled at me.

"Not my fault," I protested and pointed at Traci. "She had the Triptik."

"Don't throw *me* under the bus," said Traci. "It was *your* interpretation of the map—"

"—that you were holding *sideways*," I interjected.

Garry turned to Susan. "At least two hours."

"No way. One at the *most*," I said.

"*Regardless.* You never listen to me," said Garry.

"You rarely know what you're talking about," I laughed.

"You should *always* listen to me." Garry crossed his arms over his chest and sat back in his chair.

"Hooray for GPS!" Traci interjected, and we all laughed.

"Best vacation ever, though," I said.

"Oh, yeah." Traci smiled.

"It was the first and only time we managed to get all of the kids in one place for an extended period," Garry said.

"*Epic* vacation," I said.

"How old would your kids have been?" asked Traci. "Nicki was three. I do remember that."

Garry turned to his trusty mental calculator. "Andrea would have been nineteen which would make Chelsea fifteen and Will eleven."

"Seems like a lifetime ago," said Traci, tossing back a shot of Jameson.

"The girls thought you were the coolest dad ever," I said. "You let them bring their boyfriends along."

"Better to have them where I could keep an eye on them," he laughed. "We were all that age once. They weren't doing anything we hadn't done ourselves."

"Some things worked out. Chelsea ended up marrying Stephen," I said. "Andrea's boyfriend was fun, even if it didn't last much longer."

"I keep picturing that bright orange leash you kept Nicki on the whole damn time," laughed Garry.

"Hey, it was a *safety harness*, and I don't regret that one bit," said Traci defensively. "Gatlinburg was *loaded* with tourists and that child knew only one speed: Go."

"My Lord, the looks you got," said Garry, covering his face. "People thought you were crazy."

"Like we gave two shits about *that*," I said, laughing. "How about Will and the General Lee? I'd never seen that kid so excited." I referred to a pit stop we had made at

317

Cooter's Museum, a place honoring all things *Dukes of Hazzard*, to grab pics of Will and Garry alongside the car made famous by the popular TV show.

"Sounds like you all had a blast," said Susan.

"We did," said Garry. "A full ten days. We rented a chalet in the mountains big enough for all of us. Game room in the basement. Hot tub out back. Wrap around porch with the best damn views. We spent our days at the attractions in Gatlinburg and Pigeon Forge and met back at the chalet for dinner every night."

"I never drank so much in my life," I groaned.

Garry laughed. "Tell me it wasn't amazing."

"No, no—it was amazing. What we're doing right now always takes me there just a little bit," I said. "You always tell the best stories when you've had a few."

Traci groaned. "Yeah, all except for that last night, you asshole!" She smacked Garry in the arm.

"It wasn't my fault!" he protested. "I could have sworn I heard a bear!"

"A bear?" Susan sat forward in her chair.

"The Smoky Mountains are full of them," I said, tossing back another shot of my own. "The first morning we were there, one was eating the cover off of the hot tub."

Traci laughed, "You were *so* scared we were going to have to pay for that cover. You filmed the whole thing."

318

"Money was tight," I reminded, "We got some exciting home video footage to share, *and* we didn't have to pay for the damned thing after all, now did we?"

Traci rolled her eyes. *"Anyway,"* she said, turning her attention to Susan, "Because of that little episode, we were all a little—let's just say *alert* to the possibility of bears invading our space while we were out on that porch in the evening. The last night we were there, your husband decided it would be funny to mess with us. First, he insisted that he heard something. Then, he insisted he *saw* something moving at the far end of the porch, over by the stairs that went down to the hot tub."

"Chelsea and Stephen were inside sitting with Nicki," I added.

"Nicki was asleep," interjected Garry. "I don't want to guess what Chelsea and Stephen were probably doing."

"Andrea was hysterical," I continued. "Her boyfriend—was it Kevin?"

"Kenny," corrected Garry.

"Who's telling this story?" asked Traci, effectively scolding us into silence. *"Kenny* was trying to calm her down, but he looked like he was about ready to bolt, himself. Your *husband,* however—always the big man, told us to hang tight, he would check it out."

Garry laughed. "I didn't see any of *you* volunteering."

"No, we were sane," I said. "You drank so much you could barely stand!"

"We *all* drank plenty that night," said Garry, shrugging as he took another pull from his beer.

"*Anyway*—" Traci shot us another glare as Garry pressed his lips together before tagging me on the arm. "Big shot over there goes creeping across the porch while we all held our breaths. He got to the very top of the stairs and cried out before disappearing around the corner."

"Oh, shit!" exclaimed Susan, her eyes wide. "What *happened?*"

"Andrea was sure he was bear chow," I said. "She was hysterical."

"We all grabbed something from the porch—a chair, a broom, whatever we could find—and moved like a team to the end of the porch. Just as we got within inches of the corner, Garry jumped up from the stairwell, laughing his ass off at all of us."

"It *was* rather comical," said Garry, leaning over and resting his head on Susan's shoulder while batting his eyes winningly.

"Was it *really?*" said Traci, smiling. "He was so pleased with himself that he started doing some goofy-ass victory dance at the top of the stairs. Next thing we knew, he lost his balance and went ass over teakettle to the landing

320

midway down the flight, scaring the shit out of all of us *again!*"

"It was a loose board at the top of the stairs," Garry assured Susan, a determinedly serious look on his face. "I swear it." He went in for another quick kiss while she giggled.

"Yeah, *whatever*," said Traci. "It's a wonder you didn't break your damn neck! As it was, you broke your arm, and we all spent hours in the ER waiting for you to get patched up. We were late checking out of the chalet and that *did* cost us extra money. And poor Andrea had to do the rest of the driving for you, too."

"I'd do it again in a minute," laughed Garry, and we all broke into laughter as the memories took hold—Susan's noticeably more polite and reserved because yet again, this were *our* memories, not mutually shared experiences.

"What's the matter, babe?" Garry asked, pulling Susan close to him.

"It's nothing, really," she said. "I love when you guys share your stories. I really do. My family wasn't big on vacations, so I really don't have much to tell. But it's fine. I just can't wait until we have stories that we are *all* part of." She smiled sheepishly.

"I say we make a resolution here and now," I declared. "We need to have a fifteenth anniversary recreation of the greatest vacation ever."

"A little late for that," interrupted Traci. "Unless you think time travel is a viable option. It was fifteen years ago last July."

I waved her objection away. "Fifteenth...ish. It's still in the spirit of things. We need to get all the kids on board—"

Traci raised an eyebrow. "You expect Andrea and Keith to drop everything and fly up from Florida?" Andrea had lived in the Jacksonville area for the better part of ten years. It was where she had met and married her husband, Keith.

"I'm sure they would *want* to do it!" I continued, my enthusiasm growing as my imagination kicked in. "We are, after all, the very best people to hang out with. I'm sure everyone else will want to do it, too! *C'mon!* We can't just wait for these memories to happen; we have to *make* them."

"We might have to talk Alex into it," said Susan, but her smile indicated her interest. "He gets a little anxious traveling."

"Oh, he'll be fine," I assured. "And I guarantee he'll have fun."

"All right!" said Garry, throwing his hands in the air in mock surrender. "We'll figure it out. But not tonight. It's super late."

"But soon," I persisted, as we all began collecting our various items from the small table on the porch and headed toward the front door.

"Yes, soon," agreed Garry. "Andrea and Keith will be in for the holidays. We'll get it all figured out then."

But we never got the chance.

Garry died unexpectedly on Christmas Eve that year.

As usual, Traci, Nicki and I were spending the holidays at our own home in Grove City. My brother and cousin were due in for Christmas dinner, as were our niece, nephew and their daughter from Traci's side of the family. I was returning from a last-minute run to Kroger for some forgotten grocery items when I got a call from Garry's stepmother. I thought she was laughing hysterically—I had never heard her sound that way. For what seemed like an eternity, I couldn't follow what she was saying over the Bluetooth connection in my car, but when I could, I had a nearly uncontrollable urge to immediately disconnect the call, as if that might somehow make what she was telling me—struggling through great, wrenching sobs—untrue.

She and Garry's father were following the ambulance in their own car. The lights were flashing and rotating, but there was no sound from the siren.

We all knew what that meant.

It had been a cardiac event. No forewarning, just game over.

The service was beautiful and horrible, with all of us laughing and crying in nearly equal measure. There was quite a large turnout; Garry was an immensely popular guy. As the day wore on, faces of family and friends began to blur into one another, and exhaustion wore on all of us.

"Uncle Darin."

I felt a tap on my shoulder and turned toward Andrea, who hugged me fiercely.

"How are you holding up, kiddo?" I asked, returning the hug.

She shrugged and attempted a smile. "You know...just trying to get through it."

"I keep having these vivid dreams," I said. "I can hear his voice like he's *right there*."

"I'm jealous," she said. "I keep looking for some sort of sign—*any* sign, but I'm getting nothing. I just feel so empty."

I nodded, and we stood for a moment in silence. "I know this is super cliché, but if there's anything at all any of you need from us—"

She put a finger on my lips to stop me. "One thing."

"Anything."

"The vacation. We *have* to do the vacation. Dad told me all about it when I was talking to him about our holiday travel plans. He was so excited. I was, too! I had so much fun! I feel like he would want us to, you know—"

"Carry on?"

"Exactly. I've already spoken to Chelsea and Will, and they're on board. It might take a little coaxing, but I think we can get Susan and her kids on board, too. I don't know. It just seems..." she trailed off, unable to find the word.

"Important?" I offered, and she smiled.

"Exactly."

I nodded. It felt like the right thing to do.

Over the next few weeks, we did some painstaking research based on saved photographs from our vacation all of those years ago to track down the actual chalet where we had stayed. Once identified, we were a little dismayed to see that it was completely booked well into the summer. The earliest we could get a 10-day reservation was from late July into early August. The timing was actually fairly similar to our original vacation once I thought about it. I completed the booking with my credit card immediately so we wouldn't lose the opportunity. I knew we could all square up later.

Chelsea, Stephen and their three girls would drive from Portsmouth in their minivan, as would Will, Destiny and their two girls in their SUV. Andrea and Keith would fly into McGhee Tyson in Knoxville and rent a car to drive the remaining 40 or so miles into Pigeon Forge.

The only real persuading we had to do with Susan was related to transportation. She feared her well-worn Honda van wouldn't be up to the challenge of a round-trip drive through the mountains. My Hyundai Santa Fe had third row seating, so we struck a deal. Susan bought a cargo storage unit to attach to the top of my car, allowing us to move all of the luggage up top once we drove south and collected them. She also insisted on paying for half of the gas and wouldn't take 'no' for an answer. To be honest, we would have paid for it all. This vacation had always been meant for all of us, and it wouldn't have seemed right any other way.

Of course, it couldn't possibly feel *completely* right. Garry was gone, and there wasn't a damn thing any of us could do about that.

The first hiccup occurred before we even began. We had driven two hours south to retrieve Susan and her kids and were in the process of transferring luggage from the back of the car to the cargo storage, getting it into position on top of my car when Susan's cell phone rang. It was Will, and she put the call on speakerphone.

"We've got a problem," he said.

"What's the matter, Bub?" asked Susan, wiping sweat from her brow. The heat and humidity had already grown noticeably since we had departed Grove City.

"Destiny's been called in to work. Her store manager was in a car wreck last night and is in critical condition. They need her to run the place until they can pull some managers in from other areas." Destiny worked as an assistant manager at a beauty supply chain in Ashland, KY. She had been there for a little over a year, hired in as a salesclerk before rapidly ascending into management.

"No!" I protested. "They can't *do* this to you guys! We've had this planned for months!"

"I know, Uncle Darin," said Will. "But they're in a real bind here. And they're trying hard to make it worth our while. They're reimbursing any costs we had already committed to for the trip, *and* they're giving Dez a pretty good raise. I don't see how we can say no."

I frowned as I processed what he was telling me. I didn't have to like it to understand where he was coming from. Destiny genuinely enjoyed her job, and opportunities were few and far between in the impoverished area, despite the somewhat gruesome circumstance. I wanted to say, *'But this is for your dad,'* but knew it would be below the belt. His dad would want him to make the hard but responsible choice, which is exactly what he was doing.

"You guys will barely even miss us," Will assured.

"You got that wrong," I said. "But I understand."

"Post lots of pictures on Facebook. We'll see you all when you get back."

"I *hate* this!" Susan's shoulders sagged. "Kiss my babies for me."

"I will, Mamaw," said Will. "Maybe we can do a Zoom call when you all get settled in, too."

"For sure," I said, and Susan disconnected the call. We all exchanged shared looks of disappointment before continuing to secure the cargo storage to the top of the SUV.

The first few hours passed uneventfully. The air conditioning kept the extreme heat and humidity at bay, and the sky was a brilliant, cloudless blue. We traveled west on KY-10, the Ohio River on our right and scenic woodlands gave way to Kentucky bluegrass on our left. I drove while Traci served as my co-pilot in the passenger seat, supplying snacks and drinks as needed. Alex sat behind me, attention firmly fixed on his Nintendo Switch. Susan sat beside him, reading the latest from her favorite mystery author. Regan and Nicki huddled in the third row, whispering and laughing over TikTok videos and other internet delights. We found a station we could all agree upon on satellite radio, and settled in for the long haul, someone occasionally chiming in when song lyrics were known.

Having skirted the edge of Lexington earlier, we were nearing Mt. Vernon when my cell phone chirped through the car speakers. I pressed the "Answer" button on my steering wheel and said, "Hello?"

"He-e-e-e-ey fam-uh-lee!!!!" Chelsea sang out. We could hear her three girls in the background, chattering amongst themselves.

"Hey, little girl," I said. "How's the trip so far?"

"We got a bit of a late start," said Chelsea in what was surely a given to all of us. Chelsea was never on time for anything. Take whatever time she was *supposed* to arrive and add 1-2 hours—you'd be in the ballpark. Of course, with an 11-year-old, a 9-year-old and a 2-year-old, even a simple trip across town was an enormous undertaking, much less a 10-day trip across several state lines. "Kam is teething."

"Awww, Mamaw's poor baby," Susan said from the back seat. "Get that little punkin a popsicle!"

"We've got some in the cooler, and I froze some waffles to bring along for her to gnaw on, too. She's doing okay."

"Where are you guys?" Traci asked.

"Maybe a half-hour outside of Lexington. We've had to make a few stops already, and I'm sure we'll have to make a few more."

Stephen called out from beside Chelsea, "Peanut bladder!"

"Hush!" said Chelsea, before adding sheepishly, "I really can't help it."

"It is what it is, girlie," said Traci, just as we heard a tremendous bang and Chelsea suddenly screamed.

Susan sat bolt upright and leaned forward between the driver and passenger seats. "Chelsea? *Chelsea!*"

I unconsciously slowed and drifted to the right, my heart skipping a beat in my chest. "Talk to us, Chels. What's going on?"

We could hear Stephen barking unintelligibly as Chelsea's scream turned into frantic words, equally unintelligible. Wails from her children in the background soon joined the chorus, followed by the sound of screeching tires crunching across gravel before the call abruptly disconnected.

"Oh, my Lord," Susan said, chanting those three words over and over as she collapsed back into her seat. She patted herself on the chest as if to slow the adrenaline coursing through her veins.

331

Nicki and Regan had fallen silent, their eyes wide as they looked toward us. Regan was close to tears. Alex still wore his earbuds and was oblivious that anything had happened. He continued to mash the buttons on his handheld gaming unit with fierce determination on his face. I pulled the car to the berm of the road, shifted into Park and swallowed hard, sitting up straight. "What the fuck was that?"

Traci shook her head and shrugged, her own eyes wide.

The phone rang again, and Chelsea's number appeared on the caller ID.

"Chelsea?" My voice was loud and high-pitched in my own ears, full of panic. *"Chelsea?"*

"We're all right," Chelsea said, her voice shaky. I could still hear the girls fussing in the background while Stephen worked to soothe them. Chelsea took a deep breath and let it out audibly. *"Woo!"* was followed by a short burst of hysterical laughter.

"What happened?" demanded Susan, leaning forward again.

"I don't know, exactly," said Chelsea, her voice beginning to normalize. "Something with the car. The steering wheel jerked out of my hand and there was this loud bang."

"We heard that," I said. "It sounded like a gunshot! Is it a flat?"

"Don't know yet," she said. "I had to wrestle the wheel to get us off the road. Stephen's trying to get the girls settled and then he'll check. *Woo!*" She laughed nervously again.

"Do you guys need help?" I asked.

"No, we'll be fine. If it's a flat, we've got a spare. If it's anything else, we still have a manufacturer's warranty and roadside assistance. We'll be okay. Just later than our normal late," she laughed again, sounding almost like herself again.

I took a deep breath. Blood pounded at my temples, a full-blown headache threatening to erupt. I shifted the car back into gear and eased back out onto the highway. "Let us know just as soon as you find out what happened," I said.

"We will," she promised. "Love you guys!"

"We love you, too," I said, and we disconnected the call.

We were nearing the Tennessee border when we finally got an update. A tie rod on the front-end passenger side had broken, leaving one of the front tires listing drunkenly to the right and rendering the minivan inoperable. It was a miracle they hadn't wrecked while trying to maneuver out of traffic. The good news was their manufacturer's warranty would cover both the towing back to Lexington as well as the repair. The bad news was they would be delayed in joining us by at least a day, as the dealer didn't have all the necessary parts in stock. But the *best* news was everyone was safe and sound, albeit understandably annoyed at the latest wrinkle in our best laid plans.

"I swear, I'm beginning to think this trip is cursed," said Susan, her mood noticeably darkened by events with Will and Chelsea.

"Don't think that way. Just a couple of bumps in the road," I said, sending her a look of encouragement that I hoped looked authentic. Privately, I was beginning to share her doubts.

We decided to grab a late lunch at a Stuckey's near Knoxville. Part of me wanted to just go ahead and push through, the light at the end of the tunnel just nearly in sight. However, the kids were tired of being stuck in the car, Susan desperately wanted a cigarette, Traci needed to pee, and I, frankly, yearned for coffee. The constant sound of tires on asphalt was lulling me into a dangerous, road-weary trance. As a driver, I was a bit of a control freak—I was physically unable to rest in the passenger seat, instead working an imaginary brake pedal in the floorboard while making navigational suggestions a little too often for Traci's liking. A pit stop could satisfy everyone's needs while giving me an opportunity to refuel on caffeine for the remainder of the journey.

We had just finished trying a hapless waitress's patience while placing our brood's order when Susan's phone rang again. This time it was Andrea.

"Hey, Andi," said Susan. "Are you guys on the ground?"

Her face darkened while she listened for a moment. "You have *got* to be kidding me." Another pause while she listened. "But you guys are okay, right?" Now, we were all looking at each other quizzically. Susan listened for a bit longer, then said, "All right. You just keep me posted, okay? Have you spoken to your brother and sister?" Another pause. "Okay. Well, be careful, and hopefully we'll see you all tomorrow afternoon. I love you." She disconnected the call and looked at me in disbelief.

"What's going on?" I asked.

"About a half hour into their flight, their plane got turned around," said Susan. "A bird flew into the windshield and cracked it."

"*What?*" exclaimed Regan.

"And that's exactly why I hate to fly," interjected Nicki, nodding knowingly.

"I will never set foot on a plane," added Alex around a mouthful of French fries.

"I've never heard of such a thing," I said.

"Me, either, but apparently, that's what happened," said Susan. "There won't be another flight headed this way until morning, so they're stuck until then."

We ate for a little longer in silence before Susan excused herself and got up to go to the restroom. When I realized she had been gone more than a few minutes, I suggested to Traci that she check up on her.

Traci returned from the restroom a few minutes later and leaned in, speaking quietly, "She's a little upset, and she didn't want the kids to see it. Seems like everything about this trip has gone wrong so far."

"It *does* suck," I said, "But they're just delayed. They'll be here soon."

"Not Will and his family," Traci reminded.

I opened my mouth, but words failed me. Susan was right. The motivation for persisting with the vacation had

336

been pure, but the reality so far was entirely lacking. I cleared my throat, took a drink from my coffee cup, then blotted at the corners of my mouth with a napkin.

Susan returned from the restroom, her eyes slightly puffy and tinged red.

"Are you okay, Mom?" asked Alex.

She nodded and forced a smile. "I am," she said. "Are we just about finished here? I wanna get my ass settled down into that hot tub."

I looked at her with a raised eyebrow, my question unspoken.

"*Really*," she said. "I'm good. Just a couple of bumps in the road. No reason to let it spoil everything."

Emboldened by Susan's determination, I adjusted my own attitude. We were going to do everything in our power to have the best vacation possible. It wasn't too late to salvage things, even if some parties were unable to attend.

We paid our checks and loaded back into the SUV for the final leg of our journey.

We neared Pigeon Forge and despite our exhaustion, we decided to make another stop at a small IGA at the foot of the mountain incline that would lead us to our ultimate destination. The chalet had a full kitchen including pots, pans and dinnerware, but it was up to us to stock it with food.

"We're only getting what we need for a day or two," I reminded, as the gang got out of the vehicle, and headed for the store. "We can come back after we've had a chance to think about what we need and make a list. Don't get crazy with a lot of junk food."

"Everyone's going to be hungry before the night is over," said Traci, an audible series of cracks emanating from her spine as she stretched.

"How about spaghetti?" asked Susan. "That's pretty simple. I can cook. You've done all the driving."

"Sounds wonderful," I said, pulling a cart from the nested row just outside the store's entrance.

We split up and went after the various items we needed. More than once, I had to course-correct the teens as their penchant for snacks attempted to overtake the cart, but after about twenty minutes, we were loading our purchases into the area behind the third-row seating of my Hyundai.

"All right, guys," I said. "Final stretch."

338

We all piled back into the car and eased out of the parking lot.

We all piled back into the car and eased out of the parking lot.

The two-lane road that ascended the mountain was smooth but narrow, tree-lined on both sides by towering ancient yellow birch, oaks and pines. Occasionally, breathtaking views would erupt on the right as the dense foliage suddenly gave way to metal guardrails installed to prevent vehicles from plunging over an increasingly precipitous edge. We passed only a few other vehicles as we continued to ascend.

"Turn left in three-quarters of a mile," instructed the modulated female voice of GPS through the car audio.

"And here is the scene of the crime," said Traci, as I slowed the vehicle and turned the wheel counterclockwise. We bumped onto a narrow, pitted road that was partially obscured by tall grass on either side.

"Crime?" asked Susan absently.

"It's the turn I missed all those years ago," I said.

"It's no wonder," said Susan, squinting through her windows. "You can barely make it out. And Garry claimed *he* saw this?" She chuckled.

"I know, right?" I smiled. "But *no*—I never listen to him."

I would have given just about anything to hear his voice again.

*

After several miles of creeping and jostling along, the road suddenly widened onto a sloping, gravel expanse that skirted the rustic, two-story chalet, nestled into the wooded hillside. A wide, covered porch, supported from below by wooden posts of increasing height, ran the entire length of the house, ending where stairs led down to a landing before continuing on to the aforementioned hot tub. There would be ample room for all of our vehicles, but as we were the first to arrive, we pulled closest to the short stairway leading up to the porch and kitchen entrance. A clearing in the woods at the far end of the lot offered a breathtaking view down into the heart of Pigeon Forge, slightly obscured by dense clouds forming at our current elevation. It was largely as I remembered it, save for noticeably newer slats scattered throughout the construction of the deck rail.

Like a sad troop of zombies, we emerged from the car and began unloading the boot, starting with our haul from the IGA. Traci consulted her phone for the email with the access code to the lock box mounted to the wall underneath the porch light. Four sets of keys to the chalet doors should be waiting for us, and I held my breath, fully expecting their absence to be the next derailment of our plans. I could see she was thinking the same thing when she jangled a set victoriously with a smile before inserting one into the lock and opening the door.

It took three trips to get everything inside once we had pulled the luggage out of the cargo hold on top of the car. As wonderful as it felt to finally be at our destination, none of us had much energy left. We piled all of the luggage just inside the door, deciding it could find its way to the upstairs bedrooms after we had eaten dinner. Traci and I began unloading grocery bags into the pantry and refrigerator while Susan acclimated herself to what amenities could be found in the small kitchen. An island workspace with four bar stools separated the kitchen from the dining area. A large table capable of seating twelve ran parallel to glass sliding doors which opened out onto the deck. White slatted blinds had been pulled up to expose the magnificent view beyond. Adjacent to the dining area was a wood paneled great room with vaulted ceiling and a lazily rotating ceiling fan. Couches, loveseats and recliners, all in neutral tones, offered the ability to congregate both as a whole and in smaller groups with only a minimal amount of rearranging. Stairs at the far end led up to a walkway that bisected the house with a half-rail overlooking the rooms below. This provided access to four bedrooms, each capable of bunking four, and a community bathroom. At the foot of the stairs was a master with its own bath. If I remembered correctly, there was another half bath in the game room below. The kids sprawled out on deep brown leather sofas arranged in an "L" around a low, circular coffee table. Centered along the wall with the highest peak in the ceiling was an unlit stone fireplace crowned by a 65" Samsung LED. They didn't have the motivation to find the TV remote, much less explore its offerings.

Susan found a large skillet, placed it on the stovetop and turned the burner on before emptying a pack of ground beef into it. "I should have this all together in about forty-five minutes," she said. "Why don't you two relax?"

"Is there anything we can help with?" asked Traci, grabbing a beer from the fridge.

Susan shook her head and smiled. "Thanks, but I've got this." She glanced into the living room where Regan had already nodded off. Nicki sat beside her, thumbs flying across an onscreen keyboard while Alex, after learning the wi-fi password, had wandered upstairs to stake claim to a room where he would undoubtedly spend much of his time obliterating the same online enemies he battled at home.

"If you're sure—" I said, and Susan nodded, smiling again.

Traci and I stepped out onto the porch, admiring the view under the dwindling daylight.

"Picture perfect," Traci sighed, taking a deep breath of the fresh mountain air before sipping her beer.

I put an arm around her shoulders and pulled her close. "We needed this," I said. "All of us." I glanced back through the window of the door where Susan was industriously working the skillet with a ground beef chopper.

"I hope the others don't run into any more difficulties," said Traci, laying her head against my shoulder.

"I think we've had our fill of difficulties."

"Shhh!" She put a finger firmly against my lips. "You'll curse us."

I smiled and held my hands up in surrender.

Of course, hindsight is 20/20.

We could have avoided so much trouble if any of us had been sufficiently enthused about seeing the hot tub or what the view looked like from the far end of the porch. We might have noticed the broken pane of glass just above the knob on the door leading into the game room on the lower level.

We might have realized we weren't alone.

*

We wandered back in as the smell of dinner drifted out to the porch. Susan's cheeks were flushed as she filled a large pot with water before placing it on the stovetop and turning the burner on high. Traci went to the refrigerator and retrieved a head of lettuce and placed it on the island. "Knives? Bowls?" asked Traci.

Susan pointed to a drawer in the island and a cabinet to the left of the sink. "I can do that—"

"It's just salad—no big deal," said Traci. "You've done everything else."

I poured a healthy dose of whisky over ice and perched on one of the bar stools at the island. Despite the heavenly smells, my eyes were heavy, and I was exhausted from all of the driving. I could have skipped dinner entirely and taken a nap. Instead, I took a drink from my glass and winced as the alcohol blazed a trail down my throat, making my eyes water slightly.

"Sure does smell *dee*-licious!"

We all froze.

I turned my blurry eyes toward the great room and did a double take. A lanky man in filthy jeans and a plaid shirt sat in one of the recliners with one leg crossed casually over the other. For the briefest of seconds, I thought it was Garry. Dark, sandy hair and angular features gave reason for pause, but the smile, wide with stained, broken and missing teeth shattered the illusion.

"Who the hell—" The words froze in my mouth when I noticed the gun held carelessly in his lap, bouncing in rhythm with his jittering leg. The girls were both dozing on the couch, unaware of the stranger who sat directly across from them. Traci and Susan inched closer together behind the island, speechless at the sudden surreality in front of us.

"Oh, now, *stop*," said the stranger, his grin widening. "I was just thinking about how hungry I was, and if that don't smell like the best thing ever!"

Regan stirred on the other couch, brushing her long black hair out of her eyes. She sat bolt upright with a gasp that brought Nicki to. "Who the fuck are *you?*" she demanded, grabbing hold of Nicki's arm.

The man's grin dropped abruptly, and his eyes narrowed and focused on Regan. "What kind of trash talk is that

345

coming from a pretty little thing like you?" He let the gun swing toward Regan, and Nicki cried out.

"Leave them alone!" Susan bellowed, starting around the island but freezing when the gun was leveled in her direction.

"Oooo, we got us a mama bear, do we?" The man chuckled softly. "A mama bear can be an awful scary thing, can't she?" He uncrossed his legs and stood, his tone hardening. "I want all of your cell phones right here, right now." He pointed to the center of the great room with the gun. "We don't use our phones at the supper table."

Hot, furious tears spilled from the corners of Nicki's eyes as she lobbed her phone to the middle of the room. We all followed suit. I could almost read Susan's mind when she cast a furtive glance upstairs. She hoped Alex would see what was happening but stay put—call 911 on his cell. The hope had barely taken shape when I spotted Alex's phone sticking out of the pocket of his overnight bag along the wall behind the dining table. I saw no way to casually snag it without drawing attention. I just hoped our visitor wouldn't notice, and I might eventually get an opportunity.

"Let me introduce myself," he said, slightly bowing and pointing the gun toward his own chest. "I'm Buddy. That's B-U-D-D-Y." He seemed pleased with himself.

"What do you want?" I asked.

"A good meal. Some polite conversation." He pursed his lips. "Is that too much to ask?"

"Most people wait for an invitation," said Traci in a hollow, distant voice. All of the blood had drained from her face. I shot her a warning look. No sense in antagonizing.

"I am not most people," said Buddy, taking it in stride. "I have always found it better to do what I want and ask forgiveness later—if I feel the need." He chuckled. "You'd be surprised how very little I ever feel the need. Now come on, you two." He gestured toward Regan and Nicki with the gun and indicated the dining room table. "Dinner's ready. Get yourselves seated over yonder."

The girls moved as one, skirting the front of the couch and claiming seats as far away from Buddy as they could. He shifted his attention to Susan. "Now go ahead, mama. I believe you were about to boil up some sketty. Your pot's bubbling away over there."

Susan moved sideways toward the stove, removing the lid from the pot and dumping a box of spaghetti noodles in. She stirred the roiling water, her eyes never leaving Buddy's face. She set the time on the stove for seven minutes and stepped away.

Buddy directed his attention toward me and Traci, his smile faltering. "You two are making me nervous," he said. "Why don't you join the little ladies at the table?" We moved along the path his gun traced for us, taking seats on either side of the girls. I was within reach of the bag holding Alex's phone.

"Now," said Buddy, moving toward the head of the table. He let the gun rest against the back of the captain's chair as he leaned forward over its back. "You all know my name. How about you introduce yourselves?" He looked expectantly at Traci, who sat the furthest to the left, Nicki clinging to her arm.

"Traci." Her voice faltered.

"Well, now, how *do*, Miss Traci? See? We can be right friendly!" He favored her with a broad yellow grin. He shifted his attention to my daughter.

"Nicki." If looks could kill, this man would have been a goner.

"It is a *pleasure*, young miss! I'll bet you'd be pretty if you'd just *smile*," he looked at her expectantly, but to no avail. He sighed and rolled his eyes before settling on Regan.

"Regan," she said, her hands clasped together tightly on the table in front of her.

"Just like that little girl in *The Exorcist!*" Buddy's eyes brightened. "Don't be goin' all demonic on me!" He held up a hand in mock defense before laughing uproariously, apparently amusing himself greatly. We sat like statues, attention fluctuating between the man's mildly flushed visage and the gun he clutched loosely in his right hand. He tossed his head back over his shoulder, looking back at Susan expectantly.

"Susan," she said, stepping back to the stovetop and stirring the spaghetti again. I imagined she was trying to find a way to fling the boiling water across the room without hitting any of us or getting anyone shot. Her eyes continued to glance upward to see if Alex had been drawn out by the smell of supper, and I prayed Buddy wouldn't notice what was obvious to me.

"Well, Suzy-Q! Howdy do." Buddy pulled the captain's chair back and swung a long leg around the front of it before taking a seat. "I surely do appreciate your efforts, there. I will take me a goodly size portion if you have it to spare." While his attention was on Susan, I managed to snake a foot through the handle of Alex's overnight bag and drag it toward me under the table.

We sat in uncomfortable silence for a few moments longer until the timer on the stove announced the pasta was ready. Susan silenced it and moved the pot over to the sink where she had earlier placed a colander. I watched steam rush up around her shoulders and head, dissipating along with any hope of using the boiling water as a weapon. Robotically, she doled out six portions of noodles and topped each with a ladle or sauce. She carried the plates two at a time to the table along with silverware, serving Buddy first, then moving on to Traci, Nicki, Regan and me. Before she had a chance to sit, Buddy said, "Did I hear something about a salad?"

I could see Susan's jaw clench as she returned to the kitchen and retrieved the bowl that Traci had been preparing. She poured Italian dressing in and quickly tossed it before bringing it to the table along with a stack of salad bowls. "Anything else I can get for you?" she asked tightly.

Buddy considered briefly. "I could use one of those beers," he said. Susan went to the refrigerator and returned, planting the bottle by his plate with a thunderous crack which he ignored. He smiled up at her. "I'm gonna have to leave you a mighty fine tip! Now, go on and sit down. Eat up before it gets cold." He gestured toward the seat beside me.

Susan's eyes remained narrowed and steely as she sat. Buddy smiled appreciatively at the spread before him and began alternating noisily between the salad and spaghetti. When none of us joined in, he gestured impatiently. "C'mon! Dig in! It's even better'n it looks!" he exclaimed with his mouth full.

A rumble of thunder rolled through the mountains in the distance, the perfect accompaniment to the mood at the table.

We picked over our plates for a few minutes in relative silence, save for the occasionally slurp or belch from Buddy, who was making quick progress with his food. As he scooped a final pile of spaghetti onto his fork, he seemed surprised to see what little progress we had made with our own plates. "You all don't know what you're missing," he chastised in a sing-song cadence that managed to combine menace with childlike simplicity.

"Will you just go now?" Regan blurted out, and Buddy's head jerked in her direction, his eyes narrowing and a frown pulling at the corners of his mouth.

"Where are your gosh dern manners?" In one fluid move, Buddy was out of his chair, knocking it backward and slamming his hands down in front of Regan. I half-expected the gun to discharge as he smashed it against the table's surface. "This is *not* how you treat a *guest!"* He reached forward with his left hand and flipped Regan's plate into her lap.

Regan pushed back from the table and screamed as the hot sauce made contact with the bare skin of her legs, slapping it away. Susan jumped to her feet. "Leave my daughter alone!"

351

We watched in horror as Buddy leveled the gun at her face. "Sit down," he said. "Sit. Down." Susan slowly lowered herself back into her chair, her eyes shifting between the gun and Regan, who was now practically in Nicki's lap. Angry tears continued to flow, but she had managed to get most of the sauce off her legs.

"Can't you just leave these people alone?"

Everyone at the table turned to find a young woman standing at the far end of the living area near the top of the stairs leading to the game room below. Her scrawny arms hung loosely at her sides with fingers flexing. Her face was streaked with dirt and her limp, mousy brown hair spilled just past narrow shoulders encased in a sleeveless AC/DC t-shirt. Her jeans were far too large for her frame, cinched at the hips and almost completely covered her dirty bare feet.

"Audrey!" Buddy's face lit up like a Christmas tree. "What are *you* doing up here, sweet pea?"

Audrey regarded him with clear disdain, the muscles in her jaw clenching tightly as she leveled a steely glare in his direction. "Just stop it, Buddy. Haven't you done enough already?"

He cocked his head to the side, his face a mockery of confusion, and turned toward the girl, opening his arms wide. "I got no idea what you're talking about, sweet thing.

And didn't I ask you to stay put? Your folks are gonna wonder where you are."

"Shut your filthy mouth," she said through gritted teeth, her blazing eyes beginning to fill with tears. She was shaking now, and her hands had curled into fists. While Buddy's focus was on the girl, I seized the opportunity to kneel sideways and snag Alex's phone from his bag. I cupped it in the palm of my hand and held it in my lap underneath the table.

As if on cue, a door opened upstairs, and I watched in horror as Alex emerged from his room, already bellowing, "What am I smelling down there? Did everyone forget about me?" He leaned over the railing looking down into the living area. "Who are all these—?"

Buddy's demeanor shifted in an instant as he whipped the gun around, setting his sights on Alex. Susan cried out as Alex's words stuttered to a halt, his hands springing into the air in a universal sign of submission.

"Now, just who in the hell do we have here?" demanded Buddy, a little of his calm façade slipping away.

"Please don't hurt my baby," pleaded Susan, tears streaming down her face. The rest of us just stared like idiots, watching a scene unfold in which we had no control.

"Just how in the hell many more of you are there?" Buddy asked irritably. "Do I need to take a fucking *tour?*"

353

"Just me," Alex managed meekly.

Buddy cupped a hand to his ear, craning exaggeratedly in Alex's direction. "I'm sorry. Didn't quite catch that."

Alex cleared his throat, steadying his voice. "Just me."

"Well, then," said Buddy, allowing his menacing gaze to wander over us all while the gun stayed firmly pointed toward Alex. "How 'bout *'Just Me'* get his ass down here with the rest of us?"

He motioned with the gun, and Alex carefully made his way down the hallway toward the stairs, keeping his hands suspended mid-air and visible at all times. His eyes were all over the place, jumping from Audrey to Buddy to us and back again. As he headed toward the table, he attempted to cut a wide path around Buddy, but at the last moment, Buddy lashed out and grabbed his neck from behind, pushing him roughly forward where he crashed into the table before falling to the ground.

A series of startled cries erupted from our lips, and Susan was on her feet in an instant with her hands splayed out on the table, leaning forward with her teeth clenched and bared, her cheeks a furious crimson. "You son of a bitch," she hissed, bringing a slow smile to Buddy's lips.

"Now, is that any kind of way for a lady to talk?" he drawled before shifting his attention back to Audrey. "And *you*, little Miss Audrey—I could've sworn I left you tied up downstairs by the pool table. I told you I'd be right back just as soon as I found out what all the hubbub was about up here. I mean, I had a feelin' you were a little sweet on me, but I'm going to have to ask for a little patience here. I've got me some business to take care of here, but then I'll have all the time in the *world* for you, sweet thing."

Audrey took a step back toward the stairs from which she had ascended, her face contorted in disgust. "Stay away from me, you sick fuck," she spat.

Buddy took several steps in her direction, leading with the gun. He cocked his head and tutted his disapproval. "So much unseemly language from young ladies these days," he noted, as much to himself as to anyone else. "What would your Mama say?"

"She wouldn't say anything because she's dead!" screamed Audrey, hot tears spilling from the corners of her eyes as she took another step backwards. "She's dead because you killed her! But she would've called you a whole lot worse! And Daddy would've—"

"Daddy wouldn't do *shit!*" raged Buddy, bridging the distance between them in three long, quick strides. "Because Daddy's dead, *too*, isn't he sweet thing?"

Audrey's fear was becoming palpable as her shoulders hitched and shook. Tears were flowing freely now.

"*Why?*" she implored, all of the rage gone from her voice.

Buddy's laugh was ugly and taunting. "Why? *Why?!?* Because they stood between me, and the thing I wanted, and guess what, sweet thing? That thing was *you*."

She shook her head slowly, taking another step back. "No," she implored, opening her mouth to say more but plunging backwards down the stairs with a startled scream instead.

We stared in stunned silence as Buddy reached out to grab her arm but only caught hold of air. *"Awwww*, shit," he moaned, stomping a foot on the ground before racing down the stairs after her.

"Go!" I barked, quickly motioning the others toward the series of glass doors that opened onto the covered porch. Without hesitation, everyone began piling out onto the porch while I fumbled with Alex's phone, dialing 9-1-1 and pausing in the door frame while the others waited for me outside. I patted my pocket and was relieved to feel my Hyundai's key fob nestled within. As soon as the call connected, I barked, "Please send help! Someone's trying to kill us. He's got a gun—"

I stepped out onto the porch and tossed Alex's phone aside and fished the key fob out of my pocket, handing it to Traci.

"What are you doing?" she asked, looking from the key fob to the phone.

"I need to leave the call open so they can find us," I said. I had no idea if that was true; I was operating on know-how gleaned from television. "Get everyone to the car. I'll be right behind you."

Traci and Susan herded the kids off the porch and out into the night as another flash of lightning seared the sky. Ominous thunder followed almost immediately, rolling long and slow, rattling the boards beneath my feet. The wind had picked up, and I saw the first fat droplets of rain bouncing off the hard-packed dirt of the parking area. I looked back into the chalet and my breath caught in my throat as I spotted Buddy at the top of the stairs, scanning the room frantically for his lost quarry. He spotted me, and for a second, I froze, paralyzed by fear.

It was a paralysis broken by panic as he lifted his gun, taking aim and squeezing off a shot. I turned away from the direction in which my family had fled and ran toward the far end of the deck as the door-length glass of the patio door exploded in front of me; I could only hope Buddy would follow me and not notice the others. At last glance, they were piling into the Hyundai.

I reached the top of the stairs leading down to the hot tub and paused, waiting for Buddy to step out onto the porch. Twin bolts of lightning rent the sky angrily as the droplets of rain became a downpour. Thunder shook the wooden rail I had rested my hand upon to steady myself as I waited.

Like something straight out of a horror movie, Buddy stepped out onto the porch, unnaturally calm and leading with his gun. He started to look toward the parking area, and I screamed, *"Over here, you fucking asshole!"*

Another flash of lightning followed by rolling thunder.

Buddy's head turned slowly in my direction, and once he spotted me, his body followed suit. I turned and hammered down the stairs two at a time, jumping down to the midpoint landing before pivoting and beginning my descent down the remaining stairs. My only plan had been distraction. Give Traci, Susan and the kids the time they needed to get away safely, and with that accomplished, I scrambled for a way to save my own sorry ass. If I could just get to the bottom, maybe I could hide in the woods behind the house.

Halfway down the second section of stairs, I could see through the broken glass of the game room door and into the lighted room. Audrey's parents were inside, her father partially obscured by the pool table and her mother propped against the wall with her mouth frozen open in a silent scream as her sightless eyes stared into eternity. There was so much blood—

358

Involuntarily, I glanced back toward the top of the stairs just as Buddy appeared, brandishing his weapon in my general direction. He took another quick shot, and the rail by my hand splintered. There was no way I could make it to the woods before he'd be upon me, and his ugly smirk confirmed he knew this as well.

But then, the strangest thing happened.

The outdoor lights installed along the long porch and the path down to the hot tub suddenly sprang to life, causing both of us to shield our eyes. Their brightness continued to swell and pulse before going into a manic flicker, like the bulbs of several cameras firing off in rapid sequence. The brightest bolt of lightning yet peeled back the night, followed by thunder that may as well have been a small explosion; I could feel it through my entire body.

I looked up just in time to see Buddy topple headfirst down the stairs, bouncing and rolling over each open riser, his momentum cut abruptly short as he landed with a sickening thud against the rail. His eyes bored directly into me, and it took a long second to realize his head was turned completely around, leering over his shoulder as if he were the one playing Regan from *The Exorcist*. The gun had dropped through the stairs into the tall grass below.

I glanced back to the head of the stairs as the undulating lights continued their frantic assault on my senses, creating sunspots across my entire field of vision. I did a double-take and squinted, my mouth hanging open stupidly.

Garry was at the top of the stairs, fully engaged in the same goofy-ass victory dance from fifteen years ago. Lightning flashed again, followed by an earth-shaking boom. The lights winked out abruptly as the chalet lost power.

I looked again, and Garry was gone.

I dropped to my knees and stared up at the stormy sky, rain pelting my face and stinging my cheeks. My mind skipped through all of the improbabilities that had plagued the day, preventing his children one-by-one from being here on this horrible night, and yet we had persisted, pushing through and hellbent on celebrating a time that could never again be the same. So much for best laid plans...

Do you believe in guardian angels? I certainly do.

ACKNOWLEDGEMENTS

It is always my great privilege to have Lynne Hobstetter, Teri Lott and Traci Steele tackle the minefield of errors they may encounter after I think a manuscript is finished. With this compilation, I was also fortunate enough to enlist the talents of Cindy Hamm, super *Dwayne Morrow* fan and fellow Clay High alumnus, to provide feedback. Their remarks are invaluable, and this book would have suffered greatly without their assistance. Thank you, thank you, *thank you!* And as always, any mistakes, factual or otherwise, are completely my own.

Most importantly, thank *you* for riding along. Whether you follow me on Facebook, rate and/or review on Amazon and/or Goodreads, or bowl with me at AMF Stardust, I appreciate your support more than you'll ever know.

Until next time,
Darin Miller
Grove City, Ohio – April 2023

ALSO AVAILABLE

REUNION
Dwayne Morrow Mystery #1

CIRCUMVENTION
Dwayne Morrow Mystery #2

RETRIBUTION
Dwayne Morrow Mystery #3

DIVERSION
Dwayne Morrow Mystery #4

ISOLATION
Dwayne Morrow Mystery #5

ABDUCTION
Dwayne Morrow Mystery #6

DECEPTION
Dwayne Morrow Mystery #7

DELUSION
Dwayne Morrow Mystery #8

OVER CONSUMPTION
*A Dwayne Morrow and Jane
Bond Novella
(Co-written with V.R. Tapscott)*

OTHER WORK

HOUSE OF SECRETS
*Every Room Holds a Story
(Contributor, "Redemption")*

EQUILIBRIUM

THE LIBRARY CENTENNIAL
ANTHOLOGY
*Celebrating the Lives and
People of the SPL Community
(Contributor, "Meredith's Bad
Day")*

DID YOU LIKE ME?

☐ Yes! ☐ No ☐ Maybe?

May I ask a favor?

If you enjoyed reading this book as much as I enjoyed writing it, won't you please consider leaving a rating and/or review on Amazon, Goodreads, BookBub, or anywhere else you might see fit? It only takes a moment to leave a rating and a maybe a couple more for a short review—even a simple 'I would recommend this book!' will do nicely.

Word of mouth is the single most powerful tool in an Indie author's toolkit, and ratings and reviews help more than you may realize in growing our audience. Think of it as a gratuity you might leave a server after an evening of fine dining, but this gratuity doesn't cost a thing—only a few moments of your time.

Thank you for your kind consideration.

Amazon   Goodreads   BookBub

ABOUT THE AUTHOR

Darin Miller was born in Portsmouth but currently resides in Grove City, both of which are located in Ohio. While he has worked in Information Technology for three decades, he has *not* solved a single, solitary crime to date. He is the BookFest award-winning author of the Ohio-based *Dwayne Morrow Mystery* series, as well as an unrelated short story collection, *Broken Bits and Bobs*, and a standalone psychological horror thriller, *Equilibrium*. With equal parts action, humor, suspense and mystery, the *Dwayne Morrow* series features characters you're sure to love—and in some cases, loathe.

Stay current with updates, short stories, and other special promotions at www.darin-miller.com.